SECRET LIVES

SECRET LIVES

THREE NOVELLAS

Tom Wakefield
Patrick Gale
Francis King

First published in Great Britain 1991
by Constable and Company Limited

This edition published 1992 by Serpent's Tail,
4 Blackstock Mews, London N4

ISBN 1 85242 215 7
Set in Monophoto Sabon by
Servis Filmsetting Limited, Manchester
Printed in Great Britain by
Cox & Wyman Limited
Reading, Berkshire

A CIP catalogue record for this book
is available from the British Library

CONTENTS

The Other Way
Tom Wakefield
· 7 ·

Caesar's Wife
Patrick Gale
· 87 ·

Secret Lives
Francis King
· 159 ·

The Other Way

· Tom Wakefield ·

FOR R.T COLLIE, DAVID MCLAUGHLIN
AND ANN HANSON

'The obsession to understand things, which inevitably renders them insignificant and mediocre, is one of our unfortunate habits. If we could only allow our destiny to depend on chance and accept the mystery of life unhesitatingly, we might be able to come close to a certain form of happiness that would resemble innocence.'

Luis Buñuel

Brenda Stoneham had in her possession quite a number of things that she did not really need. In her small, two-bedroom, terraced house, the kitchen alone held three blending machines, two toasters, two microwave ovens and any number of domestic appliances which were surplus to a domestic form of heaven.

She owned three electric kettles and had marked one of them with a piece of yellow adhesive. This kettle was never plugged in as it had caused her some degree of embarrassment when it played the National Anthem before it switched itself off. If her sister or one of her neighbours called for tea there was always some discomfort about hearing 'God Save the Queen'; her sister said that it always put her in mind of a funeral or an accident at sea.

The larger bedroom in the house had become a warehouse that seemed to reflect the needs of the past decade. Time was being recorded everywhere in the form of digital, electric, cuckoo and carriage clocks. The bedroom was full of booty and modern treasures. Brenda always felt as though she were entering the hold of some stately Spanish galleon as she entered the room to add yet another object to her store.

At one time, she had begun to make an inventory: two sets of bathroom scales (Brenda hated weighing scales), a garden hose, an electric lawn-mower, thirty-four boxes of assorted talcum-powders, seventeen Bros T-shirts, five transistor radios, two spin-driers, a video-recorder, two portable television sets ... The task had proved beyond her, and when the steam iron and the duvet-set arrived she gave up the job completely. Her treasure grew weekly.

Brenda was not a greedy consumer, nor was she a frivolously addictive spendthrift. She just liked entering competitions. On average, she entered around fifteen a week. A first, a second or even a third prize had never come her way. This was why her small house had become a repository for consolation prizes.

Today was Tuesday and as Brenda buttoned up her coat she felt both nervous and excited. She re-read the letter that had plopped through her letter-box fourteen days ago. The information had momentarily startled her with its direct tone and simple use of words:

Dear Miss Stoneham,
We are pleased to inform you that you have won one of our three big ones! Yes, you have won one of the BIG THREE! Your prize will be announced on Tuesday the—of—Would you kindly send us a photograph as we like to have the snaps of our major competition winners.

> Yours sincerely,
> Philippa Bunting
> Features Editor

Brenda had baulked at this, as the only reasonable photograph that she could find had been taken over twenty years ago. After some hesitation Brenda had posted it off. 'After all,' she thought, 'it doesn't say that they want a recent one, and if I've won a car, there's no reason why a woman who is fiftyish shouldn't have driving lessons.'

She glanced at her digital wrist-watch: the newsagents should be open by now. 'I'll ask for some throat lozenges and then ask for the paper. Better to keep it all casual. Oh God, what if I've won a house? I don't want to move – this one suits me – it's fine for a large person – and me on my own. Somebody last year won a racehorse . . . I like horses but the poor thing wouldn't have room to move around in my back-yard. And where would it sleep? What if it is a four-berth caravan? Or a houseboat? Oh God . . . Oh Lord.' These worrying thoughts carried Brenda to the newsagents in a state of ecstatic anxiety.

On returning home she placed the tabloid on the table and averted her eyes from a grisly headline which said, 'Tracy did it for love'. A small-featured, small-made woman smiled out at all the would-be readers, and hanging from her chest were two enormous breasts that looked as though they were about to explode. Brenda wondered what kind of love would demand such self-inflicted deformity and quickly turned to the pages she was looking for.

'Well, nobody will recognize me,' she thought as she glanced at the pictures of the other two winners. One was a youth poised to kick a football and the other one was a young man of about thirty who smiled as he held a paint-brush.

The amateur footballer had won a car, the painter and decorator a caravan, and . . . and . . . Brenda suddenly felt nauseous, 'And young Brenda Stoneham of 33 Haymarket Street, Batsford, wins a two-week holiday amidst the exotic palm trees, sunshine and balmy breezes of North Africa.'

In order to steady herself Brenda made a pot of tea.

Half-way through her second cup she had managed to formulate a strategy of forfeiture: 'Dear Philippa Bunting, As I have won so many prizes I would like to exchange my BIG prize for a consolation prize – any consolation prize will do – if you could do this with as little fuss as possible and ...' The telephone intruded on Brenda's thoughts.

'Hello, Brenda? It's me, Moira. How are you?' Brenda's younger sister's telephone calls always began in the same way and Brenda's response always was 'Better for hearing your voice, dear.' Moira was seven years younger than her sister and, for the most part, treated her as if she were a mother. Their relationship was based on Moira's loving usage.

'Well, our Brenda, you're the talk of the town. Fancy, you're going to Africa. Lots of people asked if it was you – I remember that photograph. Taken in Torquay – just your head and shoulders. Wasn't it the year after Mum was first ill? Yes, it must have been because I had them copy the bows on the shoulders for my wedding-dress the year after. Do you remember?'

'Yes, it was in the papers. You had a bouquet of red and yellow tulips and wore a Dutch cap,' Brenda replied disconsolately.

'Oh dear, dear Brenda, we've both filled out a bit since then, haven't we?'

'Yes, yes, we have, dear.' Moira did not detect Brenda's sad, ruminative tone nor did she hear the sigh.

'What a time you'll have, Brenda. Everybody in our street is talking about it. Even Harry mentioned it and you know what my husband is like, he said that ...' Moira talked on and on and on ... and as she chattered Brenda began to feel a little better.

It became clear that Moira was very proud of her achievement. It would be cruel to disappoint her: it would be like reneging on a promise. How many weeks? Just two. Is it two or three? Brenda thought, 'The last and only time I was abroad was five years ago ... ten days ... and I longed to return after only one of them.'

As Moira talked Brenda made 'mmm' sounds and thought of the ten days in Majorca. She had shared a flat with Moira and her husband Harry. The view across the bay had looked lovely in the darkness: the winking lights, the stars, the moonlight. They had arrived seven hours late because of flight delays and it had taken them a whole day to recover from their travel exhaustion. The beach below the flat was full of sunbathers who glistened with oil and made a lot of noise. All the buildings on the hills surrounding the beach and on the land fronting the beach were modern.

Brenda had felt as though she had moved into a large, badly planned, international council estate by the sea. She had sat open-mouthed as a large contingent of German tourists had done a kind of Siegheil square-dance to some popular music. No one seemed to mind this fascistic posturing, in fact some of them ... Moira's voice had suddenly taken on more meaning: '... and it's where Dad was killed, I said to Harry ...'

'What's that? What's that you are saying, Moira?' Brenda could not keep the sharpness from her questioning. 'What are you saying about Dad?'

'Tunisia. Tunisia, that's the place where you are going for your holiday – it's where Dad was killed in the war – of course I never knew him, but ... but you did. Didn't you?'

'Yes Moira, I knew him, I knew him and he is still clear in my memory, everything about him – and yes, you are right ... he was sent there ... and he died there ... and I'm going on holiday there ... yes, it does bring a lot back to my mind ... mmm ... mm. I'll call round tomorrow afternoon. Yes, two o'clock to half past ... yes ... yes.'

Brenda returned to her unfinished tea. It was now too chilled to drink. Her father had said that it was too hot to drink, and had risen and tipped it down the sink. Him tipping it down the sink in that way had upset her mother. Her poor mother had used up all their meat ration on corned beef sandwiches; she had them all neatly wrapped in grease-proof paper and had placed them before him. There had been no external display of affection for his wife but he had lifted Brenda up from where she stood.

'His khaki uniform was rough to my legs, his breath was bad and reeked of stale Woodbines, his skin scratched my cheek, and when I winced he brushed his rough-textured jaw more fiercely into the side of my neck. Finally, he put me down. He put me down in this very kitchen, he tugged one of my plaits and told me to look after Mum.' Brenda took the remains of her tea to the sink but paused before emptying it away. She had found that one of the joys of living alone was that she could muse aloud without being considered mad.

'I did look after Mum, and I looked after Moira. I had to ... because we never saw him again. I never imagined that anybody could be killed if they were inside a tank – it still puzzles me how such a great clanking, iron thing can burst into flame. It would be like an oven inside it – so hot – and the smoke.

'I'll take the holiday; of course I must go. I can use a bit of my redundancy money for spending, but it might be cheaper to live there than it is here. Billy Wherly, the new milkman – he told me that when he was on holiday in North Africa there were beggars in the street. I said, "Billy, haven't you noticed beggars on the street here?

If you haven't you must be blind or you're just seeing what you want to see. You don't have to travel hundreds of miles to see a beggar, you don't have to travel one mile even." He's a nice lad, though I don't think he'll marry. He's too good-looking and looks much too young for his age – dresses like a teenager.'

Brenda placed her cup and saucer in the sink and looked out of the window on to the small back-yard. She wondered why the new people next door called their identical area a patio? She wandered outside and paced around the area.

'If there is room for me to walk around it, there would have been room enough for a horse but not the two of us.' She considered the future expense of the holiday in more detail.

'Perhaps I could cut back for a bit, after all I've got two months. I might not have to break into my redundancy money.' During the post-war years Brenda had been taught how to practise an elegant economy by her mother. Pilchards were cheap and nourishing and deserved more popularity than was generally accorded them. A tin of corned beef would be the basis of at least three meals for one person. Two slices with a salad. Two slices with egg and chips. Pop the rest into a stew or hash.

'I must be careful of the water. Billy told me that he had the most terrible squits and runs after he came back . . . mustn't get in the sun too much . . . not much fear of that . . . have my injections . . . tetanus, cholera . . . what was the other thing? Check my passport. Lotion to stop insects feeding off me . . . I'm sure they think I'm a piece of smoked salmon . . . plasters, sandals, aspirins . . . it's more like preparing to go into hospital. Oh God! The sooner I get it over with the better.'

*

Two months later, looking no thinner in spite of an excess of pilchards and corned beef, Brenda stood in the marble–floored reception area of a North African airport. As if to declare her generous size she wore a white cardigan that glittered on account of the gold lurex stars that were speckled all about it and a black skirt that was splattered with large white and yellow tulips. She held her heavily labelled suitcase in one hand and her raincoat in the other.

She had been informed that she was now part of some club and wore a large badge over her left breast proclaiming this. The other members of the club consisted of fifteen or twenty young men and about ten young women. The scene reminded her of some of the television programmes she watched where age seemed to exclude not only participants and performers but viewers as well.

If you were over fifty, you simply did not exist. Brenda did not mind feeling invisible in this company. Perspiration trickled down her armpits and sped towards her bra, her left ankle-strap was too tight and bit into her Achilles tendon. She made no attempt to alleviate her discomfort and stood like some pilgrim accepting of her penance.

Many of the men were drinking from cans and bottles, their mood was festive but rancorous and harsh. They sometimes launched into absurd football chants and made lewd body gestures to one another and laughed in a scornful and derisive way. They belched loudly in an exaggerated manner; this humour pleased them. It was easy for Brenda to switch her thoughts from these people.

How had it been when her father landed here? Would it have been morning or evening? A long journey by ship – had he known anything about such a place? How strange for him to go abroad and be greeted by gunfire.

'Club Palm d'Or. Club Palm d'Or members. Make your way over here, please. Over here, please. Your coach is waiting. Palm d'Or members this way, please.'

Brenda was the last person to board the bus. The lady courier seemed to view Brenda as some kind of tragic mistake. She spoke, her biro poised over her clipboard register: 'You are Brenda Stoneham?' It was as though she were addressing the Bride of Frankenstein.

'I was this morning,' Brenda replied flatly. She looked past the woman and wondered where on earth she would find a place to sit as the coach seemed full and no one on it indicated that there was a spare seat near them. Relief came from above. '*Madame, s'il vous plaît* ... please.'

Brenda looked upwards to gaze directly into the eyes of a man that looked distinctly foreign to her. His black hair and moustache were peppered with white; gold and silver teeth glittered amongst yellowed ones; the perimeters of his large dark brown eyes were criss-crossed with lines; and lettuce seeds could have been sown in the furrows of his brow. He was balanced amidst the suitcases and baggage which he had piled on top of the bus and waved a light brown arm that was thatched with hair. Even the backs of his fingers sprouted curly black tufts. Brenda smiled and first placed her case and then her raincoat into the oustretched hand. She surmised that the man's age was close to her own.

She watched him leap about the top of the bus storing and securing the baggage with a tapestry of ropes, a task he made look simple but one which would surely have confounded most men of his age. Brenda did not veil her astonishment when, with a single leap, he landed at her feet. He stood upright and dusted his trousers, then ushered her towards a seat next to the driver. He sat himself on the stairs of the bus as it drew away from the passenger-bay.

'Thank you, it's years since a man gave up his seat for me on a bus. Fancy, I've had to travel to Africa to experience something which was once a common courtesy in England. You are so kind.'

The man nodded a response to Brenda's gratitude. He could not understand the language but knew from years of observing facial expression that her statement was complimentary.

The coach journey seemed to be taking Brenda through mile after mile of burnt-out plains. In some places the soil had eroded completely to reveal outcrops of rock and stone. They seemed like man-made patternings but could not have been any use to anyone. The monotony was relieved by clumps of prickly pear which had an extra-terrestrial air about them and caused the life-void landscape to look lunar.

After an hour or more Brenda felt the air (which had been hot and oppressive) freshen. She glimpsed young boys wearing long tunics, tending goats ... bare-footed ... smiling, waving. There were palm trees, there were huge, vivid, purple and red bushes of bougainvillaea which glowed in the harsh sunlight. She saw goats – yes, she saw goats perched in the branches of pale green olive trees ... and then ... she caught her breath in wonderment. There was not just one camel but a group of four. Two rested on their haunches and looked towards some distant horizon but the two that were standing gazed with studied indifference as the coach and its passengers sped by them. Great clouds of dust from the vehicle's wheels obscured further sightings.

'It's just the Bible-story pictures come to life,' Brenda whispered to herself.

Her compatriots on the coach saw little of what she saw. Many of them were now drunk, some of them were silent and sullen, others were quarrelsome and obscenely noisy. Brenda watched helplessly as an empty lager-can was tossed around the bus. There was nothing playful about this action – it was a collective expression of contempt for both the driver and his bus. Brenda gasped as the tin ricocheted off the top of a seat and struck the luggage attendant on the side of the head.

The mishap was greeted by guffaws and laughter and shouts of 'Bull's Eye' and 'Nice one, Cyril'. Apart from feeling angry, Brenda felt deeply ashamed that she could be part of a culture which could have produced people like this. Was she part of it? The empty lager-can rolled near to the driver's seat. Brenda bent forward, picked it up and slowly placed it inside her handbag. She stood, took a deep breath as if to fill her ample lungs for a great aria and bellowed, 'Enough! Enough, I say. Enough!'

There were catcalls, a few desultory jeers, a chorus of farting sounds but her economy of words and the volume of their delivery brought some result. No more cans were tossed around.

The coach had turned down a narrow lane; a large wooden archway shaped like horseshoe spanned the turn-off. Coloured electric light-bulbs spelled out 'Palm d'Or Club' and twelve-foot-high gates were opened by rough-looking men who were dressed as desert nomads. As the coach entered the lane Brenda looked out from the window. She could see some kind of native settlement. Beyond the hundreds of conical-shaped huts there were vast stretches of white sand and, beyond the sand, the sea.

She was given little time to contemplate the beauty of these alien environs for the coach pulled up abruptly in a sun-baked dirt square. There were three white concrete buildings which had all the appearance of army barracks offices. Parked outside the offices were two Landrover cars. Brenda joined the other passengers as they assembled on the dirt square. There seemed to be no sign of life from the offices but then a voice spoke out. Brenda recognized some of the French words ... but before she could decipher any message ... the language had changed to German.

She looked up at the loudspeakers that were stuck on a flag-pole void of a flag. In spite of the heat of the afternoon a terrible chill seeped through her frame causing her to shudder.

'*Achtung! Achtung!*'

Oh God, she had once seen a film like this, only it was set in Norway. The next sequence of events brought her close to a panic attack. She began to hope that she might faint or suddenly wake up at home in Batsford.

The luggage was being taken from the bus but it was not being delivered to its owners. Instead, these items were being lodged on four hand-carts: one yellow, one green, one red and one blue.

'I'm in a concentration camp.' Brenda's unease unleashed wilder imaginings. 'They're taking all our clothes. If they start playing classical music, they will shoot everyone over fifty. There's only one over fifty but I know I can still do a good day's work. I'm a strong woman; I can put my hand to most things. Well, not everything.' Brenda closed her eyes and waited for the music and the bullets.

'Attention, please. Attention, please. Good afternoon all. Welcome to the Palm d'Or. If you are not happy now then prepare yourself for a change of mood. You will be hy-st-eri-cal in a day or two. Now please listen carefully. Please listen for your name, number and colour. Please gather round the delivery cart that is painted in your colour. Your number is the number of your house. When you are all assembled you will be guided to your accommodation.'

Brenda was momentarily relieved. 'At least I'll have a house to myself,' she thought. 'I can sit and read, and maybe knit for a while. I won't have to go out too much – it might not be too bad . . . my name! That's my name . . . Brenda Stoneham . . . yellow 316. There are four colours. If there's the same number to each colour,' Brenda frowned in bewilderment, 'if there's the same number to each colour there must be over a thousand houses. Is it possible? I wonder if there's a complex somewhere but how could I have missed seeing it?'

She looked out toward the sea. She could see the white breakers rolling towards rows and rows of inert bodies lying on the white sands. Nearer to hand were the dunes; dotted about the dunes were the conical-shaped native huts. Brenda conjectured that the housing must be beyond the barbed-wire and ferocious-looking prickly pear bushes which fenced in the native settlement. The sea seemed to be the only route outwards . . . but there was no harbour and no boats. The bay was enclosed.

After trudging behind the cart for ten minutes or more Brenda began to wonder if it might not have been better to have been shot, such was her present state of misery. The cart was being drawn by two adolescent Arab boys who wore identical robes of blue woollen material. They hauled the cart without complaint or sigh. Through all their exertions their faces remained expressionless and indifferent. Human oxen.

The cart had stopped yet again. A bronze-faced, slim, angular woman dressed in a sarong pushed her sun-glasses from her eyes on to the crown of her head, and waved a limp wrist to signify another pause in the journey. Brenda watched with doleful eyes as two more of her fellow-travellers were given two blankets, their luggage, a torch, and then despatched to a vacant bamboo hut.

'Oh, do look at the long structure to the left of the dune over there.' Brenda's eyes followed the long, thin outstretched arm.

'That is your section's toilet and washing facilities building. Water flows from 7 a.m. to 9.30 p.m.' She laughed mechanically. 'And if you want to bathe at any other time there is always plenty of sea to order.' Other people also found this funny but she continued in a more serious, almost bossy tone. 'Toilet facilities are strictly limited to the building and are available here at all times. I do urge you, for all our sakes, never have recourse to urinating or ... or ... or anything else in the club grounds or in the sea.'

There were now only Brenda and a young couple who said that they came from Walsall left in the entourage. The number of huts had now begun to dwindle and lessen in number like the outskirts of any village but Brenda drew little comfort from this. The young woman from Walsall had trod in some excrement and gave off an aroma of Opium perfume combined with shit that caused her companion to retch. Brenda felt sorry for them both.

'Three-one-three is there. That's the one for you two.' The saronged representative seemed relieved to shed the unfortunate couple. She and Brenda took in deep draughts of air after they had left.

The cart was then hauled between two large dunes

and Brenda felt as though she were about to be dropped off the edge of the world. There were just three more huts in view.

'Three-one-six.' The angular woman lifted her sunglasses and looked into Brenda's eyes as she spoke, and Brenda thought she detected a hint of compassion behind the steely blue gaze. 'And here is your hut.'

'I'm to live there?'

'Yes, you'll find it very private. It is just on the outside edge of things.'

'I've always been on the outside edge of things,' said Brenda.

'You won't feel alone – there is activity nearby. You see the arc lights near the clearing before the prickly pears? They light up the discotheque. It's open every night. Admission is free, of course. It's open to the early hours. We have an oasis bar and you can dance under the stars ...' The woman had begun to follow the hand-cart which had begun its journey back to base. She called back over her shoulder, 'All *au naturel*. I'm sure you'll like it.'

'I don't dance.' Brenda spoke to the three retreating figures and the wheels of the hand-cart. She staggered through the entrance of her hut, placed her suitcase on the dirt floor and let her blankets fall on top of it. Never had a room – a home, for that matter – looked so uninviting. She was surprised at how dark the place was. Perpetual twilight. Ouside the daylight was still startlingly bright.

An appraisal of the gloomy interior did not take very long. It possessed two single camp-beds which were separated by a steel bedside cupboard. The simplicity held no appeal for her – her surroundings were more grim and dire than she could ever have bargained for. Were they a punishment for being greedy about competitions? If so, she felt very harshly treated. She placed her torch on the cupboard top, sat down on one of the beds, covered her face with her large hands and wept.

Just three days later she sat on the same bed in the same position but found that she could not weep. 'My tearducts are exhausted,' she muttered to herself.

She raised her head and by peeping through the spaces between her fingers she looked out from the aperture of the bamboo hut and saw that it was dawn – the sky streaked with brilliant orange, red and yellow light. Slowly she let her hands flop to her sides and turned her large, moon-shaped face towards the glow, hoping that it would generate some energy to quell her present state of growing despair.

Brenda had made a thorough inventory of her captivity. The 1,100 huts which housed the members of the Palm d'Or Club were ranged along four miles of beach and cove. There were communal showers, a communal dining-hall, numerous sports and keep-fit activities, and a discotheque distanced two hundred metres from Brenda's hut which throbbed throughout the night until three or four in the morning.

In these surroundings Brenda felt, and had become, a displaced person. The rest of the population was French, German and British. Their conquered territory was enfenced by large rolls of barbed-wire and prickly pear – even the sea was cordoned. The borders of the club were patrolled by austere-faced Arab guards who carried heavy batons. They were known to the club's inmates as the 'Guardians of the Dunes'.

Brenda got up from her bed and in three giant strides

transported herself to the outside of her hut. It seemed as though she were in some way the member of an occupying army – but Brenda felt no loyalty towards the force she represented. Then she saw the houses. Not huts. Real houses, made of concrete and painted white. She raised her hand to her brow and shaded her eyes. The houses looked like a cluster of architectural shoe-boxes – they were perched on the edge of a promontory which jutted out into the sea. 'They must be six – seven – or even eight miles away.'

She looked towards the sky for help and thought of her mother's favourite picture, 'The Soul's Awakening'. As she lowered her head she was suddenly aware of how far the tide had taken the sea away from the beach.

Brenda moved quickly. There was little to pack as she had only removed some unwashed knickers and her toilet-bag from her suitcase. She must use the impulse to maintain her energy. She talked quietly to herself as though she were colluding with some fellow-prisoner who was a close friend.

'There's a space. A stretch of wet sand exposed between the fencing and the sea. It might be an unusual tide – I haven't seen it so far out before. I've got to take my chance. Must move quickly. The sea waits for nobody . . . Get there before the tide turns . . . Can't stand it here . . . I'll die if I stay here . . . I want walls around me . . . I want a chair . . . I want quiet . . . I want . . .' Brenda clicked the catches shut on her suitcase and, like all intrepid explorers, stepped boldly forward.

On her journey along the beach Brenda saw only two people who paid her no attention at all – she had almost reached the perimeter of the fencing when she saw the outstretched legs. The knees were half-bent;

there was gasping; someone was in some kind of distress. Drowning. Brenda had been taught how to give artificial respiration for swimming mishaps and she thought that the sounds indicated some kind of emergency. She had peered round the dune.

'Can I be of any . . .'

'Piss off.' The man rasped out the words breathlessly and had then proceeded to lift the legs of the woman who lay beneath him and had entered a more intensified rhythm than before. His sand-speckled buttocks rose and fell, and the gasping and horrible moaning continued.

Brenda had turned away quickly from this interrupted and anxious copulation and took up her suitcase and marched purposefully along the edge of the barbed-wire towards the sea. 'If that's sexual passion,' Brenda spoke to a seagull perched on the wire, 'if that's sexual passion then I'd rather pull a hand-cart.'

She paddled through six inches of sea-water and thought of Blackpool . . . her first glimpse of the sea. They had said she was too big to ride on a donkey. There . . . she had done it . . . just in time. She had beaten the tide . . . and she was free.

She made her way further inland and took a rest by sitting on her suitcase. It felt warmer now and even the breezes from the sea failed to cool her; her mouth felt dry from the hot spray. She licked her top lip and gleaned her own moisture from the space above it. She looked at the white buildings . . . they still looked a long way from her present position. Nevertheless, she rose to her feet and ran her fingers through her hair . . . look what Vivien Leigh had done in *Gone with the Wind*. Hadn't Gladys Aylward walked hundreds of miles across China with a child on her back? Nearer home . . .

hadn't her own mother pushed a barrow of coal in the snow just to keep the house warm?

There was room enough for one chair and a stool on one of the two tiny balconies that graced the Café des Ramparts. Immediately below the balcony were out-crops of rock and shale which tumbled their way twenty or thirty feet down to the shore. A pathway between the rocks and shale bore testament to the fact that little earth movement had taken place for many years. The rocks, the shale, the pathway were fixed from a time that few people living could remember.

Leslie Langley sat very still, eyes half closed, hands clasped together in his lap. He was relaxed but remained expectant in the same way as door-to-door salespeople await an answer from a house which is empty of people.

His spectacles were lodged awkwardly alongside an orange on top of the stool, his view of the world – myopic and astigmatic – was blurred and hazy but not unattractive. This impaired vision allowed him to view all matter, whether it was animal, vegetable or mineral, as though it were part of a gigantic Seurat painting.

Apart from gulls and the sea itself, there was little movement in the early morning and it was this universal stillness which attracted Leslie to the hour. Afternoons were for sleep. A few minutes earlier he had seen, or thought he had seen, something which caused him to doubt his own perceptions. A figure – probably some beast of burden (animals were kept for their usefulness here) – seemed to be plodding along the acres of sandy shore. It was too small for a camel, too tall for a donkey and too colourful for any living creature. He had detected great splodges of purple, yellow and green . . . what on earth?

Leslie had smiled to himself and directed his delinquent gaze towards the sky. 'It must be my age. At fifty-seven mirages are common, or at least they are to me – things are never what you thought they were. I might even still be asleep and not out here. I might be dreaming this but I don't want to wake myself up. If I lift up my arm will the effort be weightless?'

Leslie's hands remained in his lap and his ears listened for sounds . . . the gulls shrieked angrily at each other . . . and there were stirrings and bumps from the household behind him as it gradually came to life. No, he was not dreaming, he was not asleep.

The colourful beast had got nearer. Its progress was slow but persistent. Leslie admired its doggedness but was not curious enough to replace his glasses for a closer scrutiny; there was more charm to the scene without them. His reverie and sense of calm were broken by a black winged-insect which settled on his forearm, reconnoitred his wrist and then, finally, stung him on the back of his hand before flying away.

'Ouch! I suppose that's his way of saying "Hello". A greeting I could have done without.'

It was thirst that brought Leslie irredeemably back into the real world. He put on his glasses to eat his orange. He always wore his glasses when he ate oranges as once, many years back, he had been travelling by coach from London to Lancaster and had suffered agonies and partial temporary blindness in the left eye. His urgently probing finger had caused a mixture of jaffa juice and pith to spurt directly from the fruit into his eye. He now wore his glasses for peeling oranges in the same way that welders wore goggles – it was more a matter of protection than personal idiosyncrasy or taste.

His long, bony, talon-like fingers tore into the peel with adept, quick, determined movements until the fruit was revealed bald and palatable. He chose to enjoy it slowly, tearing each segment from its mooring before popping it into his mouth to let his molars complete the slow but pleasurable operation.

'Pardon me? I beg your pardon but do you speak English?' Leslie gulped down a piece of orange and blinked to make sure he was not in any trance-like state. Below him, at the point where the rocks and shale ended and the sand began, stood an unusually tall and hefty woman. He looked beyond her and saw her large footprints indelibly imprinted on the sand. She appeared to have come out of the sea as the markings disappeared into surf and rolling breakers some miles away.

His first thoughts were of goddesses, daughters or sisters of ancient deities, mother-in-law of Neptune, and that kind of thing. But appearances denied his imaginative sorties. It's true – this woman was unusually large – massive in fact – over six feet tall – broad shoulders – wide hips and strong thick legs that could have supported half a grand piano.

'Do you understand? Please answer me if you do. I am English.' Leslie detected a plaintive tremor in the woman's voice that seemed entirely out of keeping with her demeanour. She couldn't possibly have come out of the sea: she was bone-dry, there were no traces of seaweed in her tightly permed hair, no barnacles clung to her legs, and her afternoon frock patterned with huge purple and yellow daisies was entirely inappropriate to any kind of mythology.

Leslie felt that the dress was more historical as he had seen his mother wear such a garment in the late fifties. But his mother had been small and thin. Was the material called terylene?

'Please, please … please help me … help me.' The woman bent as if to lift up her case from the ground … She swayed … and then collapsed slowly on to the sand.

Leslie had approached her as if he were hoping to assist some great errant whale that had become beached and marooned. He circled about her form still holding half an orange in his right hand, gradually getting nearer so that he could see the rise and fall of purple and yellow daisies splattered across her bosom. He stood near her head and watched her slowly raise herself up to a sitting position.

'I'm thirsty.' She spoke in an empty, hopeless manner, as if she expected no response. For her part, she believed Leslie to be not only foreign but deaf and dumb.

'Eat slowly,' Leslie commanded and fed her the half orange segment by segment. 'Your arms have caught the sun.' Leslie observed the fleshy limbs and saw that the hands were undecorated but strapped to one of the wrists there was a garish digital watch with the face of Mickey Mouse stuck in the middle.

She stood and looked down on Leslie. 'I need somewhere to stay, somewhere to stay for eleven days.'

'Follow me,' Leslie responded and offered to take her case but she gently removed his hand from the handle.

'I can manage, I can manage quite well, thank you all the same.'

She followed him up the pathway and into the café without further utterance.

Brenda had – as a child – gone to the pictures with her mother to see Gary Cooper in a film called *Beau Geste*. The café interior where she now sat might well have been used for a location shot for the film. The furnishing was limited to four or five tables. Each table had benches aligned on either side of it. They were made of roughly hewn wood and looked unfinished but secure.

'Sit down. I'll order some tea.' Leslie gestured her towards one of the benches and then made his way to a doorway screened with hanging beads.

'Rashid. Rashid. Rashid, *s'il vous plaît.*' He waited near the beads looking very much at odds with his surroundings. Brenda had now settled her bulk comfortably on a bench.

From where she sat Brenda observed that the bar was well stocked. The creaking sound that stirred the quietness of the room came from a huge fan that was fixed to the nicotine-stained ceiling. The fan rotated directly above her head, breathing fresh air into an atmosphere that was already smoke-free. The whitewashed walls were hung with three large carpets which were all decorated in beautiful symmetric patterns in the Islamic tradition. The colour combinations of turquoise, purple, orange and light green were new to Brenda's eye but held great appeal. There was also a faded colour poster of a woman drinking Coca-Cola. 'Was it Betty Grable? Whatever happened to her? Got old like everybody else,' Brenda thought. 'It was nice of her to turn up here, though.'

Brenda rested her square jaw between her hands, placed her elbows firmly on the table and turned her bovine, brown eyes on the man who had come to her rescue.

'He's no Gary Cooper to look at,' she thought, as her unflickering gaze absorbed Leslie's physical details. He was a small man, the kind of small man that never got a second glance – not even out of curiosity. His khaki shorts came to his knees revealing spindly legs – and Brenda noticed that his toe-nails which peeped through his open sandals were yellow. His torso was slightly misshapen by a small paunch which gave him an appearance of early pregnancy – this was covered by an unironed, dreary dark green shirt. His hair – what was left of it – might once have been sandy in hue but now it was flecked with grey and white and 'Oh those glasses,' Brenda muttered quietly to herself. 'They make him look like an owl – wise and private birds.'

Leslie was now joined by an Arab who wore a blue and white striped shift. Leslie spoke to him in rapid French and the Arab patron nodded. From time to time the Arab would look at Brenda and nod reassuringly. When Leslie returned to the table Brenda stated her need quietly. 'I cannot stay in that place; the Palm d'Or, I cannot stay there. I cannot return to it – it would kill me.'

Leslie smiled wistfully. 'I'm sure that it would have a similar effect upon me. Palm d'Or members never call here, there is nothing in the town to interest them. Apart from us, Bolba sees few tourists. We have been here twice before.'

Brenda was slightly disappointed to hear that Leslie was not alone. (What was his wife like? Would she be joining them?) Leslie interrupted her thoughts by relaying his organizational capabilities.

'There is only one more room available here. It is next to ours. Rashid says that you may take it. It is not expensive: just over four pounds per night. I'm afraid there are no other lodging places in the town. You may look at the room before you decide ... er ... er ... it's not exactly the Ritz ... er, we are ...'

'Tell him I'll take it. As far as accommodation is concerned my situation can only improve. Tell him I am very grateful – and tell yourself too. You have been very kind.'

'Yes, of course. Ah, here is our tea. First we shall take our refreshment. I daresay you need it.'

Rashid stood alongside their table and placed a battered but elaborately designed enamel teapot next to Brenda's elbow. By its side he placed a bowl that was heaped with roughly shaped lumps of grey sugar, and two glasses. Leslie spoke rapidly to Rashid who took Brenda's suitcase with him as he disappeared through the beaded exit.

'I have asked him to telephone the Palm d'Or to give them your whereabouts. He has taken your case up to your room.' Leslie pushed a glass towards Brenda. 'Shall I be mother?'

Brenda thought that he could be whoever he liked as far as she was concerned. She mused on the excess of sugar, no milk either. 'I suppose they are short of dairy products here. So few fields. So very little grass. Poor cows.' Brenda's breasts heaved a sigh of satisfaction; she longed for a cup of tea. She watched Leslie hold the pot some height from her glass. 'How affected,' she thought.

Her thoughts turned to anguish as a stream of pale, yellowish-green liquid sprayed from the narrow spout and spilled into the glass set before her. She watched Leslie repeat the performance as he served himself. It was almost as if he were urinating in front of her.

'You don't look at all well.' Leslie plopped three lumps of sugar into his glass as he made his observation. 'Perhaps you should rest; you might have overdone things a little.'

He raised his glass and sipped and Brenda thought that she might faint. 'Mm-mmm-mm – most refreshing – it's drunk all the time here – good for the digestion too.'

Brenda thought of Mahatma Gandhi but remained

speechless. 'Are you quite sure that you are all right?' Leslie noted that Brenda's normally sallow complexion had turned a very light shade of grey. He sipped a little more from his glass.

'It's mint.'

'It's what?'

'It's mint. It's mint tea. Do try a little. It will make you feel better – take my word for it.'

The aroma from her glass banished all Brenda's fears of contracting jaundice. She took three lumps of sugar, stirred the liquid thoroughly and tasted a tear-drop of the beverage; then she cast all caution aside and swallowed a mouthful. The result was a happy surprise.

'Lovely, just like peppermint cordial. My mother drank it in her later years.' She sipped again. 'It is a soothing drink. I'm already beginning to like it. Although, I've never taken to marmalade.'

'Marmalade?'

'Yes, I've never liked it.'

'How very curious, neither have I.' Leslie was pleased to hear that he had at least one thing in common with this huge woman in a garish frock who sat opposite him.

Brenda raised her glass and pointed it in the direction of the Coca-Cola picture.

'Do I recognize that woman? Is it Betty Grable?'

'She's of that period – glorious technicolor – breathtaking cinemascope – stereophonic sound.'

'Oh, I loved those films.' Brenda spoke with the utmost sincerity and conviction.

'I don't think it's Betty Grable,' Leslie averred. 'It is a "Betty" though.'

'Hutton! It's Betty Hutton,' Brenda declared triumphantly.

'I think that you are right.' Leslie finished his tea and smiled. This companion had put him in mind of a mammoth version of Esther Williams. Did she swim just as well? She was in technicolor. He stood.

'And now, if you will excuse me, I usually take a walk about this time, *je me promène un peu*. You will probably want to take a rest. Rashid provides food at any time. His wife rarely leaves the kitchen. I've so much enjoyed meeting you. I'm Leslie Langley.' He thrust his hand forward and found that it was quickly wholly covered in Brenda's great palm.

'I'm Brenda Stoneham,' she boomed.

He paused and turned in the doorway as if he were going to say something – but only managed to nod and smile. Brenda amazed herself by her inventive spontaneity – she raised her glass of mint tea and silently toasted him as he left.

Brenda sat sipping her mint tea and spent more than an hour in peaceful, reflective self-questioning. She wondered if she had met Leslie before. There was something familiar about the inflection and modulation of his voice, his gestures, and yes, even his facial expressions. She wondered if Rashid's wife enjoyed spending most of her life in the kitchen. She wondered what Leslie's wife was like – why hadn't she chosen to accompany him on his walk? Perhaps she was an invalid? She wondered why she felt safe and secure in this place . . . in this place . . . she wondered if they sold lottery tickets here . . . she had seen a photograph of a hopelessly crippled man holding up a cheque that would change his life. A lottery prize . . . she would sell her own prizes when she got back – she had no real use for them. She wondered why her sister never complained when her husband stayed out all night . . . again she wondered why there were so many homeless people in England when everyone was supposed to be better off ... home – she wondered what her room was like and answered this question by rising from the bench and calling out, 'Rashid. Rashid.'

The beads that stood in place of a door rattled and Rashid stood before her, smilingly awaiting a bidding. Brenda smiled back and frantically searched her imagination for a mime that would convey (a) she would like to see her room, and (b) she wished to use the lavatory. Ought not the whole world be taught sign language?

'I spick English. A little English I spick.' Rashid drew encouragement from the relief reflected in Brenda's expression. 'Follow. Follow me. Follow me. This way follow please. You know Bobby Robson? This way please.'

She followed him up a narrow flight of stone steps on to a landing. At the end of the landing were two doors adjacent to each other. Rashid ushered her into the one whose door had been left slightly ajar. It was a room whose narrowness would not allow two well-made people to stand side by side. It was the kind of room that might have been allocated to a live-in barperson as part wages. An employee in such circumstances might well have sought a salary increase ... but Brenda was more than satisfied.

The bedroom's main feature was an uncurtained glass door which led out on to a small balcony; beyond this was the shore ... and the sea. Brenda noted that one chair and one small table left little space on the balcony for anything else. The room possessed one three-quarter-sized bed and a wire clothes-line.

As if to offer his prospective tenant encouragement Rashid prodded the bed which gave out sounds that might have discouraged a honeymoon couple.

'You like it?'

'Oh yes, perfect.' Brenda saw that her suitcase had been left near the glass door. 'Oh God,' she thought, 'how do you ask for the lavatory in mime?' Should she point to her bottom and then crouch, or perhaps be more discreet and make hand-washing movements?

'Follow please.' Brenda obeyed Rashid's imperative. He seemed to have a second sense with regard to his customer's immediate needs.

She was shown a toilet and a shower which were situated on either side of the short landing space. Both the utilities answered the human need in the most simple and unsparing way. The shower-room held a water tap and a bucket which was attached to a rope. The rope was connected to a pulley-wheel.

'To take a shower,' Rashid demonstrated, 'water in bucket – so. Pull up bucket on rope – so.'

When the bucket reached the top of the pulley it tipped its contents into another bucket that was fixed to the wall. The base of this bucket was patterned with holes. Rashid pointed to the gentle spray of water and was self-congratulatory with regard to his own ingenuity.

'It is good, yes?'

'Yes,' Brenda agreed, 'I've never seen anything like it.'

Nor had she seen anything like the hole-in-the-floor lavatory but this did not delay her from achieving a successful squatting position without any ill effect to her person.

Back in her room, Brenda felt the need of a rest more than external cleanliness and chose to lie on her bed rather than test the efficiency of the shower. She reached out and touched the walls of her room. Their solidity seemed to offer both comfort and privacy.

'I can walk naked in this room,' she thought. 'Nobody can see me from the sea. If they did see me it would have to be through binoculars or a powerful telescope. I don't care if they do see me through a telescope.' She took off her knickers and unleashed her brassière. 'Oh, that feels better.' She opened her case. 'I'll put them in the plastic bag and perhaps wash a few smalls later. Smalls?' She took her nightdress from the case and held it to her body. 'I've not had a chance to wear it yet.' She addressed the large cotton garment. 'I hate pastel colours. They are so half-hearted, half-baked. Nothing cheerful about them.' She struggled into the gown which flowed freely about her ankles. Now she was shrouded in bright yellow and speckled all over with a gorgeous design of red poppies.

The bed sighed as it accepted Brenda's weight; like most beds it carried secret history and information which it would never divulge. It was now past midday and Brenda was greatly relieved by the breeze from the sea that wafted through the open doorway.

She breathed in deeply, closed her eyes and listened to the gentle murmuring of the approaching breakers. She joined them in their murmurings.

'Perhaps I could take a swim later in the week. I'm a good swimmer. No, I will not swim. I vowed I wouldn't. I made a vow. Did I bring my costume? I don't think that I did . . . funny that I should think of work at this time, in this place . . . work . . . work . . . it seems a lifetime away . . . I thought that was all past but it is all with me . . . now in this room.

'I suppose I always had to be grown-up; childhood was a luxury my mother couldn't afford to offer me. There was no way that my mother could afford to keep me and my sister on a widow's pension and she got a job in a munitions factory for the last couple of years of the war. She worked on the night-shift and, for the most part, the domestic arrangements of our household were left to me. I suppose if I had been a smaller child the jobs I undertook might have drawn some comment, but I looked fifteen when I was twelve and my periods had started before I was eleven. It was my biggest secret while I was in junior school.

'School. I was always ahead of everybody else and my teacher was over the moon when I passed for my grammar. I was the first girl in our town to win a place ... and the first girl to refuse one. This was just after the war had ended and most of the women like my mother were laid off from work. I remember her words. "Women can only do jobs as good as men when men tell them they can. I suppose they'll want us to knit now. Knitting and breeding – that's what will be asked of us now."

'She was bitter about this. Later she managed to claw some work ... cleaning offices until the early hours of the morning. Very badly paid it was ... so I left school at fifteen just to earn my keep. I can see that advertisement now ... "a strong young woman would be preferred". I applied for and got a job in what was called the severe-case section of a training centre for physically and mentally handicapped children. Dear God, I needed to be strong. Apart from anything else I was forever bending and lifting. And just caring was exhausting. If it did bring satisfaction then it brought just as much fatigue to balance things out.

'My mother and me ... we weren't really like mother and daughter ... we were more like friends ... even sisters. It was as though my younger sister was our baby, not my father's child. Oh, our Moira had lots of childhood. I still don't see her as an adult.

'When I was just over twenty I was accepted as an instructor in the main part of the training centre. Our supervisor, Mrs Slater, was a kind woman who at one time had trained as a nurse. As far as the children were concerned she insisted on what she called "social training". "Hopefully some children may take their true place in the world . . . but even if they are ready to enter it . . . it is not ready to accept them." She was a woman who sighed a lot. They were good years working with her.

'My sister married at nineteen and it left me and my mother together. Oh, we did enjoy each other's company so much . . . it was never dull. We were both fond of the cinema; sometimes we went to the pictures as often as twice a week . . . and books. Books. Not only did we read them . . . but we'd talk about them to one another. George Eliot and Mrs Gaskell were her favourite writers . . . "They can make you laugh and they can make you cry . . . what else is there? Oh yes, they can make you think." She was ever so disappointed when she found out that Mrs Gaskell had been married to a vicar. She didn't like vicars as they always came on the wireless after the morning story. She said they ruined the atmosphere of what had gone before. "I have to hover over that set like a bloody moth in order to switch it off in time."

'Oh, I do miss her so much.'

Brenda opened her eyes feeling vulnerable and still, even now, in her mid-fifties . . . orphaned. Her eyes opened wider when she saw the ornamentation on the wall. She must have been too tired to notice them before. They were really lovely – so life-like and such bright, pretty colours. She thought it was a pity there were not three. There were three wild geese flying over the mantelpiece at home. Her mother had adored them. The geese weren't so well painted as these two crocodiles. Or were they newts or lizards?

Brenda half-raised her head and shoulders from the pillow to examine the emerald green figures more closely – as the bed creaked the figures seemed to vanish. There was now no trace of them. She stared at the blank wall. Had she seen the figures? Imagined them? Dreamed them? She was grateful to sink back on the pillow ... she sank back with all her weight ... further and further into the comfort of the bed ... back ... back.

In her mind it was now 1971, a year that had promised a new future but turned out to be a year that offered disappointment and low self-esteem. Brenda consciously sought to thrust the year from her mind ... she needed sleep ... but the year thrust itself into her brain, the memory of it enveloped her, and in order to expel it she spoke into the pillow.

'It was the year that training centres became recognized as schools. We were all glad of this as we knew that no child was ineducable ... hadn't many of us, in our small ways, already proved this? Overnight, Mrs Slater changed from being a supervisor to a head-teacher and I became a teacher, not an instructor. It was funny for us as we had always felt that we were teachers all along ... there were any numbers of courses which we all had to attend. The word "status" cropped up a lot and our welcome to the official world of education was publicly celebrated but professionally muted.

'I changed from being a qualified instructor to an unqualified teacher. Mrs Slater retired two or three years after the change-over and the new head-teacher actively encouraged the older unqualified teachers to leave.

'By 1980, I was the only one left and at fifty, I was the oldest adult working in that building. Young teachers came and went – sometimes as many as three in a term. I was no longer left in charge of a class. I was called on to assist countless other teachers in the organization of the day. I felt like a servant, not a teacher ... and what had once been an exciting working week now became a wearying, worrying one.

'Over a period of time, I ceased to expect any praise from Mrs Patterson, our new head-teacher. She had been studiously unaware of my existence since her arrival. Two days after my fiftieth birthday ... "Brenda, you could apply for early retirement if you wished ... you might enjoy the autumn years of your life at home. It must be such a struggle looking after your mother ... all those years ... what a sacrifice."

'I said, "It's not a struggle looking after my mother, Mrs Patterson. I do not look after her. We look after one another. It is no sacrifice being with her. She is a good friend who happens also to be my mother."

'"Ah, Brenda, you're not telling me that you have never had marriage offers ... I've always firmly believed there's a man for every woman."

'I said, "I've never sought any marriage offers. I have no complaint about the single state."

'"Marriage might have widened your experience."

'"I know some whose experience has been narrowed by it."

'Two months after this exchange Mrs Patterson dealt her final blow ... if you could call it that: she said that she was putting me to better use. I was timetabled for swimming – not for one afternoon, not for one morning, but for the whole week. Except for Friday afternoons, I spent my time escorting children to the swimming-baths and clambering in and out of the pool, and in and out of my swimming costume. I stank of chlorine and the coach drivers and swimming-baths employees referred to me as "Brenda the Blue Whale". I appealed to that woman.

'I said, "I'm sorry, it really is too much for me, Mrs Patterson. One day a week, perhaps, yes ... but not ... but not every day. I seem to be riddled with cold and I'm getting backache, real low-back pain ... with terrible spasms and ..."

'"Oh Brenda, the swimming is good for you ... just diet and lose some weight. That is the source of your back pain. Your weight. Your size. Frankly, a woman of your size is bound to have problems."

'"Yes, and you are the biggest of them."

'"Miss Stoneham!"

'"Mrs Patterson, give me an application form."

'I snatched the form from her hands and applied for the early retirement deal that very morning. After a few months it was granted and I left a year later. In my last year I refused to swim again, and in that period I held my mother in my arms as she died from rapid throat cancer. I've never thought about Mrs Patterson until now. I thought she had gone from me ... all thoughts of her ... recollections I could do without ...'

They were back, the lizards had returned ... they were so beautiful. Brenda closed her eyes seeking to retain the image, fearful that any movement might signify their disappearance. From conscious dreaming she seemed to be floating – or was it sinking? – into ... into a vast space ... so much space was all about her ... so much space all about her.

Her huge form moved with effortless agility, speed and grace. She delighted in her own body and fanned the water with her great broad tail. Sometimes she let her dorsal fin feel the air but she was always drawn back to the inviting depths of the sea below which offered her a freedom not available elsewhere.

Other creatures moved from her path and stared with glazed eyes, marvelling at her gigantic, elegant, swift progress. Even travelling at this great rate she found that she could bend and glide and change direction at will. The deeper she travelled, the more murky the light. Just at the point where she might have encountered darkness a small cod crossed her path. It turned and stared, as if anticipating some response from her. Its face bore all the familiar outlines of Mrs Patterson: the set of the mouth, those cold, dark blue eyes . . . eyes that had glared at her with such deadening effect.

The encounter was brief. It ended with one snap of Brenda's great jaws . . . the rancid taste caused her to choke and retch, and she began to make her way upwards towards the light, towards the air . . . the air . . . the air . . . air. For some reason the journey back seemed slow. Her meal seemed to have added great weight to her so that her progress was turgid. She struggled and made greater efforts to surface but the light seemed to get further away. Her mouth had become dry and had begun to fill with bile which trickled from her great jaws and . . .

The call of the muezzin, the harsh, plaintive tone, which reminded Brenda of the iniquities inflicted on Apache Indians in Hollywood Western films, summoned the Islamic faithful to pray and ended Brenda's journey into the unconscious.

She stretched and checked that her hands were not flippers or fins, laughed to herself and walked the few strides that took her on to the balcony. The sun suspended itself in a sky that reflected shades of red and apricot on to the sea. The tides had brought a welcoming, warm, gentle breeze which caused Brenda's nightdress to flap about the calves of her legs.

Westward she could see the Palm d'Or Club and she was relieved that its barbaric sounds could no longer reach her. Below her, on the shale, the club had managed to export a detritus of its charm. A broken deck-chair, empty plastic bottles of sun-tan lotion, lager cans, a deflated lilo and discarded condoms had been delivered.

A large sheet of canvas separated Brenda's balcony from her neighbours' in the next room and it was impossible to view the eastward scene without a hazardous attempt at leaning over the balcony wall. Brenda sat on her chair and breathed in the ozone. After a few minutes of yoga-like relaxation she realized the lateness of the hour. Where had the day gone? In journeys and dreams? In spite of the pseudo-spiritual tones of her reflection she became suddenly aware of her hunger. Fresh bread, tomatoes, hard-boiled eggs all entered the joys of her appetite – even cold chicken. But not fish, not fish – this was odd as she was very partial to most fish, even coley.

As she turned away from the balcony's edge Brenda heard voices from the other side of the canvas. She remained still when she recognized Leslie Langley's dulcet speaking-tone. For some reason she felt no guilt with regard to this eavesdropping: his delivery sounded to her like a quiet broadcaster . . . she was just a listener.

'I think I must have been spellbound by you . . . I know that I could not leave your presence . . . I made that half-a-bitter last the hour . . . I hadn't the money to buy another drink. I remember the beer had gone flat and its temperature had become tepid, so it was easy to take small sips from the glass.'

Brenda tried to imagine Leslie's facial expression.

She wondered what his wife looked like; she must be small or there wouldn't be room for the two of them on the balcony. Was she listening attentively? Was she sitting on his lap?

Brenda thought that now she ought to move, that she was eavesdropping, that she was invading someone else's privacy beyond all fairness. Yet, it was not as though she were going to make public anything that she overheard. She would not interrupt anything, she would not intrude, she absolved herself from all further moral implications of her behaviour by pretending that she was listening to the radio.

'I had not noticed you standing at the bar. There was no plotting of how to open up a conversation with you. I had turned quickly after collecting my beer, and you called me back. "Your change. You've forgotten your change." A shilling or sixpence was not treated cursorily in those times and I took the money from the beer-mat near your elbow. It was chance, pure chance that took me into that pub. I had called in there on my way home from the cinema. It was one of my obsessions – no, addictions would be more apt. Not the cinema. It was the star of the film I always had to see . . . yes, I had to see her in everything she did.

'It was Jeanne Moreau who drew me to her like some powerful drug. The drug culture of the sixties never touched me; at that time I could not even bear to be within yards of a cigarette, but as far as she was concerned, I was well and truly hooked. Nothing could stop me from going to see her.

'There were so many picture-houses in London then and, usually, Jeanne could be found somewhere in the city. The film had been about compulsive gambling and there were several close-ups of her face which – even when it smiled or expressed exuberance – held a degree of disdain. Or was it the hint of universal comprehension?

'I was not ignorant of that pub. I knew that it was the kind of place where, if you caught someone's gaze long enough, it might mean a quick conversation which ended in a swift sexual encounter. Previous to seeing you, I had sat with my eyes downcast, like some novice in a seminary. Someone had said, "Cheer up," and I had replied without looking up, "I'm not down. I'm not unhappy." You see, my thoughts were still with Jeanne Moreau . . . and when, at your bidding, I turned to collect my change, I looked fully into your eyes.

'"Is anything the matter?" you asked. And still, I couldn't speak nor could I avert my eyes from looking at you. There was no doubting the striking resemblance. The dark eyes which held fatigue and excitement, the shadows beneath the eyes and the full lips that turned contemptuously downwards to form the most perfect arc.

'"Are you sure that you are all right?" you asked. You seemed bemused by my astonished state.

'"I've been to the pictures." I remember blurting out the words. "It was a Jeanne Moreau film called *Baie des Anges*. She was a gambler."

'"Aren't we all. Aren't we all gamblers?" you asked.

'I said, "Has anyone ever told you that you look like her? She wore a blonde wig in the film – of course her hair might have been dyed but I think it was a wig."

'You said, "No one has ever said that I resembled Jeanne Moreau and I have never dyed my hair or worn a wig." But then, you behaved as I imagined you might behave.

'"We don't want another drink here. Shall we go to your place? I have a room near here if you live too far away but I've no milk. It tends to go off so quickly in my

room. I suppose we could drink water – I've nothing
else."

'"I'm not far away," I replied.

'You joined me and we walked in unison from that
place as if we had known each other for years, not
minutes.'

The noise of the sea breaking over the rocks and
shale had now grown louder. Its insistent action and
closer proximity began to drown some of Leslie's
quietly-spoken but alarming conversation. Brenda
strained to hear above the sound of the breakers and
the tide but had to be satisfied with a telegrammatic
narrative that was similar to a jigsaw puzzle with
missing pieces. She could not get a complete picture . . .
this did not deter her from crouching on her haunches
so that her ear could be closer to the canvas screen. 'His
wife must be very forward,' she thought. 'Brazen even.'
It was the sort of behaviour you might expect from a
tart, yet Leslie didn't seem the type of man who would
be interested in that kind of woman.

'"I don't take sugar in my tea." You pulled a terrible
face after one gulp. I thought that your expression was
exaggerated. You looked at me as though I had tried to
poison you. You pushed the cup from you and
demanded that I rinse it thoroughly before refilling it
with tea. "That's better," you said, "I'm not a sweet
person. Did you think that I was a sweet person?"

'You looked at me . . . then at your watch. "It's
stopped," you said. Not that it mattered.'

Brenda placed one hand over her mouth as if to stifle
a response. The sea was noisier now, closer, and
Brenda strained to hear some words from Leslie's wife.
The water's murmurings were so prominent that she
heard little; what she did hear came from Leslie.

'It did not seem impulsive. I felt that I had known

you always . . . we were living together three days after we had just met . . . barely parted company . . . you had so few things with you . . . you to look more like Jeanne Moreau . . . instead of auburn your hair turned out bright orange and you raged at me . . . said I had caused you to look like Woody Woodpecker . . . you called Jean an "unnatural hag" . . . and she laughed . . . the assessment was not altogether unfair . . . I think my father loved you more than I did . . . and you didn't believe in cleaning . . . those fleas . . . the man came round from the Public Health for the third time and he . . . so many men coming and going . . . it didn't seem as though he was with us all that time . . . eight years . . . why New Zealand? . . . so sexually demanding . . . three of us for eight years . . . she is a huge woman . . . colourful . . . strong jaw . . . soft large . . . I do like her . . . washed up on the shore . . . Ahmed . . . still here after all these years . . . on the bus . . . luggage . . . properly married now . . . you said . . . he fucked you for so long . . . so hard . . . that you thought your head was going to fall off and . . . we laughed about . . . Esther Williams and Betty Hutton . . . caring professions treated like delinquents . . . do they want everyone to open fish and chip shops and . . . it's Brenda Stoneham . . . very broad . . . Boadicea cut off her left breast so that she could shoot a bow . . . a rumour . . . there are some amazing queens . . . so many, being so brave . . . know how to die . . . AIDS . . . given them back a self-esteem . . . a terrible adversity turned upside down by its sufferers . . . what a history . . . feel privileged to . . . Ian, David, Martin, Danny . . . Steve . . . never thought I'd be nursing my own brothers . . . being over fifty is becoming an achievement . . . history . . . in . . . don't like . . . cropped hair.'

Brenda took advantage of the next noisy breaker to

crawl back into her room. She stood near her bed and listened to her stomach plead for food. Feeling guilty but excited, she tiptoed from the room and made her way swiftly down the stone stairway. She parted the bead curtains and entered the café.

Three men were playing a noisy game of dominoes at the table beneath the Betty Hutton picture. They looked in her direction with a momentary stare which betokened acceptance rather than curiosity, then they recommenced banging their dominoes on the table.

Rashid was at her side before she was barely seated. How did he manage to know if someone came into his café? Could he sense their presence even if they were in another room? Or was it that privacy was of little importance in this place? Brenda wondered if Leslie's wife wore make-up. If so, had time been kind to her looks? Would she look ravaged? She damn well ought to.

'You rest well? You take some sleep?'

'Yes, yes, Rashid. Yes to all you ask. I feel much better. Much better.'

'You take food now?'

'Ah yes, yes please. I would like to order some ... ' Before Brenda could ask for boiled eggs or rolls he had gone.

She felt no exasperation. She would eat whatever was placed before her. Rashid would not, could not possibly, give her marmalade – and her hunger was such that anything else that was edible would hold enchantment.

Brenda recognized the voice even though it spoke in rapid French, she bowed her head and studied the pattern on the plastic tablecloth. She heard the beaded curtain rattle and felt flutterings of anticipation in her stomach that were not connected with appetite.

'Can I join you? Would you mind?'

'I'd be delighted,' Brenda replied and looked up to greet Leslie.

'It's not that I dislike being alone, I am just not fond of eating alone. There is something inhuman about it and I have eaten alone for the past few days.'

'But your wife ...' Brenda caught her breath and closed her lips, and then managed to say, 'I had thought you were accompanied.'

'No, I am here by myself. I'm quite alone. And I have never been married.'

'Neither have I,' said Brenda.

'I never felt the need for it; it would not have been right for me. Perhaps not moral even. It was never a consideration.'

'Nor to me,' Brenda concurred and wondered why she felt so at ease sitting with this man who now reminded her of a male version of 'Old Mother Riley', with a posh accent. It was also a relief to meet someone else who talked to themselves aloud.

She watched him remove an earthenware, pyramid-shaped covering from a platter. It revealed a mountain of something which looked like rice and had at its peak a crater of meat and vegetables. It was not what Brenda's hunger had dreamed up for its appeasement but its aroma caused her to breathe in deeply and smile with satisfaction.

'It is *tajine* – a kind of lamb stew or goat stew. I'm sure that you will enjoy it,' Leslie declared. 'We have fresh dates and an orange to follow. Arabic cuisine manages to combine the simple with the exotic.'

Brenda was happy to take Leslie's word for it. She had noticed that from time to time he edged towards pomposity. Or was it formality? What he had said on the balcony was far from pompous in content but he had expressed it in formal tones. But was she not supposed to have heard it ... or was she?

'This is very good.' Brenda swallowed a third mouthful of food and felt replenished. 'It is very good, Leslie, very good indeed.'

Before the main course was entirely finished the two had lightly exchanged some autobiographical details. There were some similarities. Both had entered the working world early. Both were employed in the 'caring' professions – teacher and nurse. Both had retired early.

Leslie: 'I was made to feel ancient at fifty. The words "trends" and "style" began to make me feel sick, and who wants a sick nurse?'

Brenda: 'I felt redundant before I applied for redundancy. I was made to feel useless.'

Leslie: 'One felt guilty for having experience, and experience was often called cynicism.'

Brenda: 'Children were often referred to as "kids". I know that I could never have been a "kid".'

Leslie: 'I still do voluntary nursing two days a week but with my own kind; not relatives but my own kind.'

Brenda: 'I still visit some of my ex-pupils ... at the day centre ... one of them is nearly as big as me and ...'

Quite suddenly, Brenda's fork dropped from between her fingers and clattered on to the almost empty plate before her. Leslie watched her complexion change from its usual sallow, brownish hue to ashen-grey. He noted the anguished expression about her eyes and mouth, and saw the dark brown eyes cast downwards as if to examine some alien that had invaded her body. The look of anguish now changed to terror. Leslie watched as Brenda clapped a great hand over the bottom part of her face. She seemed to be entering some kind of panic or shame that was of enormous magnitude.

'What is it? What is it, Brenda? Brenda, my dear, what is it?'

It must have been the small term of endearment that Leslie used which gave Brenda's speech back to her. The voice she used was a small one. It was pathetic and child-like. 'I'm still in my nightdress. Whatever will Rashid... and ... and the others here think of me?' Brenda stared down at the table as she spoke; her eyes could not look about her immediate world. 'I'm so ashamed. I'm so sorry, Leslie... to let you down in this way. What must you think of...' She felt his hand rest upon her arm. The gesture both calmed and restrained her.

'Brenda ... Brenda ... Brenda, my dear,' Leslie chortled affectionately. 'Your nightdress is perfectly in order here – in fact, more in order – your mode of dress is more seemly here because it covers more of you. Many women wear shifts that are similar. Yours is – er – er – er – just a little more westernized, that's all. I do assure you, your clothing is giving no cause for concern to anyone. Why, Rashid's wife is dressed exactly as you are – er – er – but without the colours.' He patted her arm consolingly as he spoke.

Leslie's assurances acted like some kind of imme-diate absolution on Brenda who looked up from the table and smiled broadly at him.

'Thank you, Leslie. How silly of me. You know, if I had not known your past employment, I might have thought that you were a vicar. It must be your manner of speaking; it's not your choice of words.'

'I was interested in it all at one time. Pious words do tend to slip into my vocabulary. I have no belief now. Organized Christianity gets more and more like an enormous media operation. No, I don't have any belief, but I am constantly bewildered. I suppose bewilderment is a belief.'

'My mother was an atheist. I think that I am too much of a coward to be that. Yes, you are right ... I prefer bewilderment too ... I can't be told ...' Brenda's observations were cut short by three heavy thumping sounds that came from the men sitting at the other table.

'They are laying their hands. Dominoes are played with tremendous flair and flourish here – one could say with passion.' Leslie paused to remove an irritant piece of gristle from between his teeth. 'Have you? Have you had a passion, Brenda? Have you had a lover?'

'No, I have not. Not ever. I have experienced orgasm only at my own hand ... and I wasn't greatly satisfied with that.'

She began to laugh quietly, and Leslie laughed with her. 'But that does not mean that I have not loved ... I have loved people ...' Now Brenda knew who Leslie reminded her of. She bit into a date and placed the stone of the fruit on her plate ... she was now eager to share her recollection with Leslie.

'There were two of them – two handsome young men. You could even say that they were beautiful.'

'Good Lord, Brenda,' Leslie exclaimed. 'Not both at the same time?'

'Yes, almost always I saw them together. Always together. In our town, at that time, young people moved in groups. The groups were sexually segregated. Groups of young men and groups of young women would tour the town in packs, and then it was accepted that certain individuals had broken from the pack. It was then announced that the paired couple were "courting".

'There was a status to this position. I could never

hope to achieve it as I never joined a group. I was never allowed to. You see, all the young women thought that my size would put off any would-be suitors or followers. I believe both groups, the men and the women, regarded me as some kind of joke, a freak, or both.'

'Mm-mmm-mm. People can be very unkind if they think that you are in any way different,' Leslie muttered with great certainty of tone. 'But your two men? Were they in any of the groups?'

'No. Never. Oh, there were any number of girls who would have been more than happy to court with them but they would smile and nod and remain apart.'

'Just as you were apart?'

'Not really. You see, they chose to be apart. I had no choice. I was excluded by my great size. With them, my physical being didn't seem to matter. In fact, they celebrated it.'

'Celebrated it?'

'Oh, yes ... do you remember ... sometime during the early fifties ... the nation was urged to involve itself in something called the Festival of Britain?'

'I remember a little of it – I had been in London for just over a year. There was something called the Skylon put up near the Thames. It looked like a great big cigar or an outsize incendiary bomb. I can't remember joining in any jubilations.'

'We had a pageant in our area.' Brenda spoke enthusiastically. 'It was preceded by a grand parade through the town. All the surrounding villages in the Trent valley were represented and there were good prizes on offer for all the best floats. It was at this time that I got to know Colin and Don really well. That's what the two of them were called – Don and Colin. Colin's father was a coal-haulage contractor, so we had a lorry at our disposal for the event.'

'What was the theme?' Leslie asked, half interestedly.

'Well, I think it was supposed to be patriotic but Colin said that the three of us should take pride in being ourselves. He would often go on in this way, as he wanted to be an actor. It was Colin who decided that I should be Astarte.'

'Who?'

'Astarte. She was the goddess of fertility and love, and guardian of sailors and seafarers. Colin and Don were to be the sacred prostitutes of the temple ... they offered succour to those at sea.'

'I'll bet they did,' said Leslie.

'Of course, on our entrance form we just put "Britannia and her Attendants" or they wouldn't have accepted us. It was such a happy, happy time for me.'

Brenda's expression had softened and Leslie perceived a modulation in her voice that came close to rapture.

'For the five weeks leading up to the carnival the three of us could often be seen walking around the town together. Sometimes we linked arms and the other girls were stunned into gawping and gaping at the attention that I was receiving.'

'You didn't pair off with one of them? You didn't make a choice?' Leslie had now given the narrative his full attention – or, rather, the narrative had demanded it.

'Oh no,' Brenda replied airily. 'Choice did not enter it at all. That would have ruined everything.' She paused. 'You see, that was the only way that they could let their hands touch in public – by touching each other behind my back. In a way I was a camouflage to their ...' Brenda seemed to search for the right word.

Leslie suggested, 'Romance?'

Brenda shook her head. 'No, it was more than that; it was an attachment. An unassailable alignment. My mother would welcome them both to our house and all four of us would sit and talk while we made our decorations for the lorry and organized my costume. The two of them were always polite and would dutifully kiss my mother and me on the cheek before they left.'

'Did you ... or did your mother ... did either of you ... er ...' Leslie coughed, not from a dry or sore throat but from the phrasing of a question he thought might embarrass Brenda.

'Did either of you know they were homo?' Brenda interrupted without any thought for Leslie's awkwardness. 'My mother would never have used that word but she told me that "they were the other way". I prefer it to "gay", don't you?'

'I've never heard it before,' Leslie laughed with relief. 'It doesn't hold any ambiguities, I'll say that for it. Were the three of you a success?'

'We went beyond that. There was a photograph of us on the front page of the local paper. It said that we were a revelation. It said that we represented the epitome of all original, artistic endeavours. We won the first prize.'

'What was the source of your originality?'

'Well, Colin refused to offer any sops to sentimentality or pander to popular appeal; so our float was not overcrowded with small children or overdressed girls waving at relatives or friends. There was just the three of us. Colin referred to us as a weird *pietà*; we were all in silver, grey, blue and gold. We had borrowed a wheelchair from the Old People's Home and it was mounted and fixed on a rostrum, and I sat there with my crown and trident, my shoulders back, my head held high. Colin said that my role demanded perfect posture.'

'You still have it,' said Leslie.

'Apart from swimming briefs – I mean *briefs* – Colin and Don were quite naked. Their bodies were decorated with silver, gold and blue spangles. And, what was most daring – they had managed to dye their hair a pale shade of green. Colin said that they were sea-nymphs who had rejected gender. He was full of that sort of stuff but . . . but I'm telling you Leslie . . . when the other floats went past the crowds cheered and clapped. When we went by they were silent.'

'Shocked, I suppose?'

'No, awestruck,' Brenda replied with such finality that Leslie accepted her description of the reception without question. 'You remind me of them, Leslie.'

'I envy them, or at least I envy that period of their lives. I never went back home after I had completed my national service in the RAF. My mother wept and my father shouted when they found out that I was . . . that I was the other way. My father said that I was no son of his and my mother said that she didn't want any trouble on the doorstep, so I became parentless even though my parents were alive.'

'Oh Leslie, how could they do such a thing?'

'Quite easily, it seemed. It wasn't an unusual experience for people like me. Still, now, it's not that unusual for . . .' Leslie stopped talking as Brenda had begun to chuckle.

The insensitivity seemed out of keeping and he stared in silent astonishment as her chuckle rumbled on. It soon burst all boundaries and exploded into deep peals of laughter which came up from her stomach and shook her great frame. She rocked to and fro as the mirth infected her. The domino-players stopped their game. Rashid stood near the bar counter. Leslie sat bolt upright.

As Brenda rocked forward she managed to speak a little in between gasps and spasms of laughter. 'Leslie ...oh...ah...Leslie...oh...I've been sitting here... sitting here...sitting here all this time...and...ah... ah...and...I'm not wearing...not wearing...any knickers...'

She then continued to laugh, as did the domino-players, as did Leslie. Rashid moved from the bar and hovered around their table. As the laughter slowly subsided he made an announcement: 'It is good. It is good that you are all happy.'

Brenda and Leslie nodded a generous agreement to his innocent appraisal of their present state. Both of them realized that good companionship was more rare than common – and for them, far more satisfying than any holiday romance.

Leslie and Brenda accepted their joint social patterns over the next few days with very little reflection. After their breakfast, they would leave the café and make a short tour of the small town. They would return to the Café des Ramparts for a light lunch and they would spend the heat of the early afternoon in their own separate rooms.

Before sundown they would re-emerge, almost as if they had answered some inner signalling. Then, they would walk along the coastline in the opposite direction from the Palm d'Or Club. In fact, Brenda had all but forgotten that the place existed. She and Leslie saw no one from the club during their walks. The members of the club, like most conformists, could not imagine or recognize an existence away from their boundaries and their manners. Brenda was pleased that there was nothing in the town to interest them – what would they have done to the place if they had chosen to invade it?

In spite of the smallness of the town and the familiarity of particular spots, Brenda and Leslie usually managed to lose themselves every morning. They would leave the main dusty roadway, turn left and then pass through the archway that was cut into a high wall. Within minutes they entered a maze-like world of craftsmen and shopkeepers. Social life and business and commerce were all one here.

'In some ways it all reminds me of Tesco's or Sainsbury's.'

'Really, Brenda, how can you say such a thing? The comparison is absurd,' Leslie responded testily.

His occasional lapses into waspish retorts always amused Brenda, so much so that she was often guilty of engineering them.

'How can this,' Leslie encompassed the universe of the narrow street where they stood, with a papal gesture, 'how can this remind you of a supermarket?'

'All the shops in this area sell one thing. Meat. It all looks very fresh.'

'Mm-mmm-mm ... almost too fresh.' Leslie gazed sadly at three sheep tethered to a post outside one of the shops. They seemed to be bleating in foreknowledge of their fate. For their sakes, Leslie hoped that they would not have to wait for too long.

'You see, Leslie, everything that is within the maze is in sections,' Brenda extolled her perception. 'We have just come from the clothing section and now we are amidst the butchery.'

'Yes, yes, I see your point.' Leslie used his arm and forefinger as though it were a car-indicator and they turned to walk through a short alleyway which led them out into yet another narrow street. This street possessed nothing but barbers' shops.

'I wonder if there are hairdressers for women?' Brenda looked about her. 'In fact, Leslie, there are more services available here. You couldn't get a shave in Tesco's could you?'

Leslie shook his head. They wandered around in this way and finally exited from this labyrinthine, ordered world by drifting aimlessly out of it in a purposeless way. On the short walk back to the coast they paused for a time and sat under the welcome shade of an olive tree. Brenda enquired if Leslie minded being alone.

'I don't know; I think I am more used to it now. It is only in these last two years of adulthood that I have experienced it – it is one of the reasons for me being here now. I was last here twenty years ago. I was with him. I suppose revisiting this place alone was a way of coming to terms with the loss of him. Yet it's odd. Sitting here with you ... I don't feel ... I don't feel bereaved. He left so suddenly.'

'Sometimes that is better.' Brenda thought of her mother but said no more.

'He had organized a trip, a day trip to Boulogne. Most of our elderly neighbours had signed up to go on it. In my mean way, I had dreaded the outing – even the thought of travelling on the sea turns my inside green. The coach had arrived on time and he called out everyone's name to check that the company was complete. I did nothing to help him, as I felt somewhat out of place in this company of widows, widowers and elderly married couples. His instinct for neighbour-liness was so great that he would never give such matters a thought. As the coach pulled away some of them began to sing "Mademoiselle from Armentières, Parlez-Vous."'

'Sounds like fun for some,' said Brenda.

'For some,' Leslie sighed and picked some debris from inside a nostril. 'But not for me. We had not gone more than four or five miles when I realized that he had gone very silent. That was unlike him as he had a very talkative nature. I looked at him and saw rivulets of perspiration trickling down his brow and the sides of his face. His pallor had a ghostly look.

'"Get me to the hospital," he whispered. He gripped my arm very tightly and the whites of his knuckles displayed the intensity of his pain and distress. The coach drove up to the nearest casualty department and he was taken straight from the coach into the intensive care unit. Within an hour, he had lost consciousness and less than two hours later he was dead. I had never thought of him as being a likely candidate for a heart-attack. He never smoked and drank little. Later, some of the neighbours gave me presents; they had brought them back from Boulogne . . . they left them with me . . .'

On the far side of the olive grove Brenda watched as three women with scarves swathed about their heads hacked away at the earth, deepening narrow irrigation-channels with strong hoe-like implements. One of the women had some kind of bundle attached to her back. There was a distinct cry; a child's whimper.

'Life goes on,' Brenda muttered. 'Yet it would seem that it is the past that has brought us both here, not the present, nor the future. My father died in this country during the war . . . so long ago. I think my mother would have liked the idea of . . .'

A cluster of donkeys tethered to a nearby tree suddenly set up a furious braying and put an end to the retrospection.

'Are they hungry?' Brenda asked, as she and Leslie took quick flight from their noisy resting-place.

'No, no, I don't think that they are hungry.' Leslie glanced back at the creatures. 'Don't turn around, Brenda, it's nothing to worry about.'

Brenda did turn. And she did look. 'Sexual intercourse is very noisy Leslie, isn't it?'

'It can be, Brenda. It can be,' Leslie replied knowingly.

Later, in the privacy of her room, Brenda pondered over the postcard that she had addressed to her sister. Already she felt guilty for not having written earlier. The guilt seemed to increase on the realization that she had forgotten all about Moira throughout her stay at the Café des Ramparts and now she could think of nothing to say.

More out of duty than inspiration, she wrote: 'The weather has been sunny, the food is good and I have made friends with two people who are very nice. See you soon. Love, Brenda.'

Brenda let the biro drop from her fingers as though she had just completed some exhaustive educational essay. She chided herself for feeling so disconsolate. After all, she had only written a card to her sister; it wasn't as though she had signed away her body for medical research or anything like that. She remembered that form, at this time, and still she had no wish to revoke the instructions. It had been filled in and signed just two weeks before Moira's marriage.

What a drain on their meagre resources all that had been. Their entire savings, hard-earned by Brenda and her mother, had disappeared on the preparations for the wedding, and for the reception.

'Harry's two sisters would like to be bridesmaids, and his mother says that there are three cousins who can't be left out as they are her brother's favourite girls. And, of course, you will be the one representing our side at the altar. I want it to be special. After all, you don't get married every day of your life, do you?'

Brenda and her mother would have been content with a quiet registry office affair but were happy to let Moira have all the trimmings, blessings and recognition that church and state could offer.

Any doubts had been dispersed when Brenda had fingered the pale, sky-blue satin material that was to be made into her bridesmaid's dress. She was to wear a string of pearls about her throat too. She looked forward to her dress-fitting and longed to feel the soft, shiny cloth about her skin ... and then ... and then.

'Harry thinks ... er ... and I do too ... we both think that his brother's two little boys would look gorgeous as pageboys. Er ... er ... erm ... we can't order any more satin at this stage, Brenda ... and er ... I know you won't mind dropping out.'

'Dropping out? Dropping out where?' Brenda had asked awkwardly.

'I mean, we think it's better for you not to be a bridesmaid. There'll be enough material for both boys and probably quite a bit over if you gave up your allocation.' And then Moira had laughed in a nervous way and said, 'Harry says that if you stood at the altar the congregation wouldn't be able to see anybody else ... and it is our day, isn't it, Brenda?'

Brenda had sat at the back of the church, dressed in a plain bottle-green costume-suit. No one's view of the proceedings was obstructed and, apart from the corsage of fern and carnations pinned to her lapel, she might just as well have been attending a conference on developmental milestones. She had felt cold, and it was dank and gloomy. She had turned to sniff the scent of the carnations for comfort. Such pretty flowers ... flowers ... Flowers!

Her reverie now broken, Brenda got up from the chair. She was self-prompted to look for a packet of seeds. Moira had given them to her just before she had left. 'You can't forget these, Brenda. The name on the packet won't let you,' Moira had said.

The packet was still safe and secure in the sleeve of her handbag. 'Forget-me-nots' – such a pretty shade of blue – the same colour as the bridesmaids' dresses.

'Plant them somewhere special. I'm sure Dad would have liked such a little gesture. It's the thought that counts, isn't it?'

'Yes, Moira, the thought counts.' Brenda had taken the seeds from her sister and said nothing more.

Brenda turned the packet over and over with her fingertips, and read and re-read the sowing instructions. Gradually her brain was flooded with angry reverie. 'Liked such a gesture.' He would have liked no such thing. How would Moira know what he would like? He was dead before she was born. Moira had invented him.

'But ... but ... so have I,' Brenda thought. 'It's not fair, it's not fair to my mother ... or to me ... or to me.' Brenda got up slowly and deliberately from the chair and passed through the open doorway and stood on the balcony. She heard Leslie clear his throat so that his presence should be known to her. She knew that he sat not a yard away from her on the other side of the canvas screen.

The sea was still far out; the day was hot, still and silent, with just the hint of intermittent breezes. Brenda tore a corner from the tiny envelope and let the seeds fall into the palm of her hand. She extended her forearm and palm of her hand over the balcony edge and gently cast the seeds from her. She remained standing there, shoulders back, head held high, as though she were involved in some kind of militaristic ritual. She spoke out in low but clear tones, as if relieved to bear witness or give evidence.

'I have told lies, I have told lies, not only to other people but to myself. Pure chance, if chance can be pure, gave me the opportunity for coming here. And if there is a reason for me being here, it is not to remember or honour my father. No, it is to forget him. Exorcise him from my mind.

'That night, the night before he was to leave us for these shores, he had complained about the meal that my mother had set before him. She had prepared a stew. I knew that she had stood for nearly two hours for that bit of rabbit. It tasted good to me – but he was unhappy about it.

'"I come here for two days and you, you cow, you have the fucking gall to put this before me. Why didn't you put a sodding rat in the pot and have done with it?"

'He got up and pushed his chair with such force that it toppled over to the floor. Then he ... he ... he ... he stood behind my mother and ... and pushed her face into the meal that she had prepared. I can hear her pathetic whimpering, "George, George, please ... please ... not in front of Brenda." Bits of food and traces of gravy clung to her hair and face, and she looked as though she had just emerged from some shocking accident. She began to wash her face at the sink and he turned his attention to me.

'"Take no notice of her," he said but I still looked in my mother's direction. I was too afraid to look at him. "How is my little girl?" he asked, and lifted me from my chair and stood me on the table. "Not so little now, are you? You're filling out a bit." I remember his eyes, such a pale brown colour, all but yellow ... and one was blood-shot. They were not the eyes of a father ... but of an animal.

'"Now give your dad a kiss," he ordered. I stood quite still. Something seemed to have happened to me. I could not move, I could not speak, I could scarcely breathe.

'"You are just like your mother," he rasped, and then ... then ... and then he began to stroke my legs with his rough hands. He lifted my dress. "I hope that your knickers are in a better state than your mother's are ... let's have a look at them ..."

'I don't know how she did it, it was as though some power had granted her some unearthly energy ... somehow my mother managed to get herself between me and him. She had pushed this huge man aside; she held a bread-knife. "If you touch that child, I'll swing for you." I remember how quietly she said this.

'"You want to bloody swing, do you?" he shouted. "I'll show you how to swing."

'I saw him punch her heavily in the stomach. I saw her head fall forward on to her chest as she sank to her knees. I saw him clutch at the tresses of her hair. I saw him drag her by the hair from the kitchen and into the front room.

'I stood outside that room. I stood there for what seemed a whole lifetime. I heard what he did to her ... the curses ... the battery ... the injury and violence ... the humiliation ... and the rape. All this took place within the sanctity of marriage ... and my sister ... my sister was conceived in this manner.'

Leslie had taken off his glasses and placed them near to the foot of his chair. He sat with his knees held close together and one hand placed on either shoulder to form a Saint Andrew's cross across his body. Tears welled from his eyes and flowed down his cheeks. One of the reasons why Leslie had been such an excellent nurse was his innate response to the distress of other people. He did not merely feel sorry, or pity other people, he entered their suffering. This was good for them but not necessarily good for him, as he had tended to neglect his own wounds at great personal cost.

'I never saw him leave the next morning. He had left early and I was happy that there was now only me and my mother in the house. For the next few days I had to accept adult responsibilities. I remember how the instructions were instilled into me: if anyone asks, my mother is ill in bed with 'flu. She will be better soon. I paid the milkman, the baker, the rent. I did the shopping. My mother did not leave the house.

'I don't have to close my eyes to recollect those injuries. Her left eye was grotesquely swollen and completely closed. Bruises of red and purple and blue adorned the rest of her face. Her top lip ballooned outwards so that she had difficulty in speaking and her dentures had been broken. We had no meat for a fortnight as he had taken all our ration. "You promise not to tell anyone about this, Brenda. Not ever?" She held me close to her in a feverish way. "You promise?"

'I have kept that promise until now but I am glad that I have broken it. Very glad. I would like to say to my mother, "It was his shame – his shame, not ours."

'Seven or eight months after he had gone she received a letter. It was an official letter – to receive any letter in those days was an event. I stood by her, and she encircled my waist with her arm and drew me closer to her as she absorbed the contents of the typewritten note. She sighed and smiled sadly. Or was it wistfully?

'"Your father is a hero, Brenda. He won't be coming

back to us. He has been killed. Killed in armed combat. He is dead. He won't be coming back." As she began to cry she clutched me to her distended stomach. "We won't be on our own," she whispered. "I've sent off for a baby for us – for you and me."

'She placed my hand on her belly. "There, can you feel it moving? It will soon be coming out to say hello."

'We cried together in snivelling unison and we held one another very close. But ... but ... those tears ... those tears ... both mine and hers ... were not born of regret but of relief.

'I came here to let go of the past ... to shed a horror ... a trauma so terrible that it had contaminated me. Now, it has gone from me without me quite knowing how or why it has been banished. Part of it is due to the affection I have received ... or the acceptance ... or the love ... I don't know. I do know that I am well and that I have never felt larger or better in all my life.'

Brenda sat on the balcony floor, drew her knees up to her chin and chuckled.

'Letting go of the past, it isn't easy.' Brenda heard Leslie's opening words and knew that much more was to follow. She arranged her nightdress comfortably about her knees and placed her ear close to the canvas.

'I did not tell lies. I find lying very difficult, even kindly lying does not come easily to me. I did not lie. I told a story that was not fictional. I told a story of bare reportage that was void of imaginative detail. I adapted the story from someone else; it seemed to fit my need better. It was not my story. It did not belong to me. You see, bereavement was the easiest way that I could come to terms with the loss of him.' Leslie half-laughed, half-sighed and continued.

'I had only ever experienced illness in the form of head-colds or the odd bout of influenza. Two days had been the extent of any incapacity from sickness or injury, so it came as a shock to find myself bed-ridden with pleurisy. The attack left me weak and helpless. I could do little but rest, and rarely left my room for three weeks. He was . . . he was so different during this period. Perhaps it was my circumstances that dictated it.

'He saw to it that I took all my medicines diligently, he made my bed comfortable, he replenished the hot-water bottles, emptied the chamber-pot, brought me hot drinks, cooked my food and fed it to me from a beautifully prepared tray. As far as I can remember neither of us had ever cosseted one another before. We had never been interested in the domestic side of a household. Twice, or was it three times, we had the public health visit us on account of being infested with fleas. And we had never cooked for one another – not once, over a period of sharing twenty-three years of our lives together. There was quite a lot that we did not share – even our food was purchased separately and kept in separate cupboards. This new experience was enjoyable in the midst of all the pain – and he could always make me laugh.

'He would bob up and down in mock servitude, like those housemaids in old forties' films. "Would Madam be wanting anything else? If not, then I'd like to finish the dusting before the doctor arrives."

'I seemed to have been ill for so long and it was such a relief when I was well enough to get downstairs. A relief to be out of my pyjamas, a relief to be in another room, a relief to be wearing clothes – a relief to be able to make a pot of tea for myself. I asked him if he would like a cup and he said that he would prefer to make his own. I always made tea too weak, and I might forget and sweeten it. I never remembered that he hated sweet things . . . and we were back as before.

'"Sit down, Leslie," he ordered me in gentle fashion. "I have something to tell you and I don't want you to be shocked." I wondered if this was going to be more news of another death. In middle-age people that you know begin to die, and nowadays ... people who are ... men who are the other way ... consider their mortality more than most. His voice took on a sharper inflection and the next order was not gentle. "Now, you may not be upset. I forbid you to be upset." I waited and hoped that I could remain expressionless in accordance with his wishes.

'"I have been offered a flat. I have the keys and I am going over to look at it this afternoon, and if I like it I shall take it. The tenancy starts in just under a fortnight's time." He paused here, as if I should ask some question, but I could think of nothing to say. No, that is not true. If I had spoken I would have pleaded with him to stay ... I was wholly unprepared for this happening.

'"It's the other side of the river – in Lewisham. I have had my name down on this scheme for the past ten years. I'd actually forgotten about it until this letter arrived. I want my own place. I want my own kitchen. I have never seen this relationship as you have seen it ... it ... it just went on ... you may not be upset."

'I said, "If that's what you have decided then there is nothing to be done." This was the response that he required and I did not speak again.'

Brenda felt that she wanted to touch Leslie. Pat his hand or the back of his head. Any comment or observation on the complexities of half a life shared with someone would have sounded arrogant or trite. She cupped her jaw between her large hands and gazed at the canvas sheeting.

'Since I have met you, my dear, I have come to realize that I am not bereaved. I can now think of my friend with the utmost tenderness and affection. I feel no sense or trace of being wronged. No sense of being injured. I can share my life with him, even in his absence. I can see him again and not feel pained, and I can return home alone and content. I am no longer dependent. In this, you have helped him achieve his goal.'

Brenda had risen and stood with the back of her left hand touching the canvas partition. Suddenly she was aware that Leslie was addressing her directly. The 'you' could not be referring to anyone else. Or could it? Abstractedly, she began to fiddle and finger one of the corded knots which held their separation in place. Then, she recognized Leslie's long, bony fingers pulling and tugging at the knot below it. She turned and began untying her knot with both hands.

Such was the intensity of purpose of both workers that in no more than ten minutes they had disassembled the screen and rolled it neatly into the shape of a furled sail.

'I think it might have belonged to a dhow at one time.' Their work complete, Leslie breathed in deeply to express his satisfaction.

'It must have seen any number of journeys,' Brenda observed.

They sat together for a time, shared an orange, discussed the merits of Bette Davis, the teeth of Margaret Thatcher and the Crusades.

'If any Westerner visits any Arab country, try as they might, they can never be part of it, never be absorbed in its culture. In fact, they are only allowed to eavesdrop from time to time. Perhaps this accounts for the lack of understanding. Religion has always been the root of the schism between the Arab East and the West. I do not wish to embrace Islam but I see what its order represents.'

'You would not be allowed to embrace it, Leslie, even if you wanted to . . . your . . . your sexuality would not allow it. But you would not like to settle down here?'

'Oh no, this is my third and last visit. I have absorbed enough. I shall take my holidays nearer home from now on. I don't think that any Arab would view *us* as an enemy, Brenda dear, but I am sure that most, in the depths of their hearts, have since the Crusades (those barbaric, idiotic conquests in the name of Christ), viewed all Westerners with the utmost distrust whether their interests lay in oil, tourism or territory.'

Brenda drew Leslie's attention towards the sea by pointing outwards towards the horizon.

'Look, look . . . are they sharks?' Brenda recalled her dream, and felt a chill enter her bones.

'Dolphins. They are dolphins, my dear. The sailor's friend.' Leslie spoke soothingly. 'Said to be the wisest, tenderest and most innocent creatures on our planet.'

'They can't enjoy performing in captivity, then?'

'Nothing enjoys performing in captivity, Brenda.' Leslie spoke as if he had some personal experience of this and Brenda thought it best not to probe his reasoning any further.

'What about sharks?' Brenda tried to keep a sense of urgency out of her question. Leslie did seem to know a great deal about sea creatures, yet he had never mentioned any maritime adventures to her.

His answer was palatable: 'They are much maligned, unfairly so, for the most part. Most of the attacks on humans are usually a mistake.'

'A mistake?' Brenda all but felt that she had encountered first-hand experience of such errors.

'Yes, the sea is not our natural habitat, not our natural territory. A shark might mistake us for a jellyfish or a new ocean species. The taste of human flesh is not pleasant to the shark; it finds the flavour disagreeable and rancid, and rarely does more than sample it by error. People are not on its menu.'

'Oh, I know. I know,' Brenda affirmed.

Several days later, Leslie walked alongside Brenda, his arm comfortably slotted under hers, his hand gently resting on her forearm. They had become people of habit and they strolled southwards along the shoreline path which led to a small inlet some two or three miles from the Café des Ramparts.

It was late afternoon. The walk was familiar to them as they had completed it on previous occasions. This was Brenda's last evening before returning home to Batsford and, because of this, they were more aware of one another than they were of the points on the landscape which usually arrested their attention. The town's minaret on the skyline, the oleander trees, the freakish-looking prickly pear bushes, the goats, the hovering hawk – all were accepted as ordinary sightings.

Leslie, who was not conservative by nature, was bemused by Brenda's last trump card with regard to personal attire. He had wondered whether she would wear something a little chic, or even sober on this, their last night. It was true she was not wearing a dress splattered with dazzling flowers and he supposed he ought to feel grateful for this, as most of the time he felt that Brenda looked like a florist's shop window. Now, from his position at her side, he had the real sensation that he was accompanying a walking, talking traffic-light.

The design of Brenda's dress was what his mother had once described as a 'courting-frock'. It was just below the calf in length and had a sweetheart neckline, and there were buttons all the way down its centre. Simple enough in itself but it was bright orange in colour. The neckline had a three-inch red border and the hemline a three-inch green one. The large buttons down the front of the dress alternated between red, green and orange.

For her part, Brenda thought that Leslie always looked frumpish. His shirts ranged in colour from dull grey, through sluggish green, to khaki. His crumpled trousers would have fitted a man half his size again, and he would persist in carrying a battered shoulder-bag everywhere. This accessory dated back to the early sixties; it was held together by safety-pins and its appeal was historical rather than utilitarian or aesthetic.

'You are looking absolutely radiant this afternoon, Brenda. Quite dazzling.' Leslie's voice carried no trace of condescension or insincerity.

'Thank you, Leslie, and you are looking your usual trim self.'

Brenda felt that as they had told one another great truths, small lies were admissible.

They sat on some rocks near the mouth of the inlet and watched as three heavily-robed women gleaned the shore for driftwood. A battered dhow had anchored near what was left of a crumbling stone jetty. Four fishermen, whose working attire consisted only of vests and shorts, had formed a human chain to pass the creels, brimming with silver fish, from the boat to the jetty. They seemed happy and laughed noisily as they shouted to one another.

'Beautiful,' Leslie sighed and moved his head from side to side. 'Really beautiful and so unspoiled.'

'Yes, isn't it.' Brenda agreed with his appraisal but was not quite sure where Leslie's bucolic appreciation lay. Was it in the wholeness of the scene being enacted before them? Or was it the men's rugged physical presence that had moved him? The wetness of the thin cotton shorts revealed much more of the male, human landscape than was normally available to the naked eye.

'Would you like me to accompany you to the airport tomorrow, my dear?'

'Oh yes, Leslie. I hate the thought of being on that coach alone. I don't feel part of . . . I don't want to feel part of . . . oh, I don't know . . . I just don't fit in with the company.'

'Not the company, Brenda. The culture. It's the culture that you don't fit into. That's why I ordered us a place in a taxi.'

Brenda had often been surprised by Leslie in this way. It was clear that he knew that she would accept his offer or he would not have booked a cab. She was not used to people being courteous to her.

'But, Leslie, the cost? Won't it be a drain on expen . . .'

'It will be very little. There will be a group travelling to the airport. A taxi here is more like a collective car-hire service. There are eight places in the cab. We take up just two of them. Don't worry, my dear.'

Leslie's assurances did not entirely assuage Brenda's concern. If the taxi was to carry eight people it would be very crowded. Again size and space made Brenda feel guilty.

'I'm like carrying two persons – or at least one-and-a-half,' she thought but said nothing more about the arrangements.

'It seems to be getting dark earlier.' Brenda looked up at the sky.

Leslie viewed the sea and noted the increased swell of the waves. 'No, I think it is the approach of a thunderstorm. We should get back.'

They left their spot quickly and marched towards the café with determined strides. During the rush for shelter they made plans for future meetings. There was little that was prudent or cautionary about these plans. No telephone numbers or an offer of exchange of letters or cards, no vague, undated invitations, no short half-day visits. Dates were fixed, times set, social commitments confirmed.

Leslie was to spend the month of July with Brenda. 'I have always wanted to see Lichfield and Alrewas. From what you say, the Trent valley is greatly underrated. The canals of Britain offer something quite different from anything else . . . and Fradley Junction sounds so exotic.'

Brenda was to visit Leslie in London for the month of September. 'I'm looking forward to our tour of London cemeteries, Leslie – Highgate, Nunhead and Abney have such wonderful-sounding names. I do hope that they don't sell one of them before my visit. I love stone angels; they seem to look better as they get older and their gender doesn't seem to be important.'

They were sipping mint tea on the balcony when the storm broke. The thunder, the flashes of lightning and the sea in troubled turmoil offered a natural spectacle as exciting as any theatrical experience. They pushed their two chairs together and hauled the canvas sheeting over their heads and shoulders. As the storm crashed about them they viewed it as though they were sitting in the front stalls of Covent Garden; and for the first time in her life Brenda did not have to worry about obstructing someone else's view. No one was going to tap her on the shoulder.

The next day polite and formal farewells were made to Rashid, the taxi's arrival was punctual and Brenda and Leslie were the first of its passengers.

The cab-driver opened the side door and ushered them inside as though he were inviting them into his home. It was like climbing into some grotto that Walt Disney might have concocted for his version of *The Arabian Nights*.

A cyclorama of plastic flowers – of the kind that used to come free in packets of soap-powder – entwined themselves around the borders of every window, the upholstery was enlivened by multi-coloured stretch covers, and suspended from the roof by elastic thongs hung a menagerie of fluffy dolls and animals which dangled and bobbed in a state of permanent strangulation.

As the large, outdated, but well kept vehicle started Brenda murmured, 'Oh, it's enchanting, Leslie, enchanting.'

The motion of the cab had caused a velvet camel to bob up and down in front of Leslie's eyes. 'It is original, I will admit,' said Leslie as he viewed the camel's furry behind.

They collected the rest of the passengers on the outskirts of the town. A group of men were given a tearful and noisy farewell by friends and relatives. Leslie explained that all of the men were going to take up work in Europe.

'Migrant workers are treated little better than prisoners of war. They do work that others do not want. Their rights are minimal, their living conditions bleak and overcrowded, and often ...' His external anger on their behalf was cut short as the men began to pile into the taxi.

Brenda felt a tremor pass through her body, the first indication of a humiliation that she had experienced all too often before – there would not be room for everyone – they would stare at her accusingly, whisper to one another, stare again. Her bulk would place her in the dock – guilty – guilty!

With a swift but gentle sideways movement Leslie settled himself on Brenda's lap.

'I hope you don't mind, Brenda my dear, but that camel will either give me a migraine or send me cross-eyed. I can't contemplate the whole journey with it dancing before my eyes.'

By this time, the taxi was full to overcrowding but no one was left behind. Brenda encircled Leslie's waist with her great arms, as if she had held him in this way all her life. He had become such a comfort to her.

In the airport lounge, they stood apart from the Palm d'Or Club members who had formed into a band of noisy revellers whose revelry was not contagious to anyone else because it lacked goodwill. The flight-call came. Brenda bent and kissed Leslie on the forehead as though she were granting him some benediction. They spoke no further as a 'goodbye' would have been entirely inappropriate.

On the aeroplane Brenda sat next to a young couple who wore white T-shirts with highly coloured motifs declaring messages. The young man's shirt depicted a racing-driver – his message: 'Put some lipstick on my dipstick'. The young woman's displayed a brightly coloured bird – her message: 'I like a cock to wake me up in the morning'.

The couple seemed to spend most of the flight

travelling back and forth to the lavatory. Cocks, lipsticks and dipsticks seemed a fragile basis for an enduring friendship, and judging by the way that they related to one another, Brenda reckoned that this bout of joint diarrhoea would just finish off the bonding.

The set of earthenware egg-cups and the brown and white striped djellaba had looked so attractive in North Africa but had somehow lost the immediacy of their original appeal now that they were placed on Brenda's kitchen table in Batsford. They had been meant as presents for Moira and her husband but Brenda now had severe misgivings about their suitability. She doubted very much that they would ever be put to use. She surmised that this would be a pity as both intended gifts were functional and Brenda hated waste.

She had been home for just over an hour and had found her house just as she had left it – apart from the two letters. One had told her that she had won a consolation prize. Enclosed with the letter was a voucher which entitled her to collect a hostess-trolley and a set of wind-chimes at any one of a list of chain-stores. Brenda preferred the sounds of birds in her back-yard – wind-chimes sounded as if they might be unpleasantly medicinal. Perhaps she could give the hostess-trolley and the wind-chimes to Moira, and keep the egg-cups and djellaba for herself. Leslie might want to wear it about the house.

The second letter had caused her to snort with indignation. It was an appeal from the Department of Education and Science which exhorted her to leave retirement and return to teaching. There was a long list of schools with vacant temporary posts, all claiming that they needed her experience. It was like being given an accolade by someone after they had murdered you, in order to bring you back to life.

Brenda wrote this single sentence for her response on the reply-paid card: 'I have changed my life.'

Although it was only seven o'clock Brenda had changed into her nightdress. She had got used to the comfort of the flowing garment, and there was no reason why she shouldn't wear it before her bath as well as after it. She would telephone Moira just after eight.

The insistent ringing of the door-bell upset the mental order of her arrangements. No one else rang the door-bell like Moira. Three sharp buzzes – a pause – two more buzzes – then the voice through the letter-box.

'Are you in, Brenda? It's me, Moira.'

The voice always sounded impatient and fraught. Brenda floated barefoot along the hallway and managed to open the door before her sister could raise her head back into an upright position. When Moira did look up she burst into tears.

The sobbing continued unabated as she sat opposite Brenda at the kitchen table. Brenda was touched by Moira's tears which she interpreted as a reaction to her own home-coming. She waited in vain for the tiny smile and then realized that the tears represented personal anguish and not relief.

'There, there, my love. Oh, our Moira.' Brenda stood and carried her chair to Moira's side. 'There, there, don't take on so, there – there.'

She held Moira's head to her breast and gently stroked her hair. 'There, there, don't take on so. Whatever is this all about?' She carried on with the verbal and tactile soothings until Moira's sobbing had dwindled into intermittent sniffing.

'It's Harry,' Moira gasped in strangled tones.

'What's wrong? Is he ill? Has he had an accident?'

'No ... no ... no. Worse ... worse than that.'

'Oh God. Not ... not dea ...'

'He's left me.'

'Left you?'

Brenda breathed in deeply after she had asked the question. Moira nodded.

'Gone off. Gone off to live with Mrs Tatler. You know her – Sylvia Tatler – she's a widow. Her husband had a window-cleaning business.'

Moira's tears recommenced but this time she chose to talk through them. 'He's been gone more than a week. Just left me a note. He's taken most of his clothes. I don't know how he could do this. We'd only just had a new shag-pile fitted carpet laid in the lounge.'

Moira's head sagged forward as if this were the ultimate disgrace. 'I wonder if he'll come back,' she muttered into her cleavage as though she were addressing a microphone.

'Harry has stayed out before,' Brenda recollected.

'No more than one night ... well ... two nights. He was with his mates. Trust you to remember, Brenda. Oh, this time it is brazen. He might just as well have paid to advertise it all in the local paper. His car's parked outside her door and he's been out in a pub with her. You know she's older than me?'

Brenda nodded. 'Yes, she's my age. As a young woman she was nothing special to look at.'

'I shouldn't think he's interested in her face.'

'She was pleasant enough though and ...'

'Pleasant!' Moira snapped. 'What's pleasant about stealing somebody else's husband?'

'I don't think that husbands can be stolen, Moira.' Brenda spoke with quiet conviction.

'Oh, our Brenda.' Moira's exasperation and contempt could not be veiled. 'Oh, our Brenda, you know nothing. Nothing. Nothing about men. You will never know anything.' The anger she felt for her husband was easily transferred to her older sister. 'Your shape was always against you. You were meant to be on your own. No, Brenda – you know nothing of men.'

'There are more than fifty-seven varieties, Moira – and you have only known one. And I don't think that you knew him too well – even if you are married to him. Anyway, I'm not going to be on my own. I've got one.'

'Got what?' Moira asked disdainfully; she disliked dogs and cats.

'A man.'

'You – you a man. God help us. The world's gone mad . . .' Moira's crying entered a steady rhythm.

Brenda kept her arm about her sister's shoulder but was now no longer interested in her sister's suffering. She knew that it would be temporary and had begun to feel more sympathy for Sylvia Tatler than for her sister. How any woman could cry on behalf of her brother-in-law left her baffled.

'Yes, I've got a man. His name is Leslie. I met him in North Africa. Had you forgotten that I'd been away? No, that's unkind of me. I'm sorry to hear of this trouble but I'm sure that it will soon pass. Harry will have to maintain you. He's too mean for that; he'll return if you want him to. My friend Leslie lives in London.'

Moira blinked. Perhaps there were men who liked women who tipped the scales at sixteen stones? She found it difficult to think beyond the physical as to how men and women related to one another. In this, she was not unlike her husband.

'How did you meet him?' Moira asked.

'We had adjoining rooms: we shared the same balcony.'

'I hope you kept the door locked, Brenda.'

'No, I didn't. And I'm glad that I didn't.'

'Is he married?'

'Oh no, definitely not. He's not the marrying kind.' Brenda laughed affectionately on Leslie's behalf.

'Oh, Brenda,' Moira wailed and started to weep copiously as the sense of social order that she was accustomed to began to crumble further. She stopped crying on noticing Brenda's bare feet. The sight of them seemed to shock her into silence. She pointed her index finger in their direction.

'Your toe-nails. They are painted.'

'Yes, Leslie did them for me.' Brenda raised a foot for further inspection. 'Do you like them?'

'It's not you, our Brenda, it's not you at all.' Moira wondered if her sister had become a harlot. 'And why paint one nail and miss another one?'

'He alternated as there wasn't enough varnish left in the bottle. I did his big toes as they had begun to turn yellow.'

'His toes?' Moira had begun to feel deeply worried. Had Brenda taken drugs? 'Is he foreign?'

'No, he was born here. Lives in London. I'm going down to stay with him for a month. In September.'

'Stay with him ... two months ... how can you?'

'He's coming up to me first, staying here for the same amount of time. It will be a change of scene for us both. A slow shuttle.'

Moira felt terrible. First, her husband had gone off with a widow eight years older than himself and left her to tend acres of green shag-pile carpet alone. And now, her older sister – dressed in a nightgown – painted toe-nails – talking about some man who had his big toe-nails varnished – coming to live with her – in her house – then his house ...

'People aren't what you think they are. They are not what they seem to be.' Moira shook her head from side to side as she spoke, as if she regretted this insight.

Brenda plugged in one of her electric kettles. A pot of tea would help to settle things a little. Moira sat bolt upright and stared as though sightless. She seemed to have entered some kind of catatonic trance.

'It's not all bad, Moira dear,' Brenda called out from the sink. 'I've got some presents for you. I'll bring them around tomorrow. A nice surprise for you.'

'I don't want any more surprises,' Moira replied emptily.

'I've brought you a hostess-trolley.'

'It will wobble if I push it on the carpet – but I can wheel it about in the hall and kitchen.'

'And some wind-chimes.'

'I suppose I'll have to bring them indoors if the gales are like last year.'

Brenda thought that Moira sounded a little more cheerful but knew that gales or no gales, things at home would never be quite the same again.

Caesar's Wife
· Patrick Gale ·

FOR PATRICK PENDER

I

I should not have been there. The mistress should not as a rule be present at the wife's funeral, unless under such extraordinary circumstances as her being the wife's bosom friend. I was no friend of Rachel's bosom. She never addressed a single word to me. In fact, I believe to this day that she had no idea of my existence and its crucial bearing upon her own, save perhaps in some dark pouch of her shrivelled libido where she might have nursed gratitude for whoever was relieving her of the pressure of her husband's lust.

I had toyed with the charming idea of wearing my thickest veil but rejected it as being too theatrical and attention-seeking. I settled instead upon my least penetrable dark glasses, the ones with the serious tortoiseshell frames. I wore my very best black coat, the one with the delicious rustle, and my best black shoes, which have a solid gold clip about each heel. I resisted the temptation to don scarlet leather gloves, although I had a pair, bought on a macabre whim for just such an occasion. Over a silk blouse in petrol blue – she was not, after all, a bosom friend – I hung my fattest pearls. A vulgar touch perhaps, since they were the ones Tom had given me and weightier, I knew, than any bibelots in her possession, but I was nervous and they always lent me strength.

I need not have worried. As one of Europe's captains of industry, Tom commanded a horde of acquaintance in his grief. Jewish cemetery chapels are built on the excessive side of generous but even this one was filled to capacity. A fine young man I guessed to be a nephew met me at the door. He had Tom's nose. In answer to his polite enquiry I breathed, 'Oh, Rachel and I went back a *very* long way.' Impressed, he led me to a reserved seat in a side aisle. I had a good view of the Chairman of the Bank of England, the Secretary for Trade and Industry and Rachel's coffin. The flowers were banked about it so thickly that I could smell them from several feet away.

Tom of course had no idea that I was coming. He would have found it deeply offensive. I would not go so far as to say he looked right through me when he took his place but he was not a man to notice things and he did not fail me on this occasion. His silvery-blond hair had been cut that morning, slightly too short, so that he looked cumbersome and vulnerable.

Josh came down the aisle behind his father, in his wheelchair, a black blanket tucked across his lap. I had warned him I was coming, so that he would not betray my presence with his surprise. He could not resist looking for me. Recognizing me without hesitation, he smiled broadly to himself, then remembered where he was, redirected his smile towards the ceiling to stifle it, then bowed his head in sad reflection. Dear Josh.

I had expected to feel bad – the Scarlet Woman – but I didn't. I felt like family. This was unsettling so I slipped away as soon as I could after Rachel's coffin was borne outside. I thought it best not to follow the crowd to the graveside.

II

I should explain.

My involvement with Tom took up only one seventh of my time. Every Wednesday evening he came to the flat he had bought for me in Belsize Village some seventeen years before. Occasionally there was an extra visit, a bonus, on an afternoon perhaps, but he had only ever spent the night on Wednesdays. The rest of my time I passed with total success for a single woman. I had an editorial post at one of the few remaining publishing houses still in the hands of its founding family. I took on no new authors any more, contenting myself with a respectable handful who, like me, had reached the age where nobody cared for them to do anything too surprising.

I had a meeting with one of these, an unlikely bestseller called Polly Brookes, on the afternoon of the funeral. I kept on my good clothes to go into the office, to cause a stir. I normally appeared in nothing stronger than a serviceable wool suit. Kirsty, my secretary, noticed. 'You look smart,' she said, as I walked past her desk to my office.

'Death in the family,' I told her. 'No one close, though.'

'I'll bring you a coffee,' she said.

Polly Brookes was not herself. As a rule she was composed, even to a fault, like a slightly superior librarian. Normally she was the better dressed of us two, wearing her expensive togs with a pained, distressed-gentlefolk air which intensified if one paid them too fulsome a compliment. Today she had met her match but I sensed that my clothes were not the problem. We drank tea together and mulled over possible designs for her latest bookjacket. It was only when I opened a bottle of wine from my little office fridge and let her drain her first glass that she came out with the source of her anxiety. Another author had written an article which accused her books of lacking gumption.

I turned my most reassuring gaze into her doe-eyes as she perched on the sofa's edge. 'Polly, that's nonsense. Who would say a thing like that?'

'Kathy Curry.' Miss Brookes looked up from her wine glass, rekindled anguish in her voice. 'She wrote that my writing had no balls.'

'Well of course it doesn't.'

'Doesn't it?'

I topped up both our glasses. Kathy Curry was another of my authors. She was not in Polly's league but her sales figures were on the way up.

'No. I would be most alarmed if it did, Polly. People don't buy you for balls any more than they'd think of buying Kathy for the quality of her prose. You have a following, Polly, a large following, even in translation, drawn by your flawless prose style and the insights you offer into the human situations people like Kathy neglect.'

'Tales of sad old girls in Kensington?'

'No. Not "sad old girls", nothing so patronizing. The lonely. The passed-over. And not just women. Think of Pierre in *The Good Bachelor*.' I snatched a surreptitious glance at my watch as Miss Brookes drained her third glass.

'You've taken a definite and brave artistic decision', I went on, 'to write about people who don't live happily ever after, whose prince doesn't come and who are to all intents and purposes unremarkable. You take those people and force us to see that, within the narrow confines of their lives, they *are* remarkable. Their lives have drama.' God, I was good!

'Yes, well, you would say that,' she snapped. Then she set down her glass and opened and refastened her bag in the manner, I trusted, of one on the point of leaving.

'Because I'm your editor?' I asked.

'No, Because you're, well,' Polly hesitated, 'because you're one of us.'

'Who?'

'The single women, Mary. The lonely, the passed-over and all that.' She actually patted my hand as she stood. Her fingers were dry as her smile. I froze for a moment.

'Yes,' I said and smiled back, gamely. 'Yes. I suppose I am.'

'Sorry. That was uncalled for. It was the wine.'

'No. Quite all right. Anyway, it isn't just me saying that – the *New York Times* said it for over half a bloody page last month. Kathy Curry doesn't even make it into their short reviews section. Forget her.' I touched *her* hand this time. '*Forget* her, Polly. Now,' I drew her attention back to the jackets. 'You think the one with the basket of fruit is the best?'

'Yes.' She pointed. 'With the Roman typeface in that nice green.'

III

This happened all the time. People – including old acquaintances – mistook me for a spinster. A game spinster, of course, because women had to be game in publishing – fond of their food and drink, partial to gossip and smut, one of the lads – but a spinster none the less. It was my fault of course. A sexual reputation is established in one's first twenty-five years and I was a late starter. I had lost my virginity, of course, around the time when everybody else did and, like many girls, I kept quiet about this so that I could please boys and lose it several times over. I spent most of my university years in the library and sitting-rooms of an all-women college. I took a first class degree then spent a year touring Europe with my mother. She waited until Athens to tell me she was dying and we had to hurry home soon after that because her pain became too intense. I was an only child and had never known my father, just as he, I suspected, had scarcely known the woman who later called herself his widow. When she died, a month after our return, I was quite alone and fairly poor.

I joined the family publishing firm thanks to a recommendation from my tutor, whom it published. I joined as a secretary: it being a family firm, women were still expected to work their way up. Before long I was taken firmly under the wings of another secretary and her friend in the foreign rights department – confirmed spinsters both – who somehow manoeuvred me into renting a room in their Maida Vale flat. They entertained royally and often, so a steady stream of interesting Londoners passed through. Every man they allowed to come my way, however, seemed to be either gay or thoroughly involved elsewhere.

Then I met Tom. He was involved elsewhere too, of course, but we came to an immediate unspoken understanding that he could spare a part of himself for me. I was an editor by now, as recompense for having brought two authoress friends into the firm's fiction list, and I was travelling to a book fair in Lisbon. A cookery writer of ours was to give demonstrations there as part of a promotion. As the lone female on the editorial staff I was deemed the most suitable to hold her hand and keep her from the bottle. The one task was unnecessary and the other unfeasible but I held my peace because I had a fondness for Lisbon and was long overdue for a holiday. No less overdue for a rise in salary, I ensured that neither my plane ticket nor my hotel reservation spared the company's coffers.

As I fastened my safety-belt and opened the manuscript I would work on during the flight, a hostess handed me a glass of champagne. I was probably one of the only people in the first class section not to recognize Tom as he walked in and stowed his hand-luggage. His company built the engines that would hurtle us along the runway. It also built the limousines that brought him and several of our travelling companions to the airport and even the elongated shuttle buses that would ferry us across the tarmac in Portugal. His face, I would later learn, appeared regularly in the financial pages and sometimes in the social ones. Rachel's face was unknown outside the charity she chaired – industrialists' wives enjoy luxurious anonymity – but his had become public property. People could not always put a name to it but they remembered it from television interviews and articles on the economy. However relaxed his dress, the less fortunate took one look at his fading blond hair and arrogant features and smelled immense wealth. He had so often been accused of gross injustices or harassed for loans by total strangers that first class air travel was, by then, the nearest he came to public transport.

The seat beside me was meant to remain empty. This was one of the pleasures we were paying for. He should have sat two seats away. He did not smell like a smoker, however, or look like the sort of man who would prattle foolishly while I was trying to work, so I said nothing. He was the one who raised the subject.

'Oh, I'm so sorry,' he said after a few minutes. 'I should have asked you first. Do you mind terribly if I sit here instead of there? It's just that I use the empty seat as a sort of desk and, being left-handed, it's more comfortable to have it on my left-hand side. Do you mind?'

'Not at all.'

'Sure?'

'Quite,' I said.

'We could always swap sides,' he suggested after a pause. I merely smiled and shook my head. Then I turned back to the manuscript on my lap, to stifle the conversation in its infancy.

Fortunately for the course of true love, it was the second novel by Polly Brookes, who was in those days one of my 'discoveries'. Whatever I might say to her face, I always found the air of poised depression in her writing unengaging. The intelligent silence of her characters' suffering was alien to my nature. (Now, perhaps, I understand it a little better although, as you see, I still do not keep silence.)

As I say, it was an early Brookes novel. My eyes

strayed easily therefore and noticed his hands. Large hands with spatulate fingers, close-cut nails and a bright dusting of golden hairs. I watched them raise his champagne glass and saw how the hair grew thickly in the shadow of his shirt-cuff and around the thick gold strap of his thick gold watch.

However hard I try, I have never managed to keep reading at the moment when an aeroplane lurches off the runway and soars on a sickening diagonal towards the sky. I'm no Christian and I'm not a nervous person, but it's one of the few times when I pray. I lower my book, stare at the aisle climbing ahead of me or, if I'm feeling less brave, shut my eyes. Then I let my mind's mouth mutter some hasty travel insurance like:

Oh God, keep us safe this flight,
Secure from all our fears.
May angels guard us as we soar,
Till green earth reappears.

I have no shame, you see. I'm only human.

On this instance I kept my eyes open. I let the manuscript sink to my lap and glanced again at his hands. While he scrutinized the contents of a file, they had been playing with his fountain pen, nervously pulling off and clicking on its large black cap. The noise had been threatening to irritate me. Now I saw that his hands were shaking so violently that his aim was not sufficiently accurate to replace the cap. I looked at his face and saw a sheen of sweat on his brow and under his eyes. I reached out and firmly refastened pen and cap for him.

'Thanks,' he said, then dropped it. 'Sorry,' he added. He remained frozen with fear rather than stoop forward, so I retrieved it for him.

'We'll stop climbing any second,' I told him. 'When we level out it doesn't seem so terrible.'

'It seems bloody awful to me.'

'Is it that bad?'

He looked full at me and I saw that his eyes were a true, Cambridge blue. My own eyes are cow brown so I never fail to be disarmed by any intensity of blueness in others.

'You won't tell anyone?'

'I feel sure we know no one in common,' I replied. 'We'd have met by now if we did.'

The aeroplane took away his smile by dipping suddenly through an air pocket. He winced, clutching his knees.

'How on earth do you manage crossing the Atlantic?' I demanded.

'I never have,' he confessed.

'You mean you take a *boat* over?'

'No. I mean I've never been. I send someone else.' I laughed.

'Sorry,' I said. 'I shouldn't laugh, but it seems so unlikely.'

'How do *you* manage?'

'Me? Well, I just give myself up to despair,' I told him. He looked puzzled so I explained. 'Look. We're hurtling along at hundreds of miles an hour, thousands of feet in the air with only a fragile metal box between us and the infinite. We're defying every sensible physical law and every code for survival. If anything goes wrong, we die. We'll have deserved it for doing something so stupid.'

'Well that's a *lot* of help.'

'But it is. It really is. Once you admit that you are utterly powerless, fear becomes a waste of time. Give yourself up. Have another drink. Do your work and be grateful if and when we land. That rigmarole the stewardesses go through with the life-jackets and all the pointing makes things much worse, because it fosters the illusion that an emergency would give one anything to do but die as quickly as possible.'

'Thanks,' he said. 'I'll try.'

I wasn't sure if he was being sarcastic, but he did try. He opened his file and spent the flight alternately frowning and making notes in it. Occasionally the plane would dip or rise dramatically and I would catch him flinching. We smiled at such moments but we didn't speak.

As the minutes passed I became involved, willy-nilly, in the Brookes novel. It was only as we began to dive down through the clouds towards Lisbon and the plane made a series of stalling downward lurches that I thought to look round at him again. The poor man was quite bloodless with terror so I reached out and laid a hand on his to calm him. It seemed the natural thing to do. I left it there until we landed, at which point he heaved a sigh of relief and turned his hand so that our fingers meshed.

'Are you staying here long?'

'Just the weekend. Until Monday afternoon,' I told him.

'Which hotel?' he asked.

'The same as yours, I'd imagine.'

'How perceptive of you.'

'Mary Marlowe.'

'Tom Spellman.' He paused and frowned slightly. 'I should explain that I'm ...'

'It's all right,' I said. 'I saw the ring before you spoke to me.'

This behaviour was utterly out of character for me but there was no point in my telling him that, for I had given him no reason to believe a word I said. Anyway, violins soar, the screen clouds up and the sordid pleasures of the next few hours are discreetly glossed over. The narrator clears her throat.

We only had to work on our first day. Tom disappeared to power-lunch somebody while I braved the book fair. The cookery writer had barely a sober moment but was a great success. Tom didn't know the city. He thought I spent the weekend parading it for his approval when actually I was posing him a test which he had to pass. I made him leave his car at the hotel so that we could ride trams. I took him on a grimy ferry across the harbour to a clutch of unpretentious cafés where the Lusitanians gorged their well-dressed children on seafood. I walked him around the Gulbenkian with my mouth shut so as to gauge his true reactions and made him eat too much lobster with me so that we could enjoy simultaneous nightmares. I only let him use his car once, on the Sunday evening, to drive us out to Sintra. I described a precise route to the chauffeur then we sat in silence while he steered us round the miniature castles and overgrown villas beneath a lowering sky. The publishers paid for a single room where I did no more than take baths and hang my clothes.

We held hands throughout the flight home and parted without a kiss before we passed through customs. I had expected no more. I had smelt his wealth, after all, and imagined his wife; I knew my place. It took him a week to track me down. I arrived at work one morning to find a great box on my desk packed with arum lilies, like the ones we had admired in a Lisbon courtyard. (I told my colleagues these had come from the cookery writer, which the fools readily believed.) Tom and I spent five or so lunchtimes, a rash Friday afternoon – I pleaded trouble with wisdom teeth – and the first of our countless Wednesday evenings, in an hotel beside the British Museum.

Honesty has never rated as highly as invention in my pantheon of virtues but I now place a hand on my powdered breast to swear that the manner of our meeting and the glorious weekend that followed were precisely as I have described: unexpected, uncharacteristic, unrepeatable. If our brief encounter in Lisbon bore all the trappings of an unfingered paperback romance, our London assignations hailed from a second-rate *film noir* with Tom and I a cut-price imitation of Fred MacMurray and Barbara Stanwyck. Whereas Tom had been relaxed and alert in Portugal, now I saw him tense and exhausted. The need for secrecy prevented our being seen to leave or arrive together and the lack of time meant that our conversation – one of my chief pleasures before – was restricted to a minimum. The room was ugly, leaving no pleasure to our eyes but one another's bodies, which it displayed in the least flattering light. Tom seemed older and thicker-waisted than he had before and I – shorn of antiquities and culture – less worldly, less assured. These were early tutorials in an uneasy sexual education. Occasionally Tom bored, hurt or disgusted me. Frequently the glance of the hotel receptionist withered my self-esteem. Flattered by his need for me, surprised at my continuing appetite for him, I questioned, whenever we were apart, the common sense in keeping our next appointment. Then Tom sent me a note bearing an address in Belsize Park Gardens. A bunch of keys followed, under separate cover.

The flat was carved out of half the ground floor of a

mid-Victorian building. It was a recent conversion, with a brand new kitchen and – height of decadence – a bath with taps in the middle. The street was not of the smartest (it has since come up in the world) and the house was in some need of repair, but the flat was newly decorated. It had few rooms – only one bedroom – but one of these was a vast affair with high ceilings, a bay window overlooking the garden and a riot of *faux* rococo plasterwork. Standing in there, on the old parquet floor, with the rain lashing the horse-chestnut trees outside, and little fish cavorting with acanthus leaves about the ceiling, I could imagine myself in a house on the Bois de Boulogne. Even unfurnished, it felt like an interior described by Proust.

There was a pile of typed pages on the blush-pink marble mantelpiece. Beside them was a note from Tom.

Mary darling,

Herewith the papers making this place yours for the next 999 years. All you have to do is sign on the line I've marked on page five and post these to the solicitor whose name appears on page one. There's no mortgage or anything and the bills will be paid by standing order. I've opened an account for you because I thought you'd probably rather buy your own furniture and paintings and so on. You know things can't be any other way but if all this disgusts you, I quite understand. All you need do is return the key to the solicitor with the unsigned papers and I'll never bother you again. If I don't hear anything to the contrary, I'll drop by on Wednesday at seven. This place is yours and yours alone, my darling. The locks have just been changed and you have the only keys.

Tom

Naturally I had to read the note through several times. Then I read back and forth through every opaque sentence of the legal document. I walked around the flat. I opened and closed the silent doors of fitted wardrobes and peered into the glistening maws of fridge and oven. I tried lying on the king-size bed and even christened the lavatory. Then I returned to the great, Proustian sitting-room and took a pen from my bag to sign on the dotted line. I imagined my reflection in a high gilded mirror over the mantelshelf, lit by twin candelabra, in emerald silk with my hair up, and I thought to myself, '*Maîtresse*.'

IV

I took shameless advantage of there having been a death in the family to leave work a little early. I wanted to cook something for Tom – a custom I had rather let slide lately, having discovered a French restaurant which delivered. (Tom would sit up in bed like a mischievous invalid while I waited on him from covered dishes in the manner, I fancied, of Grace Kelly in *Rear Window*.)

Tonight, having drunk too much after the funeral, he would need bulky, unsubtle food in primary colours. I bought him fillet steak (I would grill myself a chicken breast), green peppercorns for the sauce and vivid French beans, which I would steam then toss, still hot, in a walnut vinaigrette. I covered a large plate with scarlet, weeping cross-sections of beef tomatoes, nestled a few naked garlic cloves among them, tossed on a pinch of coarse sea-salt and drizzled the whole with the headily fragrant olive oil Tom bought me from a specialist near Spitalfields. And then? Only coffee. No pudding. As he liked to point out, I was his 'just dessert'. If ever I made a pudding, if ever I reached for egg yolks, vanilla sugar and bitter cooking-chocolate, it was for their anaphrodisiac properties. In the code of our erotic conversation, puddings were my red camellias.

I laid out the pink cashmere dress (his favourite), shook sweet almond oil into the steaming bath-water and lay down for a soak, to soften my callouses and still my mind. He had not visited me for three weeks, not since the dismal evening when he had told me about Rachel's stroke and paced up and down the flat saying, 'What am I going to do? I don't know what to do.' He had wept like a child then and I had felt helpless since anything I said emerged, inevitably, weighted with seventeen years of envious bias.

You must understand, I had never wished Rachel dead.

The statement hangs before you, golden, pure, plump with conviction. It's a lie, of course; a slack pear of dishonesty. Watch closely and you see the first brown saggings of its skin.

I had wished Rachel dead many times. At first, in the first two years, when I ached for his touch and found the wait from Wednesday to Wednesday intolerable, I used to fantasize to myself about her being knocked efficiently to oblivion by a jack-knifing lorry or being overcome by paint-fumes (she was forever redecorating their house) or drowning, inexpertly drunk, in her swimming pool. In Tom's presence, I merely fantasized, kittenish, that she might fall in love with someone else. If she left Tom, he would appear the injured party and we two could neatly side-step blame.

As time wore on, however, I ceased to resent Rachel and found myself almost in her debt. I was not exactly on a perpetual honeymoon but my experience of Tom was inevitably more romantic and flattering than hers. I had never washed his underwear or ironed his shirts, never had to like his friends or enchant his colleagues. I had another life elsewhere. She, unless Tom had grossly underestimated her powers of deception and initiative, had not. When her husband and I clinked glasses, I mutely wished her a long and healthy life. While I reaped the benefits, she shouldered the burden. Until now.

Tom had indeed had too much to drink. He all but threw me over his shoulder on arrival and bore me to the bedroom for sex so swift that it was over for him before I had even begun to enjoy myself. Most definitely sex rather than lovemaking. I was forbearing, grateful that he was still capable in his late fifties of demonstrating such urgent, pubescent lust. I made him take a shower, however, to wake himself up and when I fed him his peppered steak at the fireside it took the desired effect. We made achingly slow love on the carpet. My way.

He was such a bear compared to me that we could sit quite comfortably on the floor with me between his thighs, leaning against his chest. We sat like that afterwards, wrapped in dressing-gowns, and ate the remaining beans in our fingers. It was a favourite posture of mine because while he leaned back against the sofa, I could hug his calves to my sides, stroking their thick hair, and feel utterly safe. I always wondered what my colleagues would say, or Polly Brookes, if they saw me in such unspinsterly *déshabillé* and abandon, wrapped in such a poundage of important male.

'How was it?' I asked at last. 'The funeral.'

'Bearable,' he said. 'Massive turn-out, of course.'

'Would Rachel have been flattered?'

'No.' He sighed. 'Poor Rachel was too cynical. She'd have said they only turned up in such numbers because of her bank balance and my name.'

'Did she have many friends?'

'Oh yes. She preferred to play several off against each other than to single out one or two to be, you know, really close.'

'She met them through her charity work?'

'Some, yes. She got out a lot, you know.'

'She wasn't totally in your shadow?'

'No,' he said, and rubbed the backs of my ears with his nose. 'You know she wasn't.'

I passed him the last bean and reached for the plate of tomatoes.

'How's Josh?' I asked.

'Exhausted. He left pretty early. He'll be coming into work tomorrow, I expect. You can ask him about it then.'

'He hates crowded parties,' I said. 'In fact I think he hates parties full stop. I can see why. If you're stuck in a wheelchair, you can't slip away from ghastly people. And even if you could, you couldn't see where the more interesting people were who you wanted to reach. Dear Josh.'

'You've got very fond of him, haven't you?'

'Of course I have. He's my best friend. And no,' I continued, hearing his cynical snort, 'his being your son had nothing to do with it. If anything, that made me steer clear of him to start with.'

'Hmm.'

We fell silent for a few minutes, listening to the hissing of gas jets in the fake coal fire. Tom straightened his legs and leaned forward to slip a cushion to the base of his spine, then he brought them in more closely about me. I knew in an instant what was coming next. I toyed with diversionary tactics but dismissed them as cowardly.

'Just think,' he said then stopped.

'What?' I asked. A droplet of sweat tickled the underside of one of my arms.

'I mean, it's awful to bring it up so soon . . .'

'What?' I asked again, knowing perfectly well.

'I could start seeing you on other nights now,' he went on finally. 'Not just on Wednesdays.'

'Yes,' I said, hugging his legs. 'Now I'm left a totally open territory.'

'Have you minded?' he asked.

'Minded what?'

'Being, you know, a mistress all this time.'

'You know I haven't. I never do anything I don't want to.'

'Yes, but it can't have been much fun.' He kissed one of my ears. 'Sometimes you must have sat there wondering when the party was going to get going. My God, when we met you were younger than Josh is now! You were so young and you gave everything up!'

'No I didn't.'

'I sincerely hope you did.'

'I kept my job,' I protested, 'I kept my friends, I kept all the things I enjoy but, in secret, I gained you.'

'But that's my point exactly,' he said. '"In secret". No one wants their lover in secret. It isn't natural. The number of times I left here and wanted to be taking you with me to show you off to people!'

'Darling,' I said, and kissed his knee. 'You're so sweet. Do you think of me as the natural type?'

I knew what was coming. I *knew* what was coming. Why were men, even adorable men, so predictable? There was always a chip too little subterfuge in their genes.

'Look at me,' he said. 'This is important.' A little stiff, I slid forward from between his legs then turned round to lean against the sofa beside him.

'What?' I asked, stifling a nervous yawn.

'I'm going to make up to you for the last seventeen years,' he said. 'I want to make an honest woman of you.'

'What a disgusting phrase!' I said. 'I trust that was a joke.'

'The wording was. Not the sentiment.'

'Oh.' I laughed, playing for time. 'Was that a proposal, then? No one's ever asked me that before.'

'Mary, I want you to marry me. I want us to live together.'

'But . . .'

'You wouldn't have to move. Not at first, at least. I'd sell the old house – it's too full of memories anyway and Josh wouldn't mind.'

'Josh would be thrilled.' I stroked his hair but he stopped me, clasping my hand in his. 'You could give him a place of his own.'

'You could keep your job.'

'That's big of you,' I said.

'You could even keep your name.'

'Bigger still.'

'Oh Mary, please. I want you with me always.'

'Yes, but why do we have to get *married*?' I pleaded. 'Marriage is so, you know, three-piece-suite.'

'I . . . Well I know it sounds pompous . . . No, it *is* pompous but it's also true,' he said, then hesitated.

'What is?' I asked.

'That I have a position to maintain. Anyway, if we were married you'd have more security.'

'I suppose so.'

'And we could have children. It's not too late.' I let out a small shriek.

'What's wrong?' he asked. He looked quite shocked.

'Tom, darling, one thing at a time. Please?'

'OK.' He reached for his wine and muttered, 'I thought you wanted children.'

'Don't sulk.'

'I'm not sulking. I'm just tired. Tired and depressed and I've spent all day bloody burying Rachel and ... Are you saying you won't marry me?'

His eyes searched my face. He looked wretched and it was all I could do not to say yes there and then and be done with it. Anything for a quiet life. A quiet, luxurious life. A quiet, luxurious, secure life. No! Rage, rage against the reading of the banns!

'I'm saying, darling Tom, that it's not a decision I can make straight away.'

'Why the hell not? I thought you loved me.'

'Oh Tom, now you're being childish.' I stood. I needed to stalk about. 'Of course I love you. Love and marriage, however, are not necessarily linked. One can make the other shrivel up and die. In some cases the two can even be mutually exclusive. You of all people should know that.' He sighed. I couldn't look at him. 'I'm sorry,' I went on. 'That was cheap. I know you loved her – at first at least. And she loved you. In her way. I'm sorry she died so soon. I really am.'

'For purely selfish reasons.' He was sharper than I thought. I hid behind a flare of anger.

'What the hell do you mean by that?'

'Don't,' he said quietly.

'What?'

'Just don't.'

'OK.'

I continued stalking, clearing away the supper things as I did so. Tom raised himself on to the sofa and arranged the dressing-gown chastely over his knees. I returned with coffee. He accepted a cup but left it at his feet, undrunk.

'I don't understand,' he said at last. 'I mean, what did you expect? Did you expect me to keep paying your bills . . .'

'I've told you,' I cut in, 'I'd be more than happy to pay them myself.'

He raised a hand. His tone momentarily icy. 'Just let me finish. Did you expect me to buy you this place, pay your bills and take huge risks to see you . . .'

'Oh huge risks. Death-defying!'

'. . . and not expect to marry you some day?'

'Tom, I hate to say this but in seventeen years you've not once suggested marrying me except in order to explain why it was impossible.'

'It was impossible to divorce Rachel.'

'Because she owned half the stock.'

'For whatever reasons, and that was not the most important one, it was impossible. But you were always on my mind. It was you I loved, you I wished I'd married and you I want to marry now. I just don't understand.'

He looked tearful. I sat beside him and took his huge hands in mine.

'Tom, listen. Listen to me. I haven't said I won't marry you. If you want a more positive answer I'll say I probably will. How's that?' Tom snorted, and took his hands away.

'It seems all too clear to me,' I pursued, angered in

my turn, 'that you *don't* understand. You see the whole
case in terms of "making an honest woman" out of me
...'

'That was a joke.'

'Whatever. As you said, you meant it in spirit. I love
you, Tom. I love you very much and I'm thrilled that
you want to marry me. But you must see that I haven't
been pining away all these years waiting for bloody
wedding bells to tinkle. I've had the best of both
worlds. Six days a week I've been a busy working
woman, enjoying all the social independence of a
bachelor. The seventh day, when I've been able to see
you, has been important and the joy it's given me has
buoyed me up on all the other six but it hasn't been the
centre of my life.'

'Hasn't it?'

'No more than it's been the centre of yours.'

'Now wait a minute ...'

'No, Tom. I'm sorry. You've had your wife, your
son, your mistress and your empire. Now quite
possibly, if you hadn't had your empire I'd have come
before Rachel. But the fact remains that I didn't. At
best I came second and in strict terms of calendar time I
came third or even fourth. By the same token you've
only been taking up one seventh of my time. I'm the
first to admit that, in crude terms, you *bought* that
seventh with this place. But you have to understand,' –
here I tried a smile but he wouldn't catch my eye, damn
him – 'if I'm hesitant about surrendering the other six
sevenths.'

Tom drained his glass and stood. He came to hug
me, his dressing gown coming adrift.

'So,' he said, 'you'll "probably" marry me.'

'Yes,' I said. 'But.'

'But what?'

'But couldn't I just carry on being your mistress? Or are you delivering an ultimatum?'

'Of course I'm not.' He kissed the top of my head and rocked me as though we were dancing. 'Just think,' he said, 'we can go on holiday together.'

'Again.'

'Yes. Again. Properly.'

'We could go back to Lisbon. Or Sintra.'

'We could rent a little palace in the hills there. And think of our life in London! We can go shopping together. We can go to the theatre. We can have friends round. Do what other couples do.'

'Tom?'

'What?'

'We don't have to be married to be like other couples.'

Now he laughed. He was exasperated but believed, deep down, that he had won me over and that I was just being difficult. Poor unsuspecting Tom. We turned out the lights and went back to bed. He was staying the night. Although he was drained of energy, I could tell, he made love to me again. He was whipping himself into a kind of angry vigour, trying to crush my will, and I enjoyed myself, letting him believe that it was thoroughly crushed. When he fell heavily asleep, however, his face in my shoulder, one of his great legs straddling mine, my will had never been more active. Josh would be back at work tomorrow. I would make him cancel any appointments and let me buy him lunch. The Son and the Mistress had urgent plans to lay.

V

The charity whose chair Rachel had filled until her death, provided financial support to the victims of medical incompetence and campaigned on their behalf for legal restitution. She had a sad interest vested in the case. Josh, the only child born to her and Tom, was physically handicapped as a result of a painkiller prescribed to Rachel during pregnancy. His upper half and his brain were untouched but he was born without feet or calves. His thighs were rounded stumps. He was one of a blighted generation. Such were her guilt feelings after his birth that Rachel had herself sterilized.

Josh Spellman's sunny nature, alert mind and seraphic good looks were Nature's compensation for mankind's negligence. By way of shoes, he had a pair of thick leather pads which strapped around his stock-inged stumps and buckled to a kind of belt. With these, he could run, play, even climb stairs and join in at football. He was one of the crowd at his nursery school and for some years afterwards, winning over the other children's doubts with his bravery and wit. Trouble arose, however, with the onset of puberty and the desperate wish for conformity that came with it. Although Josh grew no less rapidly than his friends, the difference in their heights became more painfully obvious. As their hormones got to work, other boys isolated him from their smutty conversations and magazine-fingerings, embarrassed – erroneously, it happened – that the Wonderful World of Sex would lie beyond Josh's capabilities or experience. Josh retreated into books and took to a wheelchair. No less patronizing in their assumptions, Rachel and Tom were unaware that this isolation was partly self-imposed. The wise boy had a tenacious survival instinct.

'I'm a *rara avis*,' he joked during our first private conversation, 'a thalidomide fairy. If I were albino too, I'd probably qualify for a generous government subsidy.'

Josh joined the publishers in much the way I had; soon after leaving university, because there was nothing else he wanted to do. He was interviewed by four of us and impressed us immediately with his consuming passion for books. He had read more widely than anyone else we had seen – devouring trash fiction with the same witty appetite he brought to literary biography or the demands of high art. He knew about bindings, about paper, about type-setting. Our only fear was that he might find his first editorial work too limited. We need not have worried. He proved an indefatigable reader of unsolicited manuscripts and unearthed four minor successes in his first year with us. In time, he became our poetry editor.

Tom, of course, was nervous as hell about Josh getting to know me. He rang up in a flap the moment he heard that Josh was coming to us for an interview and for weeks afterwards was convinced that his son would somehow divine our relationship. In the event, Josh needed no intuition. I told him several months after his joining us. I had to. We had become friends. I remember we had been discussing a particularly lurid novel about suburban family life in Beckenham in the Sixties, when Josh said,

'Of course, I was spared all that hair-raising

frankness at home. I honestly don't think my parents have ever had sex with each other in my lifetime.'

'Really?' I asked, pouring more apple juice.

'Really and truly. Separate bedrooms from day one. The official reason was that he tends to be up so late and likes to crash around rather in the morning. But I knew it was actually because she hates sex. She was raised by nuns and the silly woman believed every word they said. Deep down she thinks sex is wrong if it's pursued for anything but bringing lovely babies into the world for christening. You know I was only eight when she told me she had got her tubes tied and why?'

'No!'

'I was rather cross, I remember. I wanted brothers and sisters. Sometimes, in my darker moments – yes Mary, I do have them – sometimes I think that perhaps she had a *stupendous* sex life with him when they first married. I think she did it with him on garage floors and kitchen tables and every which way. I think he was quite a stud when they met – he's quite a bit younger than her, of course – and he sort of woke her up. You can see it sometimes from the way she looks at him when she's had a few too many. And then, when I was born, she reverted to her convent school mentality and decided that I was a punishment for her naughtiness. I think all my lifetime she's been trying to save her soul. No. Not a sexual animal, my Ma. And twisted! If spirits have bones, dear Mary, hers is without a straight one.'

'How does he manage?' I dared.

'Oh I think he manages very well. His own mother died young so Ma's become a sort of mother to him – someone to honour and obey. He's probably got somebody in a well-appointed love-nest somewhere. We'll never know about *her* until his funeral. She'll be the one crying in a veil, who nobody knows. She'll have ostentatiously good legs and will have dressed rather too well in order to cover her nerves.

'But Mary,' he went on, 'what about you?'

'Me?' I fancy I blushed.

'Yes. Everyone here treats you like their maiden aunt but you're not half-way old enough.'

'Thanks.'

'You're not ...' He searched for a round-edged euphemism. 'You're not a Radclyffe Hall, by any chance?'

'Certainly not.'

'Pity. But I'm not surprised. I suppose you've got a secret lover tucked away in Camberwell or somewhere.' And then Josh grinned at me with the kind of suggestive depravity only angels and small boys can get away with and suddenly the years of telling nobody seemed a tremendous strain.

So I said,

'If I told you, you wouldn't believe me and if I never told you, you'd never guess.'

'Give me three.'

'All right. One.'

'A cabinet minister.'

'Wrong. Two.'

'Your boss and mine.'

'Wrong again,' I crowed. 'Three.'

He thought hard this time and said, 'My father.'

'Wrong three times,' I replied quickly. 'Told you.' But I hadn't fooled him.

At first I thought he was joking when he said, 'It's no problem you know. Your secret's safe as the grave with me.' He said it in such a teasing way. He carried on teasing over the next few days, ringing me at my desk only to ask things like, 'He always wears flannel pyjamas with Ma. Does he keep a spare set at your place – just in case of chills?'

Then one day I snapped – he had teased me at the wrong moment, while I was clawing over a contract with my least favourite agent – and I said, 'Stop it, Josh. All right? Enough's enough. Stop it.' He raised his hands in mute apology. Later on he returned with a punnet of strawberries as a peace offering.

'Mary?'

'What? I'm busy.'

'I do love you, you know.'

'Good. What else?'

'I would never, ever tell him I knew.'

'Good.'

And that was that. We buried the hatchet, shared the strawberries and the subject was never raised again directly. We would merely make fleeting references to whether a Wednesday evening had gone well or not. I think our colleagues began to think Wednesdays were my bridge nights. At least, none of them was sufficiently curious to ask. My only penance for my indiscretion was to allow Josh to call me Ma. He told everyone it was short for Mary-Mother-of-Us-All and soon, for the least flattering but most disguising reasons, the misnomer caught on throughout the office.

Josh disliked restaurants because they so rarely made provision for wheelchairs – although he would occasionally make an exception and walk to one. He used to send his secretary out for pots of take-away food from a vegetarian restaurant in Covent Garden and invite people to lunch at his desk. Insulted at this slapdash way of entertaining, Josh's poets were always won over to it once they discerned they were among the chosen few to enter a charmed circle.

I booked him for a desk-lunch as soon as I came in, the morning after Tom's unwelcome proposal. I sent Kirsty out in a cab to bring us a meal from a Thai restaurant where I brought so much custom that my desire was law. We ate in my office because people tended to drop in at Josh's and I wanted him to myself.

'Still in mourning, as you see,' he said as he wheeled himself in. He indicated the black blanket across the lap. Normally he wore a red or bright blue one. 'Extraordinary how it shuts people up. That ghastly man from accounts – the one with the breath – was in the lift just now and he didn't say a word. I think I should revert to normal by degrees. Perhaps I should wear Black Watch tartan next?'

He put on his brakes then leaned across the desk and kissed me. 'You looked wonderful yesterday,' he went on.

'You saw me.'

'How could I miss you, dressed up like Jackie Onassis in a supermarket? Bad, *bad* woman!'

'I was going to hide myself somewhere but that nice young man insisted on showing me up to the front.'

'Yes. Cousin Martin. Hasn't he grown up *well*!'

'Poor Josh. Was it hell? Well of course it was.'

'Actually, it wasn't too bad. Rather like a wedding but cheaper. Lots of aunts I hadn't seen in ages and won't need to see again for a while. And some people said such sweet things. It was very odd but by the time I left I'd got the feeling that the old witch showed a completely different side of herself to the outside world.'

'Most people do, don't they?'

'Yes but these were people from committees and so on, people I'd never met, and they gave the honest impression that she'd been a pleasure to know. Mmm! Are those little parcels of duck?'

'Yes.'

He shut his eyes with pleasure as he bit into one. 'No one else in this building could ever get a take-away out of those people,' he teased. 'You wield such power, Madam.'

'Talking of which.'

'Yes?'

'I saw Sir again last night,' I confessed.

'Poor Ma. He was knocking it back at the get-together afterwards. He must have been wrecked by the time he got away. I hope he wasn't, well,' Josh quivered an eyebrow suggestively, 'you know ... rough.'

I saw no way to break the news tactfully so I came straight out with it. 'He asked me to marry him.'

Josh was far too well brought up to splutter his food but he registered suitable shock. 'How did you reply?' he asked after a moment.

'I said I wasn't sure but that I'd probably accept him. He didn't take it very well.'

'I bet he didn't. "Probably" is not a word he's used to.'

'Do you think I should have said yes?'

'Well of course I'd love you for a mother, Ma, but I think it's up to you.' Josh munched a moment or two, lost in thought. 'Well!' he exclaimed at last.

'What?'

'I never thought he would. I mean. Well. Somehow I got so used to the idea of him just making do with things the way they were. He was so miserable with it the first time around, it seems odd that he wants to get married again so soon.'

'I think he'd wait for a few months. I'd make him. He says he wants to make an honest woman of me.'

'I trust he was joking.'

'He said he was but, Josh, I still think that's how he thinks of it deep down. Oh Josh.'

'What, Ma? Don't look like that. You look miserable.'

'Josh, I don't think I want things to change. I wish your mother hadn't died.'

'Do you really?'

'Really.' Josh picked at some more food, evading grief. 'Of course,' he mumbled, 'you never knew her.'

'I liked things the way they were. I liked being myself, being Ma most of the time and having Tom tucked away waiting for me on Wednesday evenings.'

'Best of both worlds.'

'But if I become the second Mrs Spellman . . .'

'The very idea!'

'Quite. But if I do, I'm worried things will have to change.'

'He'd never make you give up your job!'

'Certainly not. He's already said as much. But. Oh, I dunno. Josh, I don't want to be a *wife*.'

Josh gave me his shrewdest look, the look he used to melt agents into honesty and authors into subjection. 'Is my Ma worried, by any chance, that if she becomes the Wife, someone else will have to become the Mistress?'

'No.'

'Are you sure?'

I hesitated. 'Not really,' I confessed. 'But my main fear is losing my independence. I may be only his mistress but when I fill in forms I can still write single. I like that. And yet . . .'

'You love him.' I nodded, overwhelmed with a not unpleasant wave of sad-spiced exhilaration.

Josh ate on for a while and I drank some hot-and-sour soup. Kirsty came in and left some letters for me to sign. I took a phone call from a literary scout in Amsterdam. Josh was deep in meditation, his sweet brow furrowed.

'Josh, forgive me,' I said after a while. 'I've suddenly realized how monstrous I'm being. This is the last thing you want to talk about. For God's sake, Rachel's funeral was only yesterday.'

'Ssh!' He flapped a handful of parcelled duck to silence me and flicked chilli sauce on my blotter. 'Let me eat for a bit,' he said, with his mouth full. 'I'm getting an idea.' Silenced, I waited for several minutes more. People returned from pubs and sandwich bars to congregate, chattering, by the coffee machine on my landing.

At last Josh wiped his lips and fingers on a paper napkin and sat back.

'Simple,' he said. 'It's ingenious, if a little late Henry James.'

'Tell.'

'You're the only other Ma I ever want', he explained slowly, 'but to keep you happy, we find Sir another wife.'

'Josh, really!'

'No. I mean it. Don't laugh. It's perfectly feasible. London's crawling with women who'd love to marry him; women past child-bearing age, women with careers, who want nothing better than a rich, influential husband to provide for their old age and give them a little extra social mobility. They'd snap him up.'

'I don't want him snapped up. I want him for myself!'

'You'd *have* him for yourself, all except the boring bits that the Late Lamented used to take care of. He'd be "snapped up" like a slightly-worn bargain, for the convenience of it, not for love. We could even find him a society lesbian. There are plenty about.'

'No,' I said, entering into the spirit of things, 'I don't think he'd like that. Not an open marriage – he's so fearfully respectable.'

'The Jewish streak, I'm afraid,' Josh sighed. 'I have it too. Perhaps you're right. And your side of things would be so straightforward whereas the society lesbian's extra-marital attachments could lead to all sorts of messy complications. No. Pass me your address book. What we need, dear Ma, if you'll pardon my sexism, is a good old-fashioned spinster.'

VI

As one who had long spent her days in disguise as one of the breed, my address book yielded bachelor girls in abundance, and spinsters, and 'wimmin', and even the occasional unmodified old maid. Popular as a witty, dependable single man with no visible sex life and no discernible amorous future, Josh was then able to double the list. We pored over it long and hard, like schoolboys over a chess problem or a game of Battleships. Just as bored civil servants ring each other to trade solutions to the same crossword, so, for days, the lines between our flats and desk-tops hummed with proffered names, thumb-nail biographies and character assassinations.

'Ma?'

'Josh.'

'Can we talk?'

'Yes. Your father won't be here for at least another

hour. It's so strange having him come round so often. In the last fortnight I've had what used to be several months'-worth of him.'

'How are you coping?'

'It's lovely,' I said. 'I suppose. He's moved in a suitcaseful of clothes. I think he's trying to show me how easily we could become man and wife.'

'Now Ma.' A warning tone entered Josh's voice. 'There's a very thick line separating man and wife from lover and mistress.'

'I know, Josh. I know.'

I lay down on the bed. I had just stepped out of the bath and needed to cool down before I dressed again. I used to have two quite separate wardrobes; a set of clothes to be single in and a different, noticeably sexier batch for a role as mistress. Now that Tom had expanded visiting hours beyond my once-sacred Wednesdays, my dry-cleaners could not keep up. Distinctions between erotic and motherly were being blurred. The night before I had greeted him in an ensemble much like something Rachel would have worn and I sensed the comparison cross his mind as well. He had undressed me as quickly as possible.

'How are things at your end?' I asked Josh. 'All set?'

'Table's laid, chicken breasts are stuffed, wine's on ice and my heart's aflame. I've even polished my wheels.'

'His photograph was so good-looking. How did you meet him?'

'I told you. It's a sort of encounter group.'

'And he's not . . .?'

'No, Ma. He's whole in body and in mind.'

'I know it's silly of me but it just sounds a bit kinky.'

'So? We'll have *beautiful* children. Now listen, Ma.

There's not much time and I've just had another idea for you.'

'Who?'

'Jasmine.'

'Which?'

'Jasmine Wilton.'

'No.'

'Why ever not? She's awfully nice but not too bright. She has a career, she's devoted to her country garden and she needs a man like Sir.'

'Exactly,' I pointed out. 'She needs him much too much. He might be flattered into abandoning me. Dreadful idea.'

'Sorry.'

'I was thinking maybe Pauline Savory,' I countered.

'Now there's an idea.'

'Hmm. She's so cold-blooded, she might not even mind if she found out.'

'She could even draw up a contract to protect your various interests.'

'A little vindictive, though. Remember what she did to the Goddards over the party.'

'Oh yes. She was rather a wicked fairy. It was terribly funny, though.'

'Not for the Goddards.'

'Scratch her off the list then.'

'Who does that leave?' I asked.

'Not a wonderful selection.' On our separate beds we glanced down our heavily edited duplicate lists. Judith Blake, Joan Desmond, Harriet Forbes, Ruky Delgado.

'Not her,' said Josh suddenly. 'Absolutely not her. The Stepmother from Hell.' We scratched Ruky and read on. Joely Lyons. Cathy Hobson. Margaret Creighton-Fermor. I pictured them on isolated chairs around the walls of a party. Proud wallflowers in their neglected prime. It was depressing reading.

'I know they're available', I asked, 'but are they really all in need of a husband?'

'Well, they're none of them society lesbians,' Josh said. 'My research is meticulous. Though I suppose they could always be closet mistresses like you – God knows when they'd fit a lover in. Joely and Margaret are never at home and Cathy gets lonely in anything less than a crowd.'

'No one's in need of a husband,' I told him. 'It's just a neurosis into which we have to persuade them. God but they'd be so insulted if they knew we were doing this!' Josh only chuckled.

'The other problem,' I went on.

'Yes?'

'Is that these are all women we know to have been either married or thoroughly involved at some stage of their lives.'

'They've each got a driving licence. So?'

'Well I know it's sordid but we need someone with no points of erotic comparison. I think we need a virgin.' Josh paused as though I had suggested uprooting mandrake by the light of a full moon.

'How would we tell?' he asked. 'We *can't* have them inspected.'

'Oh, you can always tell!' I scoffed.

'*Can* you? I don't think I know any any more. Even my so-called maiden aunts have one by one confessed to having had their moments. How many virgins do you know, Ma? Besides Patrick Lynton, that is.' I thought for a moment, and then it came to me. The perfect candidate.

'One,' I said. 'Polly Brookes.'

There was an awe-struck silence on the other end of

the line. 'We couldn't!' Josh breathed at last. 'Could we? She's so famous nowadays.'

'Exactly. Perfect.'

'Perfect. But how?'

'She has a new novel coming out later in the month.'

'Damn. That'll have her gallivanting all over the country giving readings.'

'Not before I give her a little launch party.'

'You're a bad woman, Ma. A bad, *bad* woman.'

'Well what would you have me do?' I asked him, plaintively. 'Should I just give up and marry him myself?'

'Never!' Josh protested. 'This is far too much fun.'

'Josh,' I pleaded, 'these are people's lives we're manipulating.' Josh turned serious. He was always convincingly grave when defending the indefensible.

'Mary Marlowe, we aren't just looking after Number One. If you married Sir and it didn't work, that would be two lives blighted. Bring Polly into the equation and it could work so well. All three of you could be happy. And if it was a disaster, he'd still have you. The two of you could escape the wreckage unscathed.'

I wondered if I could bring myself to attend Polly's wedding. I pictured myself buying them a present, choosing myself a hat.

'It's too unprofessional,' I decided. 'Polly's one of my longest standing authors. It would be like sleeping with a patient or seducing a witness.'

'Balls, Ma. However it turns out, it will be just what her writing could do with. Look on it as a creative editorial contribution. She'll be grateful to you one day.'

'Josh.'
'Mmm?'
'What do you get out all this?'
'Two stepmothers for the price of one.'

VII

Polly Brookes and I might have been close had she not been an inveterate liar. Many novelists are given to exaggeration in their conversation – their creative impulse springs, after all, from a need to restructure reality according to their own lights. Polly went too far, however. She would accuse one's answering-machine of being faulty rather than confess to having passed through a harmless anti-social phase.

'I've been ringing and ringing,' she would say. 'I've been trying to contact you for *days*.' She was incapable of answering a simple greeting with a simple formality.

'Hello, Polly. How are you?' was invariably met, not with, 'I'm fine, thanks. And yourself?' but with a catalogue of disasters. These – taxi crashes, dislocated joints, sexual harassment, dead loved ones – were of a kind that were never immediately disprovable and yet aroused one's instinctive disbelief. The maddening thing was that, despite her creative gift, she didn't even lie well. It was as though every plot-twist she thought up for a novel then rejected as too far-fetched, haunted her brain until she gave it verbal release.

A truer friend or a more honest person would have challenged Polly long ago. 'I'm sorry, Polly,' I should have said, 'but I simply don't believe you. Why is it, Polly,' I should have asked, 'that all the appalling things that happen to you, only happen when you're on your own?'

As the years went by her lies grew daring, as though to test my endurance, and came often to involve famous people she might conceivably have met. It became a fantasy of mine, as we sat in my office, or walked, chatting, out to lunch, to trip up her fictive progress with a calm negative. The results, I liked to imagine, would be as extravagant as anything in a medieval exorcism; she would let out a banshee shriek, she would scratch my face, she would turn bright green or even, like another Wicked Witch of the West, melt away leaving only a Chanel suit, a pool of steaming slime and a six-hundred-page manuscript, damp at the edges.

I never did challenge her, though. I lacked the honesty. I didn't like her enough to want to assume the responsibility of rebuilding her after the inevitable collapse. I could have liked her. She was clever, and pretty – in a Bambi fashion – and amusingly acerbic when roused. Her lies kept me at a distance, however, as they did others. Perhaps that was the whole idea and she liked herself in glorious isolation; a Norma Desmond of the literary set.

Typically, once I had set my heart on pinning her down for lunch to broach the subject of Tom, she played hard-to-get. She cancelled me twice, with last-minute excuses about a burst water-main and a mysterious cousin from Toronto. On the third attempt, she arrived so late that I had already picked my way through a salad and was on the point of returning to the office.

'Mary,' she said, hurrying forward to kiss my cheek, 'I'm so *sorry*! You wouldn't believe it. No sooner out of the house than I realized I'd locked the only set of keys inside, so I had to break a window to get in and then, of course, I had to wait until a man could come to replace the glass.'

'Poor Polly,' I said. 'Come on. Sit down.'

'He took an absolute age coming, of course, and when he got there it turned out he was only measuring the window before fetching the glass. I did try to ring you but there didn't seem to be anyone on the switchboard at all. You should have a word with your telephonists. You really should. Oh. Hello.' She turned to the waiter who had slipped to her side. 'A bottle of the Sancerre, please and, oh, yes, a *salade aux lardons*.'

'Anything else, Madame?'

'And some bread.'

Polly dismissed him with a smile then turned her huge green eyes back to me. Why *was* she still single? Could it be only her mythomania? She remained slender. Her wrinkles were small and in all the right places. She always wore her hair in a chignon, a style that had once seemed fuddy-duddy, but which now matched her age to the same perfection as her expensively *vieille fille* clothes. Her below-the-knee suits, silk scarves, low-heels and high necks were all French. Indeed, when she kept her mouth shut, she would have passed for one of those autocratic priest-esses of Paris fashion – the kind that used to sit to one side of the cat-walk at a private *défilé*, announcing each creation to *mesdames* as a mannequin brought it on parade. Perhaps it was her manner. Perhaps it was her slightly over-mobile mouth. Perhaps, after all, she kept single through choice.

'Now tell me, Mary. Tell me all.' she asked.

'Well, we've had a confirmation of the serialization offer from the *Observer*, which is good news, and your reading tour's all lined up,' I said. 'I assume Lottie has given you all your dates?'

'Some of them. Nothing for Scotland yet and I think I should go to Dublin.'

'We could drop in on her afterwards, then. If you've got time, that is.'

'Certainly. I only hope I don't get plagued by that dreadful man again.'

'Which man?'

Polly sighed. 'Didn't I tell you? He plagued me. Absolutely plagued me. He turned up to every single reading and signing – even in Birmingham – to ask difficult questions. They were very clever questions – he'd obviously read every book inside out, so I suppose I should have been flattered – but there was something sinister about him. Maybe because he knew so much about me and I knew so little about him. I asked him once how he found the time to follow me all over the place the way he did and he just smiled. Like this.' Mary imitated the fanatic's smile. She did it rather well. I grinned. Her wine and salad arrived. I let the waiter take the remains of my salad away then I filled both our glasses.

'The other thing', I said, once it was clear that she had finished, 'is that I want to throw a party for you.'

'For me? How lovely.'

'I know we usually go to a restaurant or have drinks in the office but I think that's a bit impersonal. I thought it might be fun to get some caterers into my place. We couldn't fit that many in there but I think, if we pushed the sofas to the walls, we could get about forty-five in comfortably. Obviously we ought to ask some journalists and the usual literary editors but perhaps you could draw up a list of about thirty friends of yours you'd like asked.'

'What fun!' said Polly, chasing a chunk of bacon around her plate. 'I'm not sure I can come up with that many, though. Does it matter?'

'Of course you can.'

'I don't get around nearly as much as I used to, you know. I'm getting rather dull in my old age. Most of my old friends have stopped calling.'

'Nonsense. Anyway,' I went on, watching closely for her reaction, 'there's definitely someone I want you to meet.'

'Who?'

'Darling, he's so sweet but he's rather sad at the moment. His wife had a massive stroke a few weeks ago and dropped dead out in the garden.' Polly's eyes grew larger and sadder. She clicked her tongue sympathetically.

'He'll probably be rather out of his depth, actually. He doesn't read much – he's not literary at all in fact.'

'What a refreshing change! I do get so fed up with our lot. You go out to dinner and all anyone talks about is who's writing what, who attacked whom in which review and how so-and-so is getting their own back. It's so awfully insular. What does your friend do?'

'Well, he's not really *my* friend. I mean, I've only just got to know him myself. He's Josh's father. Tom Spellman.'

'Tom Spellman? But he's a millionaire!'

'Is he? You'd never know it. He's so unaffected. I mean, he dresses very well and so on but he's terribly discreet. I think he's in cars or something.' Was I overdoing it? Polly didn't seem to notice.

'I had no idea poor Josh was his son,' she confided.

'Oh yes.'

Polly clicked her tongue again. She was evidently counting Josh as yet another of that poor Tom Spellman's misfortunes. She munched her lettuce almost greedily, then dabbed some dressing off her chin with a napkin corner. She caught my eye and smirked. 'You are a dark horse, Mary. Is he very keen on you?'

I feigned surprise. 'On me? Oh. Not at all, I shouldn't think. No. Anyway,' I flustered, stroking my necklace, 'you know how it is. I'm not really, well ... You know.' I waited until she had taken another mouthful before I said, 'No, it's you he wants to meet.'

She gestured towards her breasts, as though to say, 'Me?'

'Yes,' I said. 'Don't worry. He's not a fanatic or anything. And he certainly isn't literary. It was just that when he asked me who my main authors were and I mentioned you he immediately said how much he'd enjoyed the televisation of *A House Built on Sand*.'

'Did you tell him you'd introduce us?'

'Of course not!' Polly pretended relief. 'I simply said, "Oh well, in that case you must meet her some time."'

'And?'

'He looked quite excited. Of course, I wouldn't dream of asking him to your party if you'd rather I didn't.'

'Oh. Well. I think if there really are going to be about forty or so of us, there's no great risk. Let's be daring. Ask him.' We giggled, and changed the subject. It was that simple.

VIII

'Thomas?'

'Mmm?'

'Let's give a party.'

'Why not?' Tom said, then hesitated. 'You don't think it might be a bit soon, though? I mean, with poor Rachel and everything.'

'Maybe you're right.' I lay back on the pillows on my side and laid a hand on his chest, where the grizzled brown hair swirled. He lifted my hand and kissed it then returned it to his chest where he rubbed its palm over one of his nipples.

'Nice idea, though,' he murmured. 'Who would we ask?'

'Well, for a start I don't think we should give it as "us". Not just yet.'

'Oh.'

'I do think it's a bit soon to be doing that. But there's no reason why I couldn't throw a party here and just invite you as Josh's father.'

'Oh. I see.'

'It could be the party where we are seen to meet. Officially.'

'Your birthday isn't for ages.'

'Who mentioned birthdays? It can be a book-launch. I know. Polly Brookes has a new novel coming out in a few weeks. It's time the company gave her a proper do – she's made us enough money. I'll get caterers in – there's a firm up the road who are good – and you can come with Josh and pretend that you've never set foot in here in your life. You can have met me just once before, say, at Josh's place. How's that?'

'You *are* a devious creature, Mary.'

'*You're* the one who deceived his wife for seventeen years.'

'Don't.'

'Well you are.'

'I know. Just don't.'

'Sorry. Kiss me?'

He kissed me. His tongue tasted of toothpaste and whisky. He had always drunk whisky at bedtime but the toothpaste was a new ingredient in our lovemaking

– part of the gradual domestication process. Before Rachel's death, he never kept a toothbrush in the flat. He saw it as too momentous a step, preferring to borrow mine the morning after. He had also started bringing his work with him. He was pushing through some deal in Germany and the love-nest had become a centre of operations for the duration. It was scattered with brochures and paperwork and an incongruously cheap and ugly briefcase had begun to loiter outside the kitchen door. I kept kicking it over in passing. Its plastic made a satisfying bang when it hit the floorboards.

IX

By an unconscious irony, the florists had decorated the room as though for a wedding. The mirror above the mantelpiece was decked with a garland of mock orange-blossom, white roses and myrtle, as was the linen-smothered table where the caterers had arranged the canapés. Polly saw the resemblance too. She was the first to arrive – it was her party, after all. She walked across the hall, stood between the open double doors and chuckled. 'They've made it look like the last scene of *The Philadelphia Story*.'

'All we need is a harmonium playing "Here Comes the Bride",' I laughed. 'Happy publication day, Polly. Lovely dress.'

'Thank you. I very nearly didn't buy it, you know, because I saw Princess Michael of Kent buying one just like it.'

'Really?'

'Yes. But then I thought, we're hardly likely to go to the same parties and if we did, it would probably say she was coming on the invitation and I'd know to wear something else.'

'Of course. Champagne?'

'Lovely.'

'I've done a little display of the books on a table over here.' I showed her. 'And I've got the petty cash and a box of copies tucked away so perhaps we can mount a signing session at some stage.'

'Good,' she said. 'We can shame the people who got complimentary copies into buying one for their friends.'

The doorbell rang. As I turned to answer it, Polly tapped my arm. 'Is he coming, then?' she asked.

'Is who . . ? Oh, yes,' I said and patted her hand. 'He wouldn't miss it for the world.'

Luckily, the first guests were not Josh and Tom – which would have proved awkward. I had primed Josh that he was to create some wheelchair trouble. This he duly did and managed to delay their arrival by some twenty minutes, by which time the room was already crowded.

'Josh, darling.' I kissed him. 'And you've brought your father. I'm so glad. Hello, Tom.'

'Hello again.' Tom shook my hand, stroking my palm wickedly as he did so.

'Polly's in the corner over there signing copies,' I told them. 'She'll be so glad you both made it.'

'How long do we have to keep this up?' Tom hissed.

'Ruky, have you met Tom? Ruky Delgado, Tom Spellman.' As I left them talking, Ruky was gushing that, of course, she had heard *so* much about him.

I wheeled Josh over to the canapés and handed him a drink. 'Why did you set *her* loose on him?' he asked. 'I thought we'd agreed to keep her clear. She'll monopolize him now.'

'I can handle the Stepmother from Hell,' I said. 'It just struck me that, if he met her first, and then perhaps Joely, then Pretty Polly would make such a striking contrast.'

'Like a diamond against jeweller's velvet.' Josh delicately bit a large prawn in two. 'Ma, I hope you don't mind.'

'What?'

'But I took the liberty of asking Antony.'

'Your new friend?'

'I think he's rather more than that now. The chicken breasts were a great success.'

'Of course I don't mind, Josh. I'm thrilled. Is he here? I don't remember letting him in.'

'Well I'll stay put then. If you see him, you'll know which direction to push him in. Go and save poor Sir from Ruky.'

As I walked away, Antony emerged from the crowd. Looking even more than in his photograph like a bright-eyed evangelical, he strode smiling over to Josh and kissed him lingeringly on the lips. The effect was sensational. As he began to wheel Josh through the party, the ranks of guests parted before them with little, frightened smiles.

Tom mouthed 'save me' over Ruky's shoulder as I approached. I winked back. 'Ruky, darling, Tom's had you all to himself for far too long now,' I said. 'Besides, I'm dying for you to meet Josh's new friend.' I steered the politely protesting Ruky over to Antony and Josh then returned to find Tom draining a full glass. He was ready for Polly but I delivered him to Joely for a few minutes, to be on the safe side.

'A toast,' I called out once she had him deep in

conversation. 'Ladies and gentlemen, to *Letters Unwritten* – all success.' Glasses were raised across the room to where Polly sat behind a small fortification of books.

'All success!' people cheered, or mumbled, 'Yes' or 'Mmm'. Everyone drank the new book's health.

Ruky shouted, 'Cheers, Polly darling.' Beside her, Josh had swallowed a canapé the wrong way and was spluttering while Antony patted his back for him and held out a glass of water. I went to fetch the lady of the moment.

'How are we doing?' I asked our publicist, Lottie, who sat at Polly's side taking the money for copies.

'Sold out,' she said. 'Nothing left but these ones from the backlist. I think those copies you laid out may have ended up in people's bags.'

'Never mind. Polly, darling, come and mingle.' I wrinkled my nose at Polly to show her it was time. She stepped out from behind her table with a word of thanks to Lottie.

'Enjoying your party?' I asked her.

'Yes.'

'Who do you want to meet?'

'Oh for heaven's sake, Mary. Where is he?'

'There,' I said, indicating with a backward nod of my head for her to look over my shoulder. 'He's talking to Joely.' She craned her neck – she was shorter than me – and widened her eyes.

'Is he the tall one?' she asked. 'With the blond hair turning silver? Famous faces can look so different in the flesh.'

'That's him,' I admitted with a slight pang.

'Well? Introduce us.'

This was wrong. All wrong! She was drawing herself up and turning on her charm like so many headlamps.

She was queen of the party. She could not be refused. She would take him from me. I was mad to bring them together. I led her over.

'Joely, angel!' I kissed Joely's cheek. 'I've barely spoken to you. We must have a proper talk before you go. Polly, you know Joely Lyons.'

'Of course I do,' said Polly. 'How are you, Joely?'

'Fine,' Joely said, clasping her hand without exactly shaking it. 'The new book looks wonderful. I've already got it on order.'

'How *sweet* of you.' Polly bared her little teeth.

'And this is Tom Spellman, dear Josh's father. Tom, this is Polly Brookes – the guest of honour.'

'How-do-you-do.' Tom shook her hand warmly. 'You need another drink. Here, let me.' He took her glass and exchanged it for a full one on a passing tray. 'I expect Mary's already told you how much I enjoyed *A House Built on Sand*. Of course, I'm hopeless at reading – I never seem to find the time – but if your TV adaptation was anything to go by, it's a book I should make an exception for.'

'Well, I wouldn't say that exactly,' Polly murmured. Joely had seen someone else she knew and slipped away with a mute wave to Tom. He waved back. I took a tray of sausages from a waiter and, having offered Tom and Polly some, I too re-entered the fray.

Tom talked to no one else all evening. Josh and I could hardly believe it. One or both of us was watching them all the time. I had never seen Polly like this. She was not fluttering her eyelids or gurgling with old-girlish laughter and, to judge from his reactions, she did not seem to be lying excessively either. She was hanging with simplicity, humility even, on his every word. I ached to know what he was talking about. Tom was a darling but no raconteur. As parties draw on and reach that listless, should-we-move-on-to-eat-some-where period, a conversation of any intensity acts like a social magnet. People would drift over and stand at Polly and Tom's elbows, waiting to be introduced. Polly and Tom (how naturally their names joined hands!) would chat to them but it seemed silently understood that their conversation would continue to take precedence and the interlopers would murmur a farewell and pass on.

When Polly tore herself away at last, it was to say goodbye. 'Mary, darling, thank you so much for a heavenly evening.'

'Are you off?' I asked, glancing at Tom who was leaning on the end of the sofa, muttering something to Joely Lyons. Joely was shaking her silver mane and laughing.

'I'm afraid so.' For a moment, entirely for my benefit, Polly intensified her smile a fraction. 'Tom's sweetly offered to drive me home and buy me dinner somewhere on the way. I know you did say something about you taking me out the way we always do but I honestly think you've done more than enough. I can't get over how lovely this place looks. And the flowers!' She gestured to the fireplace with a chuckle, throwing a glance at Tom who straightened up and left Joely's side. 'Bless you for everything, Mary.'

She kissed my cheek, close to my ear, waved to one or two people then went in search of her coat. Tom walked over and shook my hand.

'Lovely evening,' he said. 'You've made it all look so nice.' I gave him a real smile – *our* smile – to show him that no one was listening and he didn't have to pretend any more but he carried on as though he hadn't noticed.

'I told Polly I'd run her home.'

'Yes. She said. She's very grateful.'

'Bye.'

'Bye, then.'

I watched him leave the room, meet Polly in the hall and steer her out to the porch. Josh saw me watching and wheeled himself over.

'I don't believe it,' he said. 'I really didn't think it would work so well.'

'We don't know for sure,' I replied. 'He might just be driving her home.'

'But Ma, he talked to no one else for the last forty minutes!'

'Maybe she wouldn't let him. Maybe he couldn't escape.' Josh looked at me cynically. I glared back. The beatific Antony walked over and laid large, golden hands on the handles of Josh's wheelchair, silencing us.

'I think we should be off,' he said. 'Mary, it was so good to meet you, finally.'

'And you, Antony. You must come again soon – just you and Josh. It isn't normally as hectic as this.' I kissed him.

'It is in its way,' Josh said, raising an eyebrow. 'Will you be all right, Ma?'

'Of course I will.'

'I'll call you over the weekend.'

Josh caught Antony's questioning glance. 'Ma's short for Mary,' he said. 'My life isn't *that* complicated. Now push me to your car.'

I kissed Josh goodnight, and Joely, and Ruky, and Kirsty, and all the other departing guests who merited it. Then I took myself off to a bistro in the village where there were always some tables laid for one, and stayed there while the caterers tidied the flat. When I returned, nearly two hours later, the empty bottles had gone, the glasses had been washed and packed away for collection. The furniture was back where it should have been and the garlands of flowers had been taken down and dismantled. All that remained to show there had been a party were two vases stuffed with white roses and myrtle, and an acrid smell of smoke, scent and wine. I flung the windows open to the cold night but there was no breeze to clear the air.

X

I had retired to bed and fallen asleep over a new manuscript when the doorbell rang. I let it ring again, to make sure it was not just a trouble-maker. The third ring told me it was Tom. I shivered as I walked across the marble floor of the hall in bare feet. I saw his bulky silhouette through the smoked glass in the front door.

'Tom?'

'Yes.' I let him in. We stood there in the semi-darkness. I tried to make out his features in the wan light from a streetlamp.

'Did I wake you?' he asked.

'No.'

'I did. Didn't I?'

'Yes. What time is it?'

'One, I think. One-thirty.'

'For God's sake come in. My feet are getting cold.' He followed me into the flat and shut the door. I turned on a table lamp then wrapped a rug around my shoulders and curled up on a sofa. The smell of the party had finally drifted out into the night. Tom shuddered and closed the windows.

'You'll catch your death,' he said.

'I was getting rid of the smoke,' I told him. 'Then I fell asleep. Sit down.' He sat on the other sofa, facing me. He looked worn and harassed; one of his most becoming expressions.

'Did you have a good dinner?' I asked.

'Not bad. I took her to Le Paradis.'

'Very nice.' He had promised to take me there but never had. I betrayed no pique.

'Did she tell you many stories?'

'Yes. She lied for about half an hour without drawing breath,' he sighed. 'Odd woman. Very attractive but odd. Then we went back to her place.'

'For coffee.'

'Yes. Coffee. Then she sort of lunged at me and we went to bed.' I froze. He saw me.

'Well what did you expect?' he asked.

'You went to bed?' I echoed.

'Yes.' He stared at me. 'That virginal bit is only a veneer, you know. She's really quite accomplished.'

'How could you!' I spat.

'It really wasn't difficult,' he said. 'As I say, she's a very attractive woman.'

'Shut up!' I shouted, jumping up. 'Shut your bloody mouth and get out.' He jumped up too. I raised my hand to hit him but he hit me first. He slapped me hard across the cheek so that the blood sang in my ears and my neck jarred sickeningly. I stumbled, gasping, to the bathroom, stubbing my toe on the way and locked myself in. He banged on the door.

'Get out!' I repeated, 'Get out get out get out!' Were we drunk? I slumped to the lavatory to nurse my toe then I looked at my face in the mirror, hair tumbling, cheek crimson, lips stiff with rage as though I had been weeping. I did not cry.

Tom stopped banging on the door and started knocking intermittently and muttering, 'Mary? Mary? What are you doing? Let me in.'

'No. What the hell do you *think* I'm doing?' There was a pause.

'I don't know,' he said. 'Let me in.'

'No.' There was a thump and I saw the door press inwards on its hinges and lock as he slumped against it.

'Mary, I didn't sleep with her. Not really.'

'Yes you did.'

'I didn't.'

'You did. You can't lie to me, Tom.'

'Yes,' he admitted after a while. 'So? I went to bed with her. You wanted me to.'

'No I didn't.'

'Yes you did.'

'This is childish.'

'*You* are childish. You throw a party then thrust woman after woman at me in the most suggestive fashion then you fly off the handle ...'

'Because you slept with one of them.'

'You wanted me to.'

I drew a breath then shouted quite distinctly through the door at him, '*I – did – not.*' I panted. I felt slightly sick. 'I ...'

'What? What, Mary?'

'I thought you might want to marry her.'

'*Marry* her?'

'Yes, Tom. Marry her. Must you repeat everything I say?'

'What in God's name gave you that idea? It's you I'm marrying.'

'Is it? Since when?'

'You said.'

'I said probably. I didn't say yes.'

'Oh this is stupid. Unlock the door so we can talk properly.'

'No. Go away. You hurt me.' I glowered in the mirror. 'I think,' I added, 'I think you've given me a black eye. How the hell am I expected to go into work tomorrow with a black eye?'

'I'm sorry.'

'Bastard. You absolute bastard. Just go away. I hate you. Go back to Polly fucking Brookes.' He fell silent a moment. I heard his breathing through the door.

'Mary, I don't understand,' he said at last.

'What don't you understand?'

'How could you be so calculating? How could you set her up like that?'

'All I did was introduce you,' I laughed bitterly.

'You set her up. I honestly had no thought of going to bed with her. It was an interesting evening and I was fascinated to meet her but. Oh God. Mary, if you'd heard her! I'd just meant to go up and see her to her door – maybe have a quick coffee with her so she wouldn't think I was running away and be hurt.'

'Jesus but you're full of shit.'

'Mary, if you'd heard her! She is so alone, Mary. So alone. I started to leave and I swear she all but fell on her knees.'

'How very flattering to your poor, detumescent ego.'

Tom kicked the door. 'Will you *stop* being so damned superior for once and listen? She begged me not to go. She pleaded. I had to sit on that sofa and listen to this ... this ... this catalogue of solitude.'

'Lies. She's a pathological liar, Tom. You must have seen that.'

'Yes, she lies. She lies to make herself more interesting, to keep people beside her. But these weren't lies. Christ, she actually wept. She clawed at me. In that big boring flat with that typewriter at one end of the huge dining-table, and all those wardrobes full of expensive clothes and that – ' he groaned, 'that awful *deadness* to it all. It was so pathetic.'

'So you ... took pity on her.'

'Yes. I suppose I did. I know that makes me sound like some egotistical ...'

'Tom, what will you do if this world-famous novelist of mine gets pregnant?'

'She won't.'

'You mean you asked her if she's on the pill?'

'Of course not.'

'You "took precautions"?'

'No. I ... I pulled out in time.'

'Oh.' I sat back on the lavatory, noticing for the first time a bottle half-full of flat champagne that someone had left beside the sink. 'Great,' I said. 'Quick thinking but hardly foolproof.'

'Let me in, Mary.'

I thought for a moment. 'Why?'

'Because I'm sorry. Because I promise that if I ever, ever hit you again I'll walk straight out of the door and never come back. Because ...'

'Well?'

'Because I want to be your husband. I don't want to end up like her.'

'Tom, I scarcely think a man of your wealth and position would ever be reduced to begging for crumbs of sexual consolation. Be realistic.'

'And you be human!' he exclaimed. The last word was distorted and, as I heard him slide to the floor outside, I also heard him quietly sobbing.

I sat in that bathroom for a long, long while. I thought of Polly Brookes and yes, I even imagined myself in her position. I thought of the proud single women I knew, and the pathetic. And I thought of Josh and Antony, of the tender carefulness with which Antony had manoeuvred his lover's wheelchair down the front steps. I did not unlock the door until Tom's sobs had subsided into gentle snores. Then I switched off the light, unlocked the door and stepped out into the corridor. I pushed gently at his shoulder with my hand.

'Tom? Come on,' I said, 'get up and come to bed. It's draughty down there.'

He mumbled something and started to get up, using my arm as a support. Suddenly he seemed to remember where he was and why. 'Mary?' he asked.

'Yes. It's me.'

'Will you . . . will . . .?'

'Yes, Tom. I'll marry you. I'll marry you after the sales conference at the end of the month. OK? Now come to bed.' He came quietly. I was in bed first. I realized as I pulled the bedding over me that I was chilled to the marrow because the heating had switched itself off hours ago. Tom hung up his suit then slid in behind me. He nuzzled the back of my neck and, as we dozed off, reached a heavy arm around my breasts for comfort.

'Mary?' he asked.

'What?'

'Good.'

XI

I did indeed have a slight black eye the next morning. I cried off work pleading, as a homage to Polly, a flood in the neighbour's flat, then had Kirsty send me a few more manuscripts in a taxi to keep me occupied over the weekend. Tom worked on one sofa, I on the other. He slipped out to a meeting on Saturday and came back with a little box from Burlington Arcade. Brown eyes are hard to match – even when bruised – so he had thought of the colours that best became me and settled for an emerald. The ring didn't fit. It was made early in the last century, for more refined fingers than mine. He offered to hurry back to Piccadilly to have it altered, assuming that such things took no longer than replacing the sole on a shoe. I kissed him and told him not to be silly and said I would take it back on Monday. It was a beautiful emerald – the first jewel I had ever owned that wasn't a mere industrial chip – but the disparity between Tom's romantic image of my fingers and their thicker, slightly crooked reality, loomed over the rest of the weekend like an ill omen.

On Monday, with the ring safely zipped into a compartment of my briefcase, I returned to the office. My bruise had turned from brown to pale green. I hid it with make-up and wore dark glasses.

'Awful conjunctivitis,' I explained to Kirsty. 'It flared up on Saturday morning and now I look like a bride of Dracula.' In all the better Sunday papers, Polly's new book had received the glowing notices that were now no surprise and I faced the weekly editorial meeting with a light heart.

The firm was based in a fine Bloomsbury town house and the boardroom (also used for occasional lunches) retained the atmosphere of an old-fashioned dining-room. I was one of the last to arrive (which seemed always to be expected of me). Josh was already at the table, as were the other four editors. He gestured at my glasses as I sat down and I repeated the story about conjunctivitis. Coffee and biscuits were passed around and, while we waited for Basil, our managing director to arrive, we began to discuss an American agent, new to the scene, who was poaching authors from his rivals then demanding extraordinarily high advances for them. After a while, when Basil had still not arrived, one of the junior editors went in search of him and met him on the stairs.

Basil's face was long when he and his secretary took their places, its naturally melancholic folds deepened into profound gloom.

'I represent, as you know, the third generation of my family to have managed this remarkable publishing house,' he said. 'After conversations held on Friday afternoon and earlier this morning, I regret to have to inform you that I shall also have represented the last.' He looked around the table at our surprised faces. 'As you cannot fail to have heard or noticed, our finances have not been of the healthiest in the last two years. The family alas can no longer afford to underwrite our more, how can one put it, *creative* losses to the extent that has always been its pleasure. After due consideration and, needless to say, much heartsearching, I have decided to accept a generous bid. From the Pharos Group.'

Now there were concerned noises. Originally a prestigious literary firm, Pharos had long since been bought out by a press baron and his tabloid editrix wife. They had steadily built up the company's finances on the less than literary reputations of several 'shopping-and-fornication' authoresses and any number of what Josh called sub-genres: book-related board games, 'novelizations' of films and television series, and even adaptations of films which had been adaptations of novels to begin with. Pharos was not a company likely to countenance our publication of new European and South-American novels, still less our

Egyptian list or the thin works of our stable of contemporary poets.

'I'm not far off my sixtieth birthday,' Basil continued, 'and I shall welcome this opportunity to retire from a field whose changes are becoming a little rapid for me. Frieda and I have long cherished a dream of moving back to Tuscany and now I can make her a happy woman.' A few of us smiled but no one was happy. I stared at Josh who stared back at me.

'Paul and Wanda Yeoward have given me their full assurances that they would not wish to make any changes to the company. Paul says he holds our list in high esteem and will regard us as a prestigious feather for his cap, not merely another firm to be broken up and sold off. The only major changes, which will of course involve the sad necessity of laying off some staff, will be the amalgamation of our accountancy and distribution departments. There is no need to tell you how this will improve efficiency.

'In a few minutes I shall be going from here to Pharos to sign the agreements though I still have a few tasks left to do about the place so I won't be disappearing for good much before the end of the week. Paul will be here this afternoon and for much of tomorrow to do a kind of walkabout and meet the staff. He'll also be wanting meetings with each of you in turn to discuss your authors, deals-in-progress, plans for next year's catalogue and so forth.

'I'm sorry to drop this on you like a bombshell – not least because I know how busy you all are getting ready for the sales conference – but you have to understand that the family's need is urgent, and Paul is not a man to be kept waiting. Thank you.' With that, Basil and his secretary left the room. There was a stunned silence until the door closed behind him and then we all started speaking at once.

I had a frantic morning, having postponed most of Friday's business. I had to claw reprint rights from one agent and take dizzying risks in a telephone auction with another. I had to smooth at least three authors' fevered brows and deal with a fourth's hysterical complaints that his new novel, well-reviewed the week before, was unobtainable anywhere in central London. In the middle of it all, Polly rang to thank me for the party and to say how fascinating but, well dear, really rather philistine Tom Spellman was – she did so agree. Lunch with a gossip-mongering – therefore superbly effective – scout we retained in America was not a welcome diversion.

I missed Paul Yeoward's walkabout – he never made it to my floor. He did however contact me in person, rather than through a secretary, to arrange an appointment for the next day. Josh was the second editor he interviewed. I returned from lunch to find a note asking me to ring him. Guessing it was about his conversation with Yeoward I chose to visit him instead. I found him clearing his desk.

'Josh? What's going on?' I asked, although it was patently obvious.

'I'm off, Ma,' Josh said. 'Or should I say, laid off.'

'*What*?'

'We're to be streamlined.'

'But Basil said . . .'

'Yes. Basil said but Yeoward also said and Yeoward owns us now. He said he was sorry but they're having to "let me go" as the least experienced editor.'

'Briony came after you did. She doesn't even have an English degree.'

'Ah but Briony brought in the money-spinning Mr

Wykeham and now she lives with him. So, if she went, Wykeham would, in all probability, go with her.'

'But you're the poetry editor.'

'Quite.' I sat on the edge of his desk watching him sling books into boxes.

'I'm also disabled.'

'Josh, he never gave that as a reason.'

'No. Although I wouldn't be surprised to find that the new offices have no wheelchair access. I'd probably have to come in via the delivery entrance like a lorry and use the service lift.'

'Who said anything about new offices?'

'Haven't you heard?'

'I was out to lunch with Venetia Peake.'

'New offices. The lease is running out here and Pharos won't renew it. It would be more efficient to have us . . . to have you under the same roof as them. Think about it, Ma. He had to choose between Briony and me. Not only does she have Wykeham, she also has legs, attractive legs at that, which can walk her leggily all over the place, to lunch, to Frankfurt, to launches, to all the places that you've been kind enough to let me avoid going. Don't look like that. I'm not being self-pitying, just realistic. To the Yeowards of this world, Briony will always represent an opportunity, I will always represent a passenger.'

I stormed up to the boardroom where Paul Yeoward was grilling another of my colleagues but I stopped on the stairs. I had no fears for my job – I was more safely ensconced than Briony and I had more influence – but I suddenly accepted the inevitability of Yeoward's decision. There was no point in storming when he had already made up his mind. It would be wiser to save my rage for questions on which he had less security; questions, for instance, of literary judgement.

I helped Josh down the few front steps and into a taxi then passed him up his boxes and his folded wheel-chair. Several people were leaning out of windows to see him go. As the taxi pulled away across the square we all waved and a slightly angry cheer went up. Genteel revolution was in the air. (It dispersed by this time the next day, however, as surely as the stench of Polly's party had left my flat.)

I returned to my desk only to snatch up my briefcase. Then I walked in a swift, decisive fury all the way across Soho to Piccadilly and into Burlington Arcade. The name of the jeweller was printed on the silk lining of the box's lid. I was served by a woman. She was discreet, motherly yet efficient – a housekeeper used to these luxuries and their attendant complications. I snapped the box shut again and slid it across the counter.

'Good afternoon,' I said, 'my fiancé gave me this engagement ring on Saturday – I believe that was when he bought it.'

'Ah yes,' said the woman. 'I remember.' She was waiting for a name, to prove I was not a thief.

'Mr Spellman,' I told her.

'That's right. He came in at about three o'clock.' She threw a professional glance at my hands. 'Would Madam like to have it altered?'

'No, thanks. Actually, I want to give it back.'

'Oh.'

'The thing is, it's difficult to give it back to Mr Spellman directly.' She nodded. She understood. 'And I was wondering whether you could perhaps just keep it in your safe or something and contact him to ask what he'd like to do with it. I assume he'll want to sell it back to you but I think it's a decision we should leave up to him.'

'Yes, Madam. That's quite all right.' Relieved, I turned to go.

'If I could just have your name and signature here, Madam.' I turned back. She was holding out a little form.

'It's just a formality, to let the customer know that the item was willingly surrendered.'

'Oh, of course.' I signed, quickly. 'This must happen quite often then?' I asked, with a short laugh. The assistant released a ghost of a smile but said nothing as she tucked the ring and my signature into a drawer beneath the counter.

XII

Tom waited over a week before visiting me again. It was a Wednesday. He mentioned the ring only to say that he had indeed sold it back to the jeweller. We had a meal sent round and slept together but did not make love. Apart from the occasional loving phone call, we then had no contact until the following Wednesday and the Wednesday after that. It was quite like old times. For a while I thought I had won. When he said, 'Of course, you do know there's always a risk of me meeting someone else?' I said, 'Yes. I know. And I know that you might marry them.'

'I might fall in love with them too,' he said. 'I might want to have children by them.'

'That's a risk I have to take,' I replied, and the subject was dropped.

Then he did meet someone else. In fact, he had met her before. I had introduced them. Not Polly – no such

Nemesis – and not Josh's Stepmother from Hell. Tom began seeing a lot of Joely Lyons; she of the silver hair and flawless skin. As her first husband had died leaving her the principal shareholder of a major West End department store, the match was an attractive one to the gossip columnists. Handsome widow and handsome widower were seen at restaurants, at the theatre, even, Josh reliably informed me, at a racecourse.

I began to spend a lot of evenings with Josh and Antony. Antony was an architect and was rebuilding his Hackney house for their joint residence. Under Josh's proud eye, he would show me drawings of ramps and wide spaces for a wheelchair and furniture and fittings that Josh could use either from his chair or at his lower standing height. Josh had told his lover nothing about my continuing liaison with Tom.

'It's not just that he's shockable, Ma,' he said, 'although he is, you know, *lipsmackingly* pure! It's more my ingrained cynicism. Telling him would be tantamount to admitting he's family and I can't believe such happiness can last.'

Tom was quite open with me about Joely. Continuing to spend his Wednesday evenings (and some Wednesday nights) with me, he said when he saw her and what they did. He told me things about Joely I had never known nor wished to find out. He asked my permission before proposing marriage to her and even offered to show me the ring – to prove, I imagined, that it was not as superb as the one he had offered me.

They announced a spring wedding. He had the gall to marry her in church. She had the decency to wear something in bluey-green. Josh bought me some red underwear especially and was peeved when I refused to wear it. I had my hair put up and wore devastating grey.

It was a beautiful day and the graveyard banks were

bursting with primroses. A lot of the press turned up, of course, as did all Joely's overly-sleek friends. I sat near the back, between Polly and Ruky. When the priest asked if anyone present knew of just cause or impediment and so on why these two should not be joined together, I nearly kept silent. For a moment I thought I could just let them go through with it as planned. I thought how perfect they looked together and how Joely's children would look up to him.

Then I thought, 'Sod this,' and I stood up. Of course everyone was astonished. Nobody ever interrupts, except in films. Ruky pulled on my sleeve to sit down again and Polly chuckled. Tom was the only one in the church not to turn round.

'I do,' I said. 'He bought us a love-nest in Belsize Village seventeen years ago and came to screw me every Wednesday in return for paying all my bills. Well, I'm still in the love-nest and he's still coming every Wednesday.'

For a few seconds you could have heard a pin drop, then Josh shouted, '*Bravissima*!' and I was surrounded by reporters.

XIII

Fantasy, of course. All the pure, idle fantasy of a frustrated will and understimulated mind. Tom *did* sleep with Polly and he *did* give me a black eye and I *did* accept his proposal. I kept the emerald however and, when I let him make the announcement after the autumn sales conference, he gave me a diamond to match. I can't wear them both at once, of course. That would be too ostentatious. I like to alternate them. No one but Josh (and Tom's solicitor) ever knew our secret. Not even Polly. We told people that Josh had introduced us, fond of me and sorrowful for his widowed father. I held my peace and let the world and his wife make the humiliating assumption that Tom had picked me in the charitable nick of time off the shelf of shame. There was some envious murmuring about funeral-baked meats, the marriage to the second wife having come at an unseemly brief interval after the burial of the first, but those who had passed for Rachel's intimates were more charitable and wished us well. I never guessed that wedding presents could be so substantial.

Josh *was* fired by our new bosses (and he *did* give me red underwear for the wedding, which I wore) but he heard no more from Antony after the night of our party. He professed no surprise and little heartache and he continued to gain inventive satisfaction through sources he thought it too indelicate to discuss. I took a week's holiday for the honeymoon (we returned to Sintra) and I never resumed my place in the office. Instead, I persuaded Tom and some of his friends to back a publishing venture Josh and I set up on our own. A family publishers.

One of our first authors, who transferred her allegiances as an act of magnanimous faith and despite promises of fat advertising budgets from Paul Yeoward, was Polly. Within seven months of the launch party thrown so fatefully in her honour at my flat, she was delivered of a novel quite unlike anything she had written before.

'My dear,' said Josh, who read the manuscript first, 'we're on to our first winner. It fairly steams.' Certain passages shocked even me, and I have read the unprintable. It was *The Industrialist*. Polly never told me what had happened between her and my husband. I never told her I knew. The book won a prize and was made into a film by some Italians which did very well on the art-house circuit, for all the least artistic reasons.

The flat, in all its Proustian decadence, we gave to Josh, who had a chair-lift installed on the front steps. In our honour, he threw mysterious parties there on the first Wednesday of every month, to which we were never invited. Tom sold the house in Oxfordshire which Rachel had redecorated so often and bought us a smaller house in Kensington. I have my own study and a dressing-room. Tom is often away on business. There is a largeish garden and a conservatory and, abetted by Josh, I have become something of a hostess. Our little company did not stay little for long and I have few hours left for reflection. There are times, however, often on quiet Sunday evenings, or in the silence after Tom has yet again mentioned the possibility of children, or at the end of dinner parties where most of the guests have been guests of his, when I feel less than I was.

Secret Lives

· Francis King ·

I

'Mrs Clive?'

'Yes.' Oh, hell! Receiver to ear, she stooped to pick up the wooden spoon which, in her scurry to get to the telephone before the answering-machine clicked and whirred into action, she had knocked to the kitchen floor. 'Who is it? ... This is Anna Clive. Who is it?'

'This is Ossie, Mrs Clive.'

'Ossie? ... Oh, *Ossie*!' She had never got used to the westernization of Osamu into Ossie. She rarely called him anything but Osamu. 'How are you, Ossie?'

'Is this a bad time?'

That day, as she had rushed out to shop, rushed out again to the post office to buy Wilfrid some stamps, rushed to the dentist, rushed home to let in the plumber, rushed to her voluntary work in the hospital library, and then rushed home again to prepare supper, all times had been bad. 'No. Oh, no. Not at all.'

'I do not wish to disturb you. But something terrible, very terrible has happened. And I can think of no one else.'

'What is it?'

She had not seen or heard from Osamu since, some four or five months back, he had moved from Kensington to Highgate. Before that, it had always been in Holland Park that they had met, she striding out impatiently, and he seated composedly on a stool, an easel before him and a brush in his hand. Briefly she would halt; briefly they would chat.

'Brian has died. He died today.'

Receiver still to ear, she edged over to the stove and switched off the gas above the grilling steaks. Wilfrid loathed overcooked steaks. 'Brian?'

'My friend.'

'Oh! Oh, dear! Oh, I am sorry.'

She had never met Brian. She had never even heard his name until now. My friend: that was how Osamu had always referred to him. Next weekend my friend is taking me to Brighton. My friend is away on business. My friend did not like the picture which you liked. My friend has bought a house in Highgate. My friend is again in hospital. Yes, that was the last reference to my friend. And now he was dead.

'I am alone. He died this morning. I am alone, Mrs Clive. And this house . . . it seems too big, too quiet, too – different.'

A silence, ominous, even eerie.

'Isn't there anyone you could ask to be with you? Anyone you could visit?'

Another, even longer silence. 'I regret – there is no one.'

'That's terrible, Osamu!' Already she knew what was coming.

'It is difficult to ask this. Mrs Clive, please forgive me. But . . . I have no other friend. In London, in England I have no other friend, no other true friend. Would you – please, *please* – would you come and sit with me? For an hour, half an hour.' Before she could answer, the high, metallic voice went on: 'Please take a taxi, Mrs Clive, if you do not wish to drive in your car. I will pay taxi. I do not wish to inconvenience you.'

'Oh, there's no need for that. But thank you for thinking of it.' Yes, she would have to go, even though she would miss *The Maltese Falcon* on television, would not be able to water the garden, and would be deprived of a promised early bed.

'Then you will come?' He sounded so surprised that she realized that all along he had expected a refusal.

'Yes, of course, I'll come. Just as soon as supper is over.'

'There is food here. I cannot eat. I bought food but I cannot eat.'

'That's sweet of you. But I have to feed the family as well as myself.' His own family were presumably all far away in Japan. Did he have any contact with them? And if he did, had he told them of 'my friend'? Probably, almost certainly, not.

'Then you will come?' he repeated, as though fearful either that he had not properly understood her or that she would change her mind.

'I'll be with you in, oh, an hour, an hour and a half. Will that be all right?'

'Thank you. Thank you, Mrs Clive. That will be fine.'

The steaks were overcooked; but jaws champing while he gazed at the file propped against the salad bowl beside him, mercifully Wilfrid did not notice. The wireless was on, so that Joanna could listen to Mahler's Resurrection Symphony from the Proms.

'Does that have to be so loud?' Wilfrid asked at one moment, scowling across at the set.

Joanna did not answer. Her eyes had a misty languor, her cheeks were flushed. She had been reluctant to leave her cello practice when Anna had called her down. Standing at the bottom of the stairs, Anna had felt the rasping notes as though they were emery paper rubbing up and down somewhere deep within her.

'You've eaten hardly anything,' Wilfrid glanced up from the file to comment.

'Not hungry. Too hot.' Anna jumped to her feet, carried her plate over to the sink and emptied what was left on it. Her hand reached for the switch of the waste-disposal. 'Anyway, I must fly.'

'Fly?' He was not really interested; once again, head tilted sideways, he was gazing at the file.

'That Japanese boy – the one I told you about – the one who had the exhibition in the Ice House. He rang me just now. An SOS.'

Wilfrid was not listening. Joanna was not listening. There was no need to explain the nature of that SOS.

At one traffic light and then another she looked in the *A to Z*. When she had finally located the deep-eaved Victorian house, set far back from the main road, it was far larger than she had imagined. She parked the car in front of the garage, its doors shut. There were no flowers, only neat, glossy shrubs in the front garden up which she then walked.

It was a single house, not flats. That, too, surprised her. Must be worth at least half a million, she thought. She pressed a handkerchief to the beads of sweat which she could feel along her upper lip, and then, handkerchief still damp against the palm of her hand, rang the bell.

The door opened so quickly that he must either have been waiting in the gloom of the cavernous hall or else have seen her from a window. But oddly the door opened only a fraction.

'Yes? Who is it?' The metallic voice struck her as unusually high, as though with apprehension, even fear.

'It's me. Anna Clive.'

'Ah, Mrs Clive. Come in. Come in.' He put his head round the door; then slowly, as though in reluctance, opened it.

Several inches taller than him, ample, sweating in her light-blue cotton dress, Anna edged in.

'Poor Ossie.' On an impulse, she put an arm round his narrow shoulders and hugged him to her; then she felt him resisting this contact and at once let him go.

There were some good pieces in the ground-floor sitting-room. There were also a number of his pictures, some of which she had seen while he was painting them in the Park. Although so literal, the pictures – of the Chestnut Walk cruelly dishevelled in the aftermath of a gale, of some children clambering over a fallen tree, of ducks on the pond – had a certain vapid charm. She wished that, when they had visited the exhibition in the Ice House, Wilfrid had not dissuaded her from buying one. Throwing money away, he had said; but two days later he had insisted on buying an electric hedge-trimmer, which he had then never used, preferring the old, rusty shears.

Its windows all shut despite the heatwave, the room had about it an oppressive smell, as of flowers long dead. But there were no flowers, fresh or dead, to be seen. Anna was always buying flowers for the Kensington house; she loved flowers, pausing to sniff at roses as they trailed over neighbours' fences in the street and even getting pleasure from cupping some particularly spectacular bloom in a hand.

She was thirsty; and even if she had not been thirsty, she could have done with a drink. But Osamu offered her nothing. He pointed at an armchair and said 'Please'; then, when she had sat in it, he said 'That is Brian's chair.' She found pathos in the present tense; then she wondered whether he had used it merely because he was a foreigner. He stared at her intently. His face had never seemed more narrow or more pale; he was twisting his left hand from one side to another in his right.

'Was it sudden?'

He blinked, shook his head. 'Expected. He was ill last year – remember I told you?'

'Oh, yes.'

'Pneumonia. Then other things, many things.'

'How old was he?'

'Fifty-five. Fifty-five next August. August twenty-fourth.'

'How sad!'

She wanted to take that perpetually twisting left hand in her own and hold it still.

'Sad. Very sad.' He caught his lower lip between his teeth. Then suddenly, without any warning, he let out a wail and precipitated himself out of his chair to fall on his knees before her. He put his left hand on one of her knees, his right hand on the other. Then he lowered his head on to her lap and she felt his whole body jerking against hers, as though in an orgasm. He was crying. She now knew that that oppressive smell, as of long-dead flowers, emanated from him, a distillation of his grief and the self-neglect resulting from it.

She tried to console him, one hand stroking hair which was stiff and dry to the touch, as though he had only recently sprayed it with lacquer. 'Osamu! Osamu! Don't do that! Don't!' But wasn't it better that, previously so much in control of himself, he should now totally abandon that control?

Eventually he straightened, his cheeks glistening with the shed tears in the gradually darkening room. 'He died in my arms.' There was a defiant pride in his voice. 'I do not care about doctor, about nurses. He died in my arms. Blood. I do not care. Blood on my trousers, shirt. I do not care.'

'How terrible!'

He was staring over her shoulder, out of the window, as though at some waiting presence, invisible to her from where she was sitting. There was a look of spent exaltation on his face, such as one sees on the face of a winning athlete as he breasts the tape.

'His father is not there. Can you believe this? His father knows that he will die any time, any time. But he goes to his club to sleep and then he goes again to his club to have lunch with a friend. Can you believe this? So he dies in my arms. His father is not there. His father arrives after he has died.'

'Where is his father now?'

'How do I know? Maybe still at his club. We meet for the first time last week. We are not friends. Not at all!'

'Then how long were you and, er, Brian together? I thought . . .'

'Four, five years.'

'And yet you . . .?'

'Brian did not wish it.' Again he caught his lower lip between his small, white teeth. 'Strange.' Then, as though expecting her to contradict him, he added: 'True.'

'But his father – his family – knew about you?'

He shook his head. 'Nothing. Damn-all.' Damn-all. She imagined that Osamu had learned that from Brian. 'They know about me only last week. Before that they know nothing. . . . A secret life.' He gave a small smile. 'Now they know everything.'

'But how . . . why?'

He pondered, head tilted and his left hand once again twisting from side to side in his right. 'Another time I will tell you.' He laughed. 'A long story. Brian is very conventional man. Maybe you think that Japanese are very conventional but Brian is more conventional than any Japanese.' Again, as though he thought she was about to contradict him, he added: 'True.'

'I wish I had met Brian.'

He stared at her. 'Maybe you will get on with each other. But I think – maybe not.'

'Oh!'

'You are not conventional lady.'

'Aren't I? My daughter and son think I am!'

Suddenly he seemed no longer to wish to talk about his friend or his death. He began to question Anna about her life, as he had never done before. It might have been she, not he, who was in need of comfort. What exactly was it that Wilfrid did? How old was Joanna? And there was a son too, wasn't there? Had they always lived in that house of theirs on Campden Hill? Did they own it or did they rent it? Anna answered all these questions as best she could; but she kept wanting to say 'But I came here to talk about you, not about myself and my family.'

All at once he jumped up from the chair opposite to her. 'I think you must go home.'

Not sure whether to be offended or relieved, she laughed. 'Must I?'

'It is late. You have far to travel.'

'But I've been here such a short time. Isn't there anything I can do?'

'You have done a lot for me.'

'I hate to think of you alone in this house.'

He gave a little shudder. 'I must become accustomed.' He hesitated. 'Now this house seems to be – haunted. I feel ...' He put a long, pale hand to his narrow forehead, thumb and forefinger massaging it. 'He seems ... Here. Everywhere.'

On an impulse she said: 'Why don't you come back with me?'

'Back with you?' He frowned in seeming bewilderment.

'You could spend the night with us. Philip – my son – is away in Germany. You could have his room.'

He laughed, as though this were a joke, then shook his head vigorously. 'No. Thank you, Mrs Clive. My place is here.'

'I do hope you'll be all right.'

'I will be all right.'

'If you should want a chat, then, please, don't hesitate to ring. Any time. Any time, day or night.'

He gave a little bow. 'You are very kind.'

'In any case, I'll ring you tomorrow, if I may. To make sure that everything is well with you. But I haven't got your number. Could you give it to me?'

'You do not wish to telephone. It is bother for you.'

'Of course I want to telephone. Please – let me have the number.' She clicked her bag open and took out her address-book. 'Your surname *is* Kawasaki, isn't it? I've always thought of you just as Osamu – or Ossie.'

'Yes, Kawasaki.' He came close to her and then, in a voice so soft that she could hardly hear him, he told her the number. 'There is also a machine. If I am not here, you can speak to the machine. Tomorrow I have so many things to do. I must procure death certificate, register death, arrange funeral, see lawyer. Many, many things.'

'Won't his – Brian's – family help with all that?

He seemed dubious. 'Maybe father.' Then: 'Not their business,' he said, the metallic voice suddenly sharpening. 'My business. I am executor.' He hesitated and then added: 'I am sole beneficiary.'

'Oh. I see.'

'I think you are surprised.'

'No. Oh, no.' But she had been surprised. 'Well, if the family are not going to help you, do please call on me ...'

'Mrs Clive, you are very kind. Very good. When I first met you in the Park – do you remember? It was raining and we both sheltered under some trees – I thought, "This is a good lady." ' Suddenly he bowed, took her right hand in his, and raised it to his lips. The lips felt dry on her skin.

As he walked with her to the car, she said: 'So this house is now yours?'

'This house is now mine.' Suddenly his face froze into a stoical grief. 'But what use is it to me? What use? Now?'

'Well, I suppose it helps, helps just a little, to know that he wanted you to have it and everything else.'

He shook his head. His face was still frozen. 'It does not help.'

Driving down Highgate Hill, the air mercifully cool on her forehead and bare arms after the heat of that sealed room in which they sat facing each other, she in one heavily-upholstered armchair and he in another which he had pushed away from the wall with jabs from now a knee and now an arm, Anna said aloud to herself first 'Thank God!' and then 'Well, that was an ordeal!' She often talked to herself in the car when driving alone, as she also did in the kitchen when working alone. 'But why me, why me?' Then she answered herself: 'Because there was no one else, you chump.'

She saw the name of a street and, on an impulse, braked, swerved across the road, and entered it. Behind her the invisible driver of a bug-like van hooted. 'Sorry, sorry, *sorry*!' It was years – how many? twenty? twenty-five? – since she had driven down this street, with its dim lighting, its stunted trees and its mean little houses. As one descended the hill so one also made an equally precipitous social descent. Two black youths, one holding a bicycle, stood under a lamp-post, arguing about something, faces thrust towards each other and hands gesticulating. Then, as she drove slowly past them, they burst into laughter. The argument could not have been about anything important. An old man in a cap was hobbling along on crutches. A cigarette drooped from one corner of his mouth, his eyes were screwed up in effort or even pain.

This was the house, number 17. Its appearance now was little different from its appearance all those years ago when, tremulously eager, she used to ring the bell and then, with beating heart, wait for the middle-aged, stooped, emaciated man to open the door to her.

'Anna!'

'Jack! I could think of nothing all today but seeing you!'

'I wish I could say the same. But I had to think of so many other things, even though I didn't want to.'

He always had that dampening way with her, cool when she was ardent; but somehow, paradoxically, his restraint only had the effect of making her passion blaze up more fiercely. A composer, whose compositions were rarely performed – he was bitter about that, making ungenerous remarks about the successes of other composers unknown to her but known to him – he also taught music at a nearby secondary school.

'Is she out?'

'Of course she's out! I'd hardly be opening the door to you if she were in.'

His wife, whom Anna had never met or even seen, worked as a nurse at the Royal Free. It was when she was on night duty that Anna made the long journey up from the minuscule flat which she shared with another girl in Earls Court. She would so much have preferred Jack to visit her there; but something – an unwillingness to undertake that long journey? embarrassment first at the presence of someone else so close to their love-making and then at the use of a bathroom that that someone else might be waiting to use? a desire to be on his own territory rather than on hers? – made him always insist: 'No, you come to me.'

'But suppose she were suddenly to return?'

He shrugged.

'Or supposing one of the neighbours said something?'

He shrugged again.

She laughed, half apprehensive and half delighted. 'You like to live dangerously!'

One evening, the autumn fog making her cough as she stood on the doorstep, he seemed preoccupied as he let her in. This time there was not that delighted 'Anna!' He said 'Oh, hello,' and then, when she had entered, thrown her arms around him and kissed him, he nodded and said, as he had never said before, 'That was nice, very nice.' He might just have eaten a chocolate which she had given him. When she began to mount the stairs up to the bedroom, he caught hold of her hand and stopped her.

'No, no, Anna.'

'Why not? Why ever not?'

'Because ... Oh, come into the sitting-room and let me explain.'

She at once thought that it was something to do with her. Never for a moment had she apprehended that it was something to do with what later, in superstitious terror of naming, she was to think of as It.

'It's a bit worrying, of course. But I'll only be in hospital for five or six days.'

'And I can visit you there?'

'Well, no, it might be better not. You see – I'll be at the Royal Free. And she ... well, she might pop by to see me while you were with me, or some nurse on my ward might gossip to her ...'

'I do hate it that everything has to be so secret between us.'

He laughed. 'Oh, I rather like secrets. Fun.'

'Fun?'

'Somehow – our meeting like this – no one knowing – no one in the whole world – makes it all so much more exciting.'

She did not tell him that she had spoken about the affair to her sister, to her mother – both of them disapproving – and to the friend with whom she shared the Earls Court flat.

There were other, longer periods in the Royal Free. There were the treatments which left him nauseated, afflicted him with a deathly weariness and caused his already thinning hair to fall out so much that, on her last two visits, he was wearing a cap, heart-breaking in its jaunty tilt above his grey, bony face. By then they had long since ceased to make love. 'Sorry, pet. I'm just not up to it.' On that occasion she sat with one arm around him. From time to time she would raise his hand – it was cold, damp, seemed totally nerveless –

and place first one finger and then another in her mouth.

On her last visit he told her of his decision. 'No point in dragging out the whole awful business.'

Aghast, she pleaded with him. As she became increasingly hysterical, so he became increasingly detached. When she clutched at him, the tears by now streaming down her cheeks, he gently but decisively, hands on her forearms, pushed her away from him and then moved over from the sofa to a chair. Later, tucked down in a corner of the sofa, his wife was to find the ball of a tear-sodden handkerchief. She had said nothing about it. The confirmation which she had for so long both craved and dreaded had now come too late. Always meticulous in the hospital or in her home, she put the handkerchief in the washing-machine with his soiled bed-linen from the night before, and then she ironed it and kept it for her own.

'I've had a reasonably happy life, you know. I can't really complain. I'd like to have had more success with my music, of course. I think I was unlucky there. And I'd like to have had children. Your children,' he added, 'since Jean could never have any. But how wonderful to have met my last and only love' – his tone was joking but she was certain then, as she was always to be certain, that really he meant it – 'before going into the dark. These past two years have been the best of my life.'

'The best of mine.'

'But you have so many ahead of you. There'll be many better for you.'

'No, Jack, no. Never. My first and only love.'

'Nonsense!'

He told her how he would do it. 'I have my Lethe kit ready. I've had it ready ever since I saw my mother die in perfectly ghastly circumstances. Jean is going to a conference at the weekend. You know, she's interested in this Est nonsense.' Anna had not known; they rarely spoke about Jean when they were together, it was easier to forget her existence. 'First it was Subud, now it's Est. Ridiculous. But things like that keep her happy. Est or something like Est will keep her happy after I've gone.' On Saturday morning, after she had left the house, he would take the pills along with the whisky which would make their action that much quicker and more potent. 'I've laid in an extremely expensive malt.' He smiled at her. 'Oh, don't look so horrified. It's as easy as, well, falling off the proverbial log. One falls off into nothing. And it *is* nothing.'

'Do you want me to be with you?'

'With me? When?'

'When you do it.'

'Are you crazy?' He laughed, and the laugh then changed into the dry little cough, as though grains of sand were lodged in his throat, from which he had recently been suffering. 'Of course not! I couldn't subject you to that. And in any case think of the risk!'

'The risk?'

'You could be prosecuted. You might end up in a gaol.'

'I wouldn't mind. What would that matter?'

He shook his head decisively. 'No, dearest, no. Sweet of you to offer. But . . .' Again, no less decisively, he shook his head.

Soon he was telling her, 'Now I think you'd better leave.'

'Oh, but Jack – '

'Please.' He put his head on one side and smiled at her with an extraordinary sweetness. '*Please*. A quick goodnight. Yes?'

Briefly she held his emaciated, sour-smelling body

close to hers. Then he was gently prising himself free.

'Thank you, Anna. Thank you.'

She ran out of the house and down the hill to the bus-stop. There was a bus standing at it, disgorging some noisily drunken passengers: two stout old women, a stout old man and a youth with a small grey-and-white mongrel on a lead. 'Ta-ta, dear!' she heard one of the stout old women call out to the boy, and then all four of them burst into laughter for no apparent reason. Anna felt a terrible exhilaration seething within her, as well as the weight of a terrible desolation.

The next Saturday morning she got off the bus where she always did, and trudged up the hill. The air was raw; the sun, a squashed, yellow-orange ball, was low on the horizon. She walked down the street, not worrying now, as she had always worried in the past, that some inquisitive neighbour might see her, wonder about her, even report on her. She stood, on the opposite side of the road, and gazed at the house. How *empty* it looked. It had never looked empty like that on all those other evenings when she had approached it. But he was in there now, as he had been in there on all those other evenings. Perhaps even now he was cupping the pills in his hand, raising the glass of neat malt, throwing the pills back, gulping, swallowing . . . Perhaps even now . . . She hurried away up the road and then hurried back. Again she looked at the house. Empty. Totally empty. Briefly she had an impulse to rush to the door, ring the bell, smash a window if the bell was not answered, climb in, summon the police, summon an ambulance . . . But what would be the use? It was right what he was doing. It was terrible but it was right.

. . . Now twenty-three years later, Anna, her arms folded over the wheel of her car and her head tilted sideways, stared across the road at the same house, identical with all the other small, mean semi-detached houses in the same row. The house no longer seemed empty, as it had on that Saturday morning all those years ago. There was no light in its windows, all its curtains were drawn; but she sensed a teeming life within it – parents, grandparents, children, dogs, cats, rats, mice, beetles, flies.

She groaned. Then she whispered the name 'Jack.' Again: 'Jack.'

In recent years she had thought only fitfully of him; and she had never thought of him with this overwhelming grief. It was as though a love-letter had lain for a long time in the gutter into which it had been chucked, the grime gradually obliterating the words written in it, the rain gradually causing them to fade and blur; and then suddenly, in the hand which had retrieved it, those words miraculously, cruelly thickened, acquired a fresh focus, grew bigger, at last burst into scorching flame.

Before going into the narrow sitting-room, in which she could hear Wilfrid typing, Anna mounted the stairs to the bathroom. Stooping over the basin and using her right hand as a scoop, she splashed cold water on to her face again and again. She felt a burden of unshed tears behind her eyes, the pressure building up and building up. But she was determined to deny herself the relief of actually weeping. 'Life's a bitch,' she muttered to herself. Then she gave a little laugh. Where had she read that or heard that? It was not the sort of thing that she herself would normally say.

Meticulously she dried first her face and then her hands, easing back the cuticles one after another on the towel. Competent hands. That was what Jack had once called them, holding them in his own. 'I love your square, strong, competent hands.' Surely he had had enough competence from brisk, bouncy Jean without also wanting it from her.

She could see the light on under the door of Joanna's room. On an impulse she knocked, calling out at the same time: 'May I come in?' In the last year sixteen-year-old Joanna had become jealous of her privacy, sometimes even locking the door.

'Yes! Come in, come in!'

In her pyjamas, feet bare, she was curled up in the armchair under the open window. Her shed clothes were scattered on the floor around her. The cello was leaning against the wall in a corner, with a recently framed Chirico print, *Interno metafisico*, propped, unhung, against the wall beside it.

Joanna looked up from the score which was resting on the arm of the chair. Her face, mouth open to reveal small, pointed teeth, was radiant.

'How are you, darling? I just looked in to see.'

'Oh, I'm so happy, so happy. I've got it right. At last I've got it right.'

Anna lowered herself on to the bed. 'What have you got right?'

'The prelude to Bach's sixth suite. A real pig. I've been working on it for, oh, weeks and weeks. And now it's right, absolutely right. It was while you were out, I tried it again, and then suddenly, suddenly . . . Like first learning to ride a bicycle or keeping afloat for the first time in water . . . Marvellous!' She gave a clear, delighted laugh.

'Oh, I'm so glad!'

'But you don't really know what I mean, do you? Do you, Mummy darling?' She jumped up off the chair, lowered herself on to the sofa and then, having put an arm round Anna's shoulder, pressed a cheek to hers. 'It's funny that you're so totally unmusical. And Pop too. Where do I get it from?'

It's funny that you're so totally unmusical. That was what Jack would often say to her. Out of loyalty she would go to concerts at which works of his were going to be played. She would sit near the back, and of course she could never betray, by even a greeting or a smile, that she knew him, let alone that they were lovers. Later he would say: 'No use asking you for your opinion.'

'But I enjoyed it.'

'Did you? Did you really? Well, then, you enjoyed it as a non-gardener enjoys wandering through a garden.'

'Isn't that one way to enjoy a garden?'

'Well, your great-grandmother was musical,' Anna now said defensively.

'You mean because she used to appear in those amateur productions of Gilbert and Sullivan?'

'Well, surely you have to have some musical sense to be able to sing Buttercup and Katisha.'

Again Joanna gave her clear, delighted laugh, and again she pressed her cheek against her mother's. 'Oh, I do love you!' Suddenly, straightening her body and turning her head, she looked closely into Anna's eyes. She put up a hand and took a lock of hair between her forefinger and middle finger. She began to caress it. 'What's the matter?'

'The matter? Oh, nothing. I suppose I'm a little depressed after my visit to that Japanese.'

'Japanese? What Japanese?'

'The painter. The one I used to talk to in Holland Park. The one you met once when we were walking there. I had to go up to see him in Highgate – that's where he now lives. His – his friend had just died, died today.'

'Highgate! But that's a ghastly journey! Oh, the things you take on! It's not as though you even knew him well. Is it?'

'It seems I know him better than anyone else in England. The poor little thing seems to know no one else.'

For a while the two women continued to talk of Osamu.

'Rather attractive, in a girlish way,' Joanna said of him.

'I suppose he's gay,' she said later.

'Yes, I rather think he is.'

Both of them laughed.

'No use to you then,' Joanna said in joke. 'Or to me,' she added. 'I wonder if he's musical.'

'I remember mother telling me that, when she was a girl, to say a man was musical was a politer way of saying he was queer.'

Eventually Anna got off the bed. 'Well, I must leave you to get some sleep.'

'Oh, I don't feel at all sleepy. I never feel sleepy when I'm happy.'

'Well, I feel sleepy.' But what she felt was not sleepiness but an ineluctable tiredness.

'Milk drink?' she opened the door of the sitting-room to call to Wilfrid.

He looked up from the typewriter. 'Oh, darling! You're back!' He was genuinely glad to see her; not in the least exasperated, as he so often was when she interrupted him in his work.

'Oh, don't work so hard,' she said, as she so often said.

'I must get this draft ready for tomorrow. The

Jackass insisted.' The Jackass was Jackson, his boss in the Ministry. 'Where have you been?'

'Oh, I just felt that I wanted a breath of air.' She did not know why she told the lie, instead of revealing to him that she had been up to Highgate to attempt to support Osamu in his bereavement. As so often, Wilfrid had hardly been aware that she had been out of the house. 'It's so stifling indoors. So I took the car and drove down to Chelsea Harbour.'

'Wish I could have come with you.' He drew a deep sigh and then sucked in his lips.

She crossed to the desk, leaned over him and put her lips to his cheek.

He twisted round in the chair, grabbed her hand. With sudden urgency he said: 'Let's go to bed.'

She laughed. 'And what about that draft?'

'Oh, fuck the draft. I'll get up early and finish it tomorrow.'

'And what about a milk drink?'

'No milk drink. Come – to bed, to bed!'

It was as though he knew both that she was in need of comfort, and that to go to bed with her was the best way to provide it for her.

II

When inquisitive people asked Osamu why, at the age of twenty-four, he had chosen to come to England, he would tilt his head first to one side and then to the other, suck in a deep breath, and answer slowly: 'I think – I think because I wish to find myself.' But he had really come to England because he wished, not to find himself, but to escape from the image and the expectations which others had of him.

His beloved father, whose son he was by a late second marriage, had died when he was only six. Osamu had been told by his mother to summon the still vigorous old man to luncheon from the garden of the inn, on the foothills of Mount Hiei in Kyoto, which he, she and his grown-up son by his previous marriage ran with an efficiency so tireless that it was both one of the most successful and one of the most expensive in the area. The old man had been pruning a persimmon tree. A fine drizzle, lingering like fragments of cobweb on the skin of Osamu's bare legs and arms and the back of his neck, was occasionally pierced by a brilliant shaft of sunlight. '*Papa, papa!*' he called, as he walked between bushes aglitter with frecklings of rain. '*Papa!*' Suddenly there was a panicky urgency in the cry. He knew, he knew already that something terrible had happened, long before he saw his father, far ahead of him, lying, like a bundle of abandoned clothes, under the persimmon tree. He was humped face downwards and the back of his grey summer kimono showed a dark triangle where the drizzle had soaked it. His hand, its long nails meticulously buffed, was still gripping the clippers.

After that, the previously boisterous child became a still and silent one. Grave and self-possessed, he would take himself off to school, carry out the duties in the inn which his mother and his always kindly but never affectionate half-brother assigned to him, and settle to his homework. But all that really interested him was his drawing. First he worked in the traditional manner with a brush, once his father's, imported from Szechuan, an ink cake and an ink stone, also once his father's. Then, tidying a room in which a French woman tourist was staying, he had found a sketch-book open on a pallid depiction of the Golden Temple, with a box of water-colours beside it. She returned to the room at the moment when he was kneeling on the floor by the sketch-book, brush in hand, staring down at her painting. He might have been about to attempt to improve it or at least to modify it. She smiled with sweet indulgence and addressed him in French. Totally unable to understand her, he jumped in terror to his feet and with a gabbled 'Excuse me, excuse me!', scuttled from the room. When the time came for her to leave the inn, she asked for the boy and then, when he had been pushed towards her by his mother, held out the paint-box and three brushes as a gift. From that time onwards he painted in the Western manner despite the disapproval of his mother, his half-brother and his other relatives.

When he was eleven, an English student stayed for three days at the hotel. Each time that he returned to his room at the close of a day of sightseeing in the damp heat of July, this youth spurned the *yukata* left out for him as part of the hotel amenities, and preferred, having stripped himself and then gambolled and snorted in the Japanese bath, to sit in nothing but Y-fronts, the paper-shutters pushed wide, so that anyone in the darkening garden could see him. He could speak some Japanese, since it was oriental languages that he was studying at Cambridge. '*What is your name?*' '*How old are you?*' '*Do you go to school?*' Standing before him, his arms pressed rigid to his sides and his face slowly darkening, Osamu would feel an intense embarrassment combined with an excitement no less intense. The Englishman had a mat of hair on his chest, a dark mole on the side of his pugilist's nose, and acne on his shoulders. Osamu's mother and his half-brother had both commented that his feet smelled; but the odour, permeating the room from the socks which he would leave lying under the television set or in a corner, only served to excite Osamu.

On his last day in the inn, the Englishman beckoned to Osamu to join him by the window, where he was standing, looking out into the garden. 'See that bird? What is it? I've never seen a bird like that.'

Slowly edging round to join the Englishman by the window, Osamu glimpsed a flash of green and orange. Then he could see nothing.

'Beautiful! So beautiful! There are so few birds in Japan.'

The Englishman put his arm around Osamu's fragile shoulder, as though it were the most natural thing to do. 'And you are beautiful,' he said. 'Like a bird. Like an exotic bird.' He hugged Osamu against his hirsute body.

Osamu let out a little bird-cry, pulled free and ran from the room.

He never saw the Englishman again, except from far off. On that last occasion, with ferociously beating heart he stood at the window of another room at the opposite end of the house, while the Englishman, his heavy, sullen face already flushed with the heat of the early morning, clambered into a taxi. Osamu's mother and his half-brother waved goodbye to him, as they waved goodbye to all their guests, however little liked, but the Englishman did not wave back. Later, Osamu learned that the Englishman had been surprisingly generous. In the envelope which, with discretion unexpected in a foreigner, he had handed to them, was a 'present' far larger than even a rich Japanese businessman would normally give. A small part of this 'present' was made over to Osamu, since he had so often waited on the foreigner.

Soon Osamu learned the knack of making himself almost invisible. He could be seen by those who needed him for something; but at other times he would, in effect, dissolve. Long after he had taken himself off to England, schoolmates of his would try to remember him and would find that they could barely do so. As, totally absorbed in the task, he squatted to paint in the garden, on the verandah that ran around the house, or in the corner of a room still awaiting its guest or guests, his mother, his half-brother and all the other people who serviced the hotel were seldom aware of his presence. Even at meals, silent while everyone else chattered, he was hardly there for them.

Having passed into university and graduated, he opted, against the wishes of his mother and half-brother, now married, to continue to work in the hotel. Meticulously he would draw up the accounts; and no less meticulously he would supervise the preparation of meals in the kitchen. When foreigners came to the hotel, they would find him disconcerting in the cool formality of his treatment of them. He would rarely look at them, preferring to look either down at the *tatami* or out into the garden, as he listened to their questions and requests or spoke a few words in answer. But little that they did escaped him. He was adept at overhearing them and spying on them through the paper screens.

Once, drunk, one of these tourists, a lean, red-haired, red-faced, middle-aged Australian missionary, put up a hand and laid the back of it on Osamu's cheek, as Osamu stooped to place a tray before him on the low table beside which he was squatting. Osamu jerked upwards and stood rigid, the tray resting on his palms. The man laughed and then caressed Osamu even more intimately. Osamu did nothing. He remained standing there, motionless. The man lowered his hand, then raised it again to take the tray from the boy. He rocked forward on his bony haunches, took up the chopsticks from their tray, tore off their paper envelope, and snapped them apart, as though he were severing a wishbone. He began to eat, as Osamu left the room.

From time to time someone – his mother and half-brother acting in concert, an uncle, a friend of the family, a rich client of the inn – would arrange a *miai* or marriage meeting for him. Accompanied by her parents, the girl would arrive at the agreed theatre, temple garden or beauty spot. Osamu's air of self-possession would totally belie the turmoil of emotions – apprehension, dread, shame – within him. He would talk to the girl with the same cool formality with which he talked to foreign guests at the inn. So what did he think of her? – the question would come later. He would shrug, and then he would either say merely, 'I do not think that we are suited,' or he would say nothing.

When, at the end of a long day of coping with the loud, exigent demands of a party of German tourists, he announced to his mother, his half-brother and his half-brother's wife that he wished to go abroad to study English, he realized that, so far from their being opposed to the idea, as he had expected, they were all three secretly relieved. If he could speak perfect English on his return, then that would be a great asset in the inn, his half-brother said. And if he did not wish to continue to work in the inn, his mother took up, then fluency in English would open up all sorts of other occupations to him. Perhaps he would find an English girl to marry, his half-brother's wife said with inno-cent-seeming malice, knowing that he would find nothing of the kind. 'Oh, no, no, no!' his mother protested to that. He must come back and marry a nice, Japanese girl with a generous dowry.

When they saw him off at the airport, did they realize that they would never see him again?

Osamu certainly realized that he would never see them again.

In England, he registered at a school of English. There were other Japanese students there; but he spoke to them only if they spoke to him, and then only in the most perfunctory manner. To the overtures of a Turkish student, a big, shambling man in his thirties, with a taste for garishly coloured shirts and with jowls which, by mid-afternoon, were already heavily sha-dowed, Osamu responded more readily. Between classes, the two of them used to sit in the little café attached to the school, with Osamu leaning close to the Turk to help him with whatever in the previous lesson he had failed to understand.

One day the Turk said: 'How about coming out with me this evening?'

Osamu felt excitement buzzing within him like a swarm of bees; but of this excitement he gave not the smallest indication. He looked down into his empty coffee-cup as if considering the invitation. Then he looked up and nodded. 'All right.'

The Turk went on to say how he had persuaded two other of the students in their class – attractive Spanish twin sisters, with large mouths and quantities of dark, shiny hair piled on top of their heads – to come along too. That would be fine, the Turk explained, very fine, that would make two couples, and they would not quarrel about who had which girl since they were so exactly alike.

After the next class, the last of the day, Osamu told the Turk that he would not, after all, be able to join him and the two girls. He had forgotten, he lied, that he had agreed to work that night at the hotel, owned by Ugandan Indians, in which, without a work-permit, he earned two pounds an hour for four hours of work each morning. From then on he avoided the Turk, arriving after the first class of the afternoon had started, so that the Turk had no opportunity to place himself beside him, as in the past. When the Turk asked him to have a coffee with him in the break, Osamu would say sulkily that he was going to stay in the classroom, there was something he wanted to study before the next lesson. Soon the Turk had made another friend, a middle-aged banker from Brazil. He no longer even greeted Osamu.

It was in a pub for homosexuals, known as 'The Elephants' Graveyard' because of its largely elderly clientele, that Osamu met Pete. Osamu, feeling unaccountably lonely one evening, on his return from school to his small room in a lodging-house in a street off Ladbroke Grove, decided on an impulse that he would visit this pub, of which he had read in a magazine for homosexuals, found crumpled and smeared with grease-stains on the back seat of a bus. Since it was Saturday night, the pub was full. Osamu edged to the counter, ignoring a bosomy hustler in a lacy, open-necked pink shirt, who greeted him with a 'Hello, there!' as though they were old friends. Then, after having uncomplainingly waited while two voluble, grey-haired men pushed ahead of him, he eventually murmured 'A glass of beer, please.'

'What sort of beer?' The barman, who had already complained to the two men that he was 'rushed off his feet', was truculent.

'Er – bitter, please.' In a restaurant to which he sometimes took himself, he had heard someone order bitter and had then seen the glass of beer.

'Pint or half?'

'Excuse me?'

'How much do you want? Pint or half?'

Behind him a voice said: 'Do you want a small glass or a big glass?' That was Pete, who had been a foreman with British Leyland in Cowley and who had, as a young man, lost three fingers of his left hand in an industrial accident for which he believed, as he was often later to grumble to Osamu, that he had not been properly compensated. Pete was now porter of a block of flats in Kensington High Street, from time to time emerging from the dank basement, in which he had two rooms, to wrestle with dustbins, to give what he called 'a spit and a polish' to the communal parts, or to take in laundry, registered parcels and deliveries from such stores as Fortnum and Mason, Harrods and Peter Jones. Pete had recently had a heart-bypass operation, which made him wheeze at any physical exertion.

'A small glass.'

'Where are you from then?' Pete asked, when the barman had impatiently banged the glass down on the counter and Osamu, scrabbling in a purse, had at last assembled the right number of one-pee, two-pee and five-pee coins. ('Just broken open your money-box, have you?' the barman had sourly quipped.)

'Japan.'

'An ex-mate of mine survived being a prisoner of your crowd. Skin and bone he was, when he was released. He showed me a photograph. Shocking!'

Osamu had buried his face in his glass.

'Mind you, I don't hold that against you. One can't visit the sins of the fathers on the children.'

It was an inauspicious beginning to what was to prove an unsatisfactory affair.

After a halting conversation, from which Pete was constantly distracted by the greetings of other regulars and which Osamu would certainly have terminated if he could have thought of any way of doing so without seeming rude, the barman eventually called time.

'Well, I appear to have been stood up,' Pete said. 'Something that happens all too often when you reach my age.'

Osamu, who had never heard the idiom 'stood up', asked uncertainly: 'You are meeting someone?'

'Not now, I'm not! So why don't you come back to my place for –' Pete gave a roguish grin – 'for a night-cap?'

'A night-cap?'

Pete did not explain. 'I have my bus just round the corner,' he said, puzzling Osamu even more.

It was loneliness and a determination to *do it* – at long last, somehow, somewhere, with someone, anyone, however unattractive and inappropriate – which took Osamu back in Pete's battered Metro to the basement flat crammed with cages containing canaries and budgerigars. 'My little family,' Pete declared of the birds, having whistled at one through his teeth and then repeated to it over and over again 'Who's a pretty boy then?', without getting an answer. 'Sit yourself down,' he then told Osamu, who was standing in the centre of the little room, looking fearfully about him.

After Pete had handed him a tumbler of sweet red wine ('My own brew, and not at all bad, though I say it myself') and Osamu had sipped at it, the two men, seated side by side on a sofa which sagged in the middle, slid towards each other, against their true inclinations, and so slid into a relationship which was to last for several weeks. Osamu was repelled by the tattoos on Pete's forearms, by the three puckered little stumps on his left hand, by the jagged, purple scar on his chest, by the way in which his greedy kisses tasted of alcohol and nicotine, and, worst of all, by what he thought of as his lack of education. Pete confided to his friends at the Elephants' Graveyard that, though Osamu was a nice enough little chap, he just did nothing for him in bed. Rough trade, as they knew, was his ticket, he would add. There was the further problem that, in Pete's absence, Osamu was constantly tidying things up – 'I like a bit of mess, it makes the place look more like home, if you see what I mean.'

Osamu was therefore ready for Brian on that autumn day in Holland Park. He had often dreamed of someone like him, even at those moments when, obese and sweaty, Pete was nibbling one of his ears, pinching one of his nipples, or thrusting an exploratory hand between his legs. For so many years he had longed for a Brian – kind, elegant, well-mannered, discreet, at once a father and a lover; and there, suddenly, he saw him, in a beautifully-cut grey cashmere coat, a trilby hat of darker grey and shiny black brogue shoes. Over his arm was the malacca handle of a perfectly furled silk umbrella. He was tall and slim, he had a small moustache the colour of his coat, and there was a signet-ring on the little finger of his left hand. He appeared to be about to walk past Osamu, who was seated, brush in hand, on his stool in front of his easel; then, as though on an impulse, he halted. He leaned forward, he inspected the half-finished canvas on which a shaft of light slanted through the golden leaves of a chestnut tree on to a squirrel nibbling at the nut held in its paws. 'Yes, I like that. I like that a lot. Nice. But where's the squirrel?'

'The squirrel?'

Brian pointed at the canvas. 'He's there. But – ' he pointed towards the sunlit stretch of woodland – 'I don't see him there.'

'He has gone. I paint him from memory.'

'Where are you from?'

'Japan.'

'Japan! Then I'll give you a hundred yen for that.' He indicated the picture with the end of his umbrella.

Since a hundred yen represented a sum of about fifty pee, Osamu felt as though the stranger had suddenly punched him or kicked him. His face darkened; he tilted his head down and away. 'Sorry. Too little.' He could barely get out the words.

Brian laughed. 'That was a joke! Oh, lord! That was meant to be a joke . . . But seriously, I'd like to buy the picture when it's finished. You must just name a price.'

'You really wish to buy?'

'I really wish to buy.'

'I will give it to you.'

'Certainly not! I wouldn't dream of such a thing! . . . How much do you want for it?'

Head on one side, Osamu sucked in his breath. He still wanted to give the picture to the stranger; but, having been trained from infancy that to accept a present meant also to accept the obligation eventually to give a present or at least to do a favour in return, he could understand why the offer should have been so strenuously resisted. 'Usually I am paid twenty pounds,' he said. In fact he had never sold a single picture in England. From time to time in Japan, a foreign guest, seeing him at work, had bought a picture off him for less than the cost of a room in the inn for a night.

'But that's far too little! I'm afraid you've been done.'

'Done?'

'Cheated. I'll give you fifty. How about that?'

'You are very kind,' Osamu mumbled. 'Too much. Much too much.'

'Nonsense! The picture will be worth all of that.'

Brian drew out his wallet and extracted a card from it. Then, with a silver pencil, he inscribed his address and telephone number beneath the engraved: *Sir Brian Cobean QC*. Osamu wondered why he had not had these details printed. Brian held out the card. 'When the picture's finished, give me a ring.'

'It will be finished tomorrow.'

'Tomorrow?' Brian laughed. 'Are you sure?'

Osamu nodded gravely. 'But then it must dry. By Saturday it will be ready for you.'

'Well, if that's the case, why don't you bring it round to me some time early on Saturday evening? I'll be at home at about, oh, half-past six. I live just round the corner.'

'I will come at seven. Is that suitable?'

'Most suitable. Seven it is.'

At that period Brian occupied a flat on the top two floors of a large Georgian brick house off Campden Hill Square. The house belonged to a former lover, first encountered at Eton, who had married, been divorced and then married again, while pursuing a political career with unrelenting energy and ambition but little success.

Osamu was terrified by the size of the house; by Brian's disembodied voice asking over the entryphone, 'Who is it?' when he had rung the bell; by the stout, cross woman who, coming down the staircase as he was about to mount it, demanded: 'Which flat do you want?'

But Brian's eager welcome at once put him at his ease. 'Come in! Come in!' He had taken off the jacket of his suit and was wearing a dark-blue silk dressing-gown. Osamu, used to the smallness of rooms in Japan, was amazed by the length, the breadth and the high ceiling of this one. He was also amazed by so much furniture, so many pictures, so many bibelots, so many books.

'Let me see it! I'm so excited.'

Osamu untied the string about the picture, and then removed the brown paper in which it was wrapped.

Brian, who knew a lot about paintings, did not really think much of this one. But he said 'Oh, it's terrific!' and then: 'We must decide where best to hang it. In my bedroom, I rather think.' If it were in his bedroom, then few people would be in a position to look critically at it and wonder why on earth he had bought it.

Osamu sat on the edge of a chair which seemed to him, like the room, extraordinarily spacious. Brian brought him a glass of pineapple juice – 'No, no, thank you, no alcohol, no alcohol!' Osamu had protested in panic, knowing how even the smallest amount of saké turned his face bright red. Then, having poured himself a gin and tonic, Brian sat down opposite Osamu. He smiled the smile, gentle and coaxing, which Osamu, with a terrible mixture of longing and grief, was so often to remember after his lover's death. 'Tell me all about yourself.'

When Osamu was clearly at a loss how to obey this command, Brian prompted him with a number of questions. Being naturally truthful, Osamu answered with the truth – except that he described himself as Pete's lodger, not his lover, when Brian asked him where it was that he was staying.

'Are you lonely in England?'

'Yes, I am lonely. It is easy for a foreigner to be lonely.'

'It is easy even for someone English to be lonely.' Although he was never lonely, Brian wanted to imply to Osamu that he often was.

From time to time Osamu had been still gazing around the room in wonder. In a pause, while Brian was refilling his glass, he said: 'Beautiful apartment.'

'Thank you. But I have so many possessions that it's terribly overcrowded. My wife inherited a lot of this stuff from an aunt of hers.'

My wife. Osamu felt as though, while he was blithely strolling through Holland Park, a truck had suddenly lurched out of the woodland and struck him down. 'You are married?'

'Was. My wife – died.'

Later Osamu was to hear the story of how Brian's wife had fallen from the window of a hotel in Agadir, when the two of them had been on holiday. 'I think that she must have had a sudden giddy spell,' Brian was to say, in a tone suggesting that he was still trying to convince himself that this was the truth. 'That's what the doctor and the, er, police decided.'

Now he stared down into his glass. Then: 'There's a photograph of her over there.' He pointed towards the Georgian desk at the far end of the room.

Osamu gazed across at it. 'Beautiful,' he said, feeling an obscure jealousy for the blonde woman posed against a trellis of roses in full bloom.

'Yes, she was beautiful. Very beautiful. Poor dear.'

Eventually Brian said: 'Well, let's hang the picture. Let's see if we can find a place for it in the bedroom.'

Brian climbed up on to a step-ladder and Osamu, standing below him, handed him picture-hook, nails, hammer, picture.

Brian asked if the picture was straight. He continued to fuss: 'How's that?' How's that?'

Osamu said, 'A little more to the left' and then, 'A little more to the right.'

Brian descended from the steps. 'Yes, I like it, I like it a lot!' He turned to Osamu, put a hand on his shoulder. 'And I like you a lot.'

Osamu swallowed. Then in almost a whisper he said: 'I like you a lot.'

After it was over, they lay side by side on the bed. Out of a sense of modesty, Osamu had pulled a corner of the crisp linen sheet over his slim naked body; but Brian exposed the whole of his muscular one. Brian was smoking a cigarette, fitted into a holder which, he explained, had a filter. 'I wish I could give up smoking, it's such a filthy habit. But . . . I'm afraid I have no will-power.' In declaring that, he was deceiving both Osamu and himself.

'How old are you?' Brian asked.

'Twenty-four.' Then, greatly daring, Osamu asked: 'How old are you?'

'Fifty-one.'

Impulsively, Osamu jerked over and kissed him on the mouth.

When they were both dressed, Brian said: 'We'll meet again, won't we?'

'I hope.'

'But Ossie – ' already he had begun to call Osamu that – 'there's something I must tell you. I'm a lawyer, you know. What we call a QC – a Queen's Counsel.

Any day now I may become a judge. I have to be terribly, terribly discreet. Careful. No one must know about us. You understand that, don't you?'

'I understand. I do not speak to anyone.'

'Good boy! But there's more than that ... We – we can't really be seen in public together. You see, it would be difficult to explain to friends, colleagues ... If, for example, we were at a theatre together – or at a concert – or in a restaurant ...'

Osamu nodded. 'I understand. I understand very well.'

'Here it's all right – because my friends, Jeremy and Lucy, the friends who own this house – well, they know all about me ... But ...'

'I understand.'

'I *loathe* secrecy. But it's one thing to come out of the closet when there's nothing much to lose and quite another ...'

'Secrecy is good.' But even then Osamu did not believe that.

The two agreed to meet at the same time on the following Saturday. 'But it'll have to be a quickie, I'm afraid. I have to go to a farewell dinner for a colleague. He's been elevated to the Bench. Made a judge. He's younger than I am,' Brian added.

As Osamu was hurrying down the stairs, Brian called out after him. 'I forgot this, I forgot this!' He was waving a fifty-pound note in a hand. Osamu had never seen one before but he guessed what it was.

'No, no! Please! *Please*!'

But Brian raced down the stairs to where he was leaning against the banister, and pushed the note into the breast-pocket of his jacket. 'Thank you,' he said, kissing Osamu on the forehead.

Osamu then felt, against all reason, that the note was

payment not for the picture but for what the two of them had done on that wide, deep bed.

He was overcome by a terrible sadness and guilt.

Late that night, Osamu listened in disgust from their shared bed as Pete, having returned drunk from the Elephants' Graveyard, stumbled and banged about. 'Who's a pretty boy then? Who's a pretty boy? . . . Oh, fuck you, if you don't want to give me a civil answer!' Eventually the bedroom door was pushed open, and Pete staggered towards the bed. He groaned as he collapsed on it, and then he put out an arm and attempted to draw Osamu towards him. 'Who's a pretty boy then?' he asked the Japanese, as he had repeatedly asked the budgerigar.

Osamu pulled free. 'Sorry.'

'What's the matter with you? I only want a little cuddle. That's all. A nice little bedtime cuddle.'

'Sorry. I have headache.'

'A *headache*! Christ! What are you? A bloody slit?'

But he was too drunk and too sleepy to persist any further. He turned away from Osamu, belched, grunted, and was soon snoring loudly.

After their third Saturday meeting, Brian told Osamu: 'Oh, I do wish we could set up home together.'

'I wish too.'

Brian thought for a moment, hugging his knees as he sat up in bed. 'There's one possibility. But it wouldn't really be fair on you.'

'Tell me.'

'Well, you could clean for me, for a proper wage, instead of cleaning at that hotel for a pittance. And we could then pretend you were my houseboy. You could live in.'

'Live in?'

'Yes. There's a little room beyond the guest-room. With a loo and shower beside it. You could have that. Carmen – my daily – is returning to Spain next week. I was about to try to find a replacement for her . . .'

'Maybe you are joking?'

'Joking? Of course not! . . . So you'd like to come to live here?'

'It is my dream.'

'Even though there'd be cleaning to do and some-times even a little simple cooking . . .'

'I do everything. *Everything*.'

When Osamu told Pete that he had got himself a live-in job and would therefore be moving, he expected recriminations. But, like Osamu's parents when he had told them of his wish to leave Japan for England, Pete was relieved. 'All right, old sport. I'm sorry to lose you, but no doubt, taking one thing with another, it's the right decision.' Later he was to confide in one of his friends at the Elephants' Graveyard: 'There was not much point in having the little bugger around if he was no longer willing to play along. And with him there, it was a bit dicey to take anyone else back.'

As a leaving present, Pete presented Osamu with a Saint-Laurent tie. He had bought it, seemingly brand-new, from the Oxfam shop in Kensington High Street for £3.50; but he had then found it so broad that he had never worn it. Osamu presented Pete with a cotton kimono, far too small for him, which Pete then tried to pass on to a truculent and therefore potentially dangerous Irish labourer, picked up in the street, a few weeks later. It was also far too small for the labourer, who threw it back at Pete – 'I don't want this bloody thing!'

'No hard feelings,' Pete said to Osamu as they took their leave of each other.

'Sorry?'

'Oh, never mind!'

There were, indeed, no hard feelings.

Brian would frequently remark to Jeremy and Lucy or to his homosexual cronies that the wonderful thing about Ossie was his *tact*. Instinctively he always knew which of two roles he must play: companion or houseboy. No less instinctively he always knew when Brian was busy and therefore wished to be left alone, and when he wanted company.

Osamu was often by himself in the flat. Brian would come home late; or, having come home, he would give Osamu the most perfunctory of greetings before rushing to have a bath, to change his clothes and then to go off to Covent Garden, the Coliseum or Glyndebourne, to a theatre or to a dinner-party. 'Oh, I do wish you could come with me! I feel so bad about it!' And he did really wish it; and he did really feel bad about it. Already he was in love with Osamu, finding himself thinking dreamily of him in the middle of an aria in the opera-house or a soliloquy in the theatre; while some colleague was holding forth about his latest case in the club; in a taxi speeding home from a dinner-party; while waiting to be served in a shop; while having his hair cut at Trumpers.

During Brian's frequent absences, Osamu would yet again hoover the carpets and yet again polish the furniture; study the cookbooks on a shelf in the kitchen and then set about preparing elaborate dishes for the next day or the day after that; clean the silver, press Brian's many suits, polish his many pairs of shoes. Once, long after midnight, Brian came home to find the Japanese seated at the kitchen table, his eyes bleary as he rubbed at one of a pair of Georgian candelabra. There were other pieces of silver, already glistening, before him. 'Oh, Ossie, Ossie! It's far too late to be working! What are you doing? You really are a marvel.'

Tired but grateful for the praise, Ossie smiled up at him. His carefully kept hands were black with polish.

'Come to bed! Forget about all that silver and come to bed!'

'I must just finish this.'

'Nonsense! I want you in bed – in my bed.'

Sometimes Brian would say: 'Oh, I wish all this secrecy wasn't necessary. If you were my Japanese wife, no one would think anything of it.'

'Unfortunately I am not a wife.'

Once each month Brian would go north to spend the weekend with his widower father, a retired major-general, in Yorkshire.

'I wish that I could meet your father.'

Brian laughed. 'Out of the question! He's very conventional. A pillar of the local church and a pillar of the local Conservative Association. He's got no idea that I'm gay. If he knew, he'd never see me again.'

'Yes, I see. I understand.' But Osamu believed that, if only he could meet Brian's father, then somehow both he and Brian's homosexuality would be accepted.

That Christmas seemed interminable to Osamu. Brian went off to stay with his father for a week; Jeremy and Lucy had a succession of rowdy parties but never thought of asking Osamu down for a meal or even for a drink. Soon there was nothing left to do in the flat, so he either sat, hour after hour, in front of the television set, or, in an overcoat and scarf which Brian had insisted on buying for him at the Scotch House, he painted in the icy Park.

'Did you have a nice time?' Osamu asked when Brian returned.

'It would have been far nicer if you'd been there with me. My father and I are fond of each other. But the sad and dreadful thing is that we have nothing at all in common.'

'Like myself and my family.'

Twice, within a few weeks after that, Brian took himself abroad. Once he travelled to a legal congress in New York; once on holiday to stay with friends in Athens. On each occasion Osamu would find himself wondering whether this man whom he so much loved was, perhaps at that very moment, being unfaithful to him.

'I think that New York is full of beautiful boys,' Osamu said, trying to make it sound like a joke, after the first of these visits.

'Yes. But none as beautiful as you.'

'Greek boys are very beautiful and passionate,' he said after the second of these visits.

'And very mercenary!'

When Easter came round, Brian announced that he was going to take Osamu with him to the villa, a few miles south of Florence, which he had rented for two weeks. For the first week, a 'gay chum' of his, who worked for the BBC, would be with them. For the second week, the two of them would be alone. 'I do so hate this life of secrecy. In Florence we'll spend all our time together.'

This was not wholly accurate. Twice in the first week, the 'gay chum' and Brian went out to dinner-parties, given by anglophile members of the Florentine aristocracy, to which Osamu was not invited. 'Be thankful you've not been invited. You'd be hideously bored. There's no society as provincial as Florentine society.'

In the second week, things were far better. There were no longer those long conversations – about music, about art, about books, about literature – between the two Englishmen, from which Osamu felt himself to be cruelly excluded. No longer did the BBC producer irrupt into the kitchen, telling Osamu that to boil pasta it was necessary to have lots and lots and lots of water in a *very* large pan, that pesto sauce should never, never be heated, that balsamic vinegar was so much more adventurous than the ordinary kind.

'I don't think you really liked Jim,' Brian said, when they had returned to the villa after driving their guest to Pisa airport.

'Yes, I like him.' But the tone made it clear that he hadn't.

'He liked you. A lot. Even though he well might have been jealous.'

'Jealous?'

Brian laughed. 'Well, years and years ago, back in the mists of time, he and I had a little ding-dong together.'

That last week was a wonderful one for Osamu. With infinite patience Brian instructed him about every church, museum, gallery and villa which they visited. Constantly he was buying Osamu presents: a pair of shoes, a cashmere sweater, a shirt, a watch. Constantly he was making love to him: in the pearly light of dawn; after luncheon on the terrace, when they were both stupefied from having drunk too much Chianti; late at night when, by some miracle, they awoke at precisely the same moment, as though by arrangement, and turned to each other.

Their villa, owned by an impoverished marchesa, half Italian and half American, surmounted a hill. On the hill opposite, there was an even older and grander villa, occupied – so the marchesa contemptuously told them – by 'a *nouveau riche* Jew', owner of factories in Pistoia and Prato, who had recently bought it. Each morning, as Brian and Osamu ate a late breakfast on the terrace before the arrival of the maid on her scooter, a helicopter used to hover, buzzing angrily, over the opposite hill and then creak down on it. 'Oh, that bloody thing! Why does every morning have to be disturbed by it?' In the evenings the same helicopter would bring its owner back to his villa, and again Brian would exclaim: 'Oh, that bloody thing! That bloody thing!' But Osamu found the giant bird, glittering in the early sunlight of the morning or the late sunlight of the evening, immensely exciting. He would watch it, a hand shielding his eyes, as its blades flashed, flashed, flashed.

Two days before their holiday was over, on a Sunday, they met the stout, yellow-faced owner of the helicopter, as they emerged from the gate at the end of their drive and he, across the narrow road, emerged from the gate at the end of his. He had with him the silvery ghost of a dog, a Weimaraner, on a lead. He was wearing a panama hat at a jaunty angle, a white silk suit, and pointed white-and-black shoes. He smiled at them and raised the stick on which, clearly lame, he had been supporting himself. In all but perfect English he then addressed them. He was sorry that he had not made their acquaintance earlier. The marchesa had spoken of them to him. That evening he and his wife were giving a party – perhaps they had noticed the workmen putting up coloured lights? There would be food, music, dancing. He would like to invite them. He was a great lover of England. He had spent so many happy times there. Many of the guests would be English.

Brian accepted. Then, as he and Osamu continued down the hill to the little shop at which they regularly bought bread, wine, fresh pasta and the most delicious cooked foods, he said: 'Do you really want to go to that party?'

'You are going?'

'Yes, I'll have to go – though I don't in the least want to go. Mimi' – this was the marchesa – 'might be offended otherwise. But *you* don't have to go. You could give it a miss. I should think it'll all be the most awful bore.'

Osamu sat out alone on the terrace, the evening darkening around him, and watched as the high gates of the property opposite swung open automatically and yet another huge car, often with a uniformed chauffeur at the wheel, zigzagged up the hill. He could hear the distant music. The multicoloured fairy-lights glittered in the trees.

He had agreed not to go to the party because he knew that Brian had not wished him to go. No doubt Brian had feared that there would be prominent members of the British colony among the guests: the consul, the director of the British Institute, retired notabilities who had made Tuscany their home.

For the first time Osamu felt a vague resentment and rebellion.

When Osamu answered the telephone, the call was person-to-person from New York.

'For you.' He held out the receiver. 'Mr Eliot

Gottfried. I think.' He still had difficulty with foreign names at a first hearing.

'Eliot Gottfried? Never heard of him.' Brian put down his book. Then he remembered: Eliot Gottfried was the stockbroker friend, never met, of George Morris, the young architect whom he had picked up in the Metropolitan Museum. Gottfried and George lived together in Gottfried's duplex on South Central Park. George had often talked of the duplex – he had himself 'handled' the conversion, each of the three bedrooms had its bathroom *en suite*, there was *the* most enormous roof-terrace, perfect for parties in the summer, there were these three Jackson Pollocks, this David Hockney portrait of Gottfried and George together, this truly fabulous Gwen John. But George had never asked Brian there, preferring instead to meet him in his hotel.

Osamu listened, as he tidied the Sunday papers which Brian had scattered over the floor. He had sensed a tension in Brian's voice as he had picked up the receiver and said: 'Brian Cobean here.'

'Oh, God! But that's terrible . . . But when did he first fall ill? . . . Yes, I see . . . Well, I wish I could help but . . . My father knew him and that's how I met him . . . But I'd hardly call him a friend . . . Well, not at all really . . .' The conversation went on and on and round and round. Glancing up, Osamu could see that Brian's face had become extraordinarily pale, even leaden. There were large drops of sweat on his forehead. Then Osamu saw a drop of sweat on the tip of Brian's nose. That drop splashed down on to his shirt-front.

'Well, give him my love . . . Please . . . Yes . . . And say that I'll be thinking of him – and praying for him.' Osamu thought those last words odd. Brian had often told him that he had lost all faith during his second year at Eton.

Brian put down the receiver and then stood there, extraordinarily still, his eyes wide. 'God!' It was almost a whisper. Then: 'What a bloody fool!'

'What is it? What did he want?' Suddenly, for no reason he could have given, Osamu felt a terrible apprehension.

'You remember George, don't you? George the architect, George from America.' Brian was now walking back to the sofa with the weary stiffness of someone who has been trudging over a mountain all through the day.

'Yes, I remember him.'

How could Osamu not remember him? During George's visit some four months before, he had been convinced that beneath the crust of formality with which the two men behaved to each other, there was heaving and bubbling a lava of passion. At the church of St George in Bloomsbury Way – 'my patron saint' – George had held forth first about Hawksmoor and then about the building ('Look, just look at that six-column Corinthian portico! *Mag*-nificent!') with such eloquent enthusiasm that, against his will, Osamu had been rapt. Later George had played some Scarlatti sonatas on the grand piano, from time to time exclaiming 'Oh, shit, shit!' when he hit a wrong note. Later still, he and Brian had gone off to a performance of *The Trojans* together. 'Oh, I do wish you could come too!' Brian had exclaimed, as Osamu, sitting on the bed, had watched him tie his black bow-tie. 'But the Garden is exactly the sort of place where I run into colleagues.'

Osamu had thought bitterly: 'So he is willing to be seen with George, but not with me.'

Now Brian said: 'He's dying.' Then, since Osamu made no response, merely staring at him, he repeated with an odd fretfulness: 'George is dying.'

'Dying! But he ... he is so young. Almost my age.'

'Even the young sometimes die. Didn't you know that?' Brian was speaking as though he hated, not loved, Osamu. 'And that fool wants me to ask the Archbishop of Canterbury to pray for him. Can you imagine! There are people dying all over England, all over the world, and he thinks that, if I ask him, the Archbishop will pray, will pray especially for George. Whom he's never met. Who probably hasn't been to church for years and years. And what good will the Archbishop's prayers do? Will they do any more good than anyone else's? Has that Archbishop got a special line to God? Is that man crazy? George must have told him that I'd told him – I can't think why – that I'd met the Archbishop with my father. But he's not a *friend*! Is that man crazy?' he asked again. 'Bloody idiot!'

Later, Osamu was to understand the craziness that drives one to seek for any solution, however preposterous, to the problem of how to keep a loved one who is dying alive. But now he merely shook his head in answer to Brian's question.

'Poor little George!'

Then Brian put both hands up over his face. His body began to shake.

Osamu did not go to him. He merely watched him.

III

All his life Andy Cobean had had a dread of hospitals. Now eighty-six, he had fortunately never been obliged to spend even a single night in one; but the illnesses of others – his parents, his wife, his children, his friends, his men and their families – had repeatedly forced him to do what he hated to do. Typically, he had never spoken to anyone of this dread; and only his wife, so acute in all her perceptions about him, had ever guessed at it.

In retirement he now drank little, after years of drinking too much. But that day the thought of what lay ahead had driven him first to gulp three whiskies in succession before luncheon at the bar of the In and Out, and then to finish off most of a bottle of claret during his meal with a retired colonel, even older than himself, who kept protesting, covering the top of his glass with a shaky, mottled hand, as though he were about to crush it: 'No! No! For God's sake! No! Strictly against the orders of my quack.'

Near to the hospital there was a pub, which on that day of exceptional heat had vomited out on to the pavement a number of sweating, dark-suited young men with brief-cases, loud voices and braying laughs. Having passed the pub, Andy turned back and strode into its almost empty interior. He ordered a double Scotch – neat, no ice. He raised the glass and swallowed.

'Much cooler in here than outside. Why does everyone want to stand out on the pavement?'

'Search me.' The barman, not in the mood to talk, shrugged and moved off.

The drink had made Andy's mouth even drier; and it had done nothing to still the churning of his bowels. *You're too old for this sort of thing*. But he did not know if by that he meant that he was too old for trekking all the way from Yorkshire to London and then trekking from the club to the hospital, or too old for experiencing this kind of panic.

As he marched down the hospital corridor, he

suddenly thought: He might have asked if I wanted to stay in his flat. It's not often I come up after all. Once in a blue moon. Would have saved me a bob or two. I'd have looked after the place, he knows that. I may not be as finicky as he is but I'd have looked after the place and left everything shipshape. Odd. It's as though he didn't want my life to get entangled with his.

'Well, old boy, how are you getting on?'

So that he could breathe more easily, Brian had been propped up in bed. There were no flowers in the room, although many had arrived for him. Beside him an oxygen cylinder gleamed in the sunlight slanting through the window.

'Oh, I'm better now, thank you.' A wan, embarrassed smile. 'They eventually found the right antibiotic.'

Andy dragged an upright chair towards the bed.

'Wouldn't you rather sit in the armchair?' Brian did not want his father so close to him. Irrationally he was convinced that the old man's proximity, like the proximity of the flowers, would make breathing even more onerous.

'This is fine.' Andy put out a hand and placed it over his son's. They seldom touched each other. He exerted a slow, gentle pressure. 'I got a fright when that couple – that couple below you – never remember their names – phoned to tell me ...'

'Jeremy and Lucy McAllister. I once brought them to lunch with you, when we were driving up to the Edinburgh Festival. Don't you remember?'

'Of course I remember their coming.' Andy was proud of his memory. 'But I can't be expected to remember everyone's name, now can I?'

'No, you can't. Of course you can't.'

'When do you expect to get out of here?'

'In four or five days. I hope.'

'Then you'll have to take things easy.'

'Yes, I'll have to take things easy.'

The likelihood was that he would have to take things easy for all of what little now remained of his life.

'Like me, that's something you've always had difficulty in doing. You drive yourself too hard. Just the opposite of your brother. He never drives himself at all, just ambles.'

'How are things at home?' Although he so rarely went there now, Brian still referred, out of habit, to the large, bleak house on the moors outside Ilkley as home.

The old man drew in a deep breath and began to tell him. At last the tide of panic had begun to ebb inside him. He could even begin to examine all the coiled and rubbery apparatus which surrounded the bed, instead of trying not to notice it. There had been a row with old Parkinson, who had originally come to the house as gardener's boy, who had then become sole gardener, and who had eventually grown so crotchety and pig-headed that Andy was always on the point of dismissing him. 'I really think that this time I must make up my mind to give him his cards.'

Brian laughed and then began to cough. 'You've said that so often! Would you find anyone else?'

Andy stroked his chin. 'Yes, that's the problem, of course. A big problem. One hears of all these people on the dole, but try to get someone to come and do a job of any kind . . .'

Andy went on to speak of the local elections; of the 'new' vicar – in fact he had been in the parish for almost three years – who was full of damn-fool ideas, like expecting the congregation to kiss each other or shake each others' hands; of a scheme to drive a new road through a neighbouring valley, where he would now often walk for hours on end, alone but for his two red setters.

Eventually Brian tilted his head back on the mound of the pillows and closed his eyes.

'I'm tiring you.'

'I'm sorry. I tire so easily.'

'I'd better be on my way. I brought you two half bottles of champagne.' Andy stooped for the plastic bag resting against the armchair in which he had declined to sit. 'You may not feel like them now, but some other time ... And there are some peaches here, peaches from the greenhouse. You always liked peaches, didn't you?'

'You shouldn't have bothered, father.'

Suddenly Brian was moved by the thought of the old man carrying peaches up with him in the train from the country, in addition to his luggage.

'I'm planning to make for home this evening. I'm having dinner with Bonzo Robbins at the club – as silly an ass as ever but I have a kind of affection for him – and then I'll catch the midnight train.'

'I hope you have a sleeper.'

'God no! Waste of money. I expect I'll be able to find a carriage to myself. I'll just curl up in a corner.' He hesitated. 'I'd like to stay – until you've totally recovered – but there are these elections coming up and I've also got to sort things out, one way or another, on the Parkinson front.'

'Yes, of course, father. I'm all right now. Nothing to worry about. Nothing at all.'

'You were never all that strong. Like your mother. Do you remember when you had measles during your first half at Eton? You were terribly ill, you almost died.'

Brian laughed. 'Well, not really, father. But I did feel pretty rough for a day or two.'

One hand on the door-handle and the other stroking his white, clipped moustache, Andy said: 'If you want to convalesce in Ilkley . . .'

'Thank you. Yes, I'll think about it.'

'No trouble. No trouble at all. And Trenchie – Mrs Trench, the new housekeeper – she's first-class, you know, for all her disapproving manner. Produces even better grub than at the In and Out.'

Brian was relieved when his father had gone. He had arrived much later than arranged and had therefore also stayed much later. At four Osamu had said he would come; and Osamu was always so punctual that Brian imagined him sitting out in the hall until his watch showed him that it was precisely the hour. It would have been disastrous if the two of them had coincided.

Head now turned sideways on the pillow and eyes fixed on the gleaming oxygen cylinder, Brian yet again considered whether to tell Osamu the truth or not.

Then he decided: 'Better not.'

When Osamu arrived, exactly at four, Brian said: 'My father brought two half-bottles of champagne, so let's drink one of them.'

'Is that good for you?'

'I'm sure it's good for me. I'm feeling much, much better. So – let's celebrate!'

Even now, after so long of living with Brian, Osamu rarely drank; and in any case he did not care for champagne. But he went out and asked one of the nurses for two glasses and then, watched by Brian, he opened the bottle. Some of the champagne fizzed over his hand. He raised the hand and licked at it, the taste unpleasantly sour on his tongue. He looked up.

'You are truly better?'

'Yes, I'm truly better.'

Andy was able to lie outstretched across one seat of the carriage. He had removed his jacket, neatly folding it up before laying it on the rack, his tie and his shoes. Opposite to him, like a mammoth bolster propped up in one corner, was a menacing-looking, middle-aged woman who turned out, when he spoke to her, to be a tourist from Brittany. He told her that he had memories of fighting in two wars over French soil; but her interest was merely polite. Each time that he himself awoke, her eyes were open. Although he could well afford a first-class ticket, he never bought one – 'No point in throwing money away,' he would often remark.

Half-awake and half-dreaming, his body curled up and a hand under his chin, he suddenly felt an unreasoning apprehension about the son whom he loved, whom he had never understood, with whom he had so little in common, and whom he now saw more and more rarely. As so often in the past, he wondered: Is he telling me the truth? He had sensed a despair behind that embarrassed, wan smile. Was he iller than he had revealed? It was foolish to have these morbid thoughts. Such thoughts only came to one when one lay sleepless in the early hours.

The Frenchwoman suddenly drew a deep, audible sigh, as she gazed out at a bare landscape lightening to a pearly grey as the day broke. Perhaps she too, seemingly so invulnerable in her massive self-possession, was also having morbid thoughts, Andy told himself.

*

Osamu had prepared carefully for Brian's convalescence. At the Barkers summer sale he had bought, with his own money, a blue-and-white striped deck-chair, with an extension for the legs, and a cold-box in which to keep drink and food. He imagined in detail how they would spend their days together.

... Rising early, he would prepare something light and tasty for a picnic meal. Then, loaded with deck-chair, easel, folding-stool, cold-box, the newspaper, a book – well, if he had to make two journeys, it wasn't all that far – he would walk with Brian to that area of Holland Park, above the Chestnut Walk, where unaccountably few people ever went. He would put out the deck-chair under a tree and settle Brian in it.

'Is it better for you in the sun?'

'No, this is fine.'

'You are right. At this time of year the sun is not so good. . . . Do you wish to talk with me or read?'

'I want to talk with you.'

Osamu would set up his easel and open the folding-stool. He would perch on it.

'That's going to be the best picture you've ever painted.'

'You think so?'

'I know so.'

Later, they would travel to East Anglia, where they had recently spent a holiday as happy as their holiday in Florence. If Brian was well enough, they would take the car. If not – since Osamu himself could not drive – they would be extravagant and hire a car to get them there. Brian, unlike his father, enjoyed being extravagant. When he bought some antique or picture for a price which astounded Osamu, he seemed to be exhilarated not so much by the acquisition of a beautiful object as by the sudden lightening of his pocket. They would stay in Dedham, at that hotel with the carp pond. It was near enough to Flatford Mill for Brian to walk there and back without strain or tiredness. There was a converted barn in the grounds, in which painting courses were conducted; so, while Brian read or slept in the garden, he himself could be painting.

... The reality was far different. In the immediate aftermath of his return from hospital, Brian wished to do little but sit in front of the television set. Yet in the past he had so often said to Osamu, as he was preparing to leave him alone in the flat: 'How can you bear to sit there watching that mind-numbing rubbish?' Now the two of them watched the mind-numbing rubbish together.

'I wish I had more energy,' Brian would say from time to time.

'Wouldn't you like to go into the park?' Osamu would coax.

'Oh, no, not today!'

'Wouldn't you like to go away for a little?'

'No, I much prefer to be at home.'

Osamu wondered when Brian would return to work. There were all kinds of indications – visits or telephone calls to his doctor, an ever increasing number of medicine bottles in the bathroom cabinet, trekking to the lavatory two or three times in the night – that he was still far from well.

One day Brian announced that he was going up north, to Ilkley, for a week. 'My father keeps pressing me. My brother, his wife and his two children will be there.'

'I wish I could come with you.'

'I wish you could too. But ...' He shrugged. 'You know how it is.'

Osamu knew how it was.

'Are you well enough to travel alone?'

'Of course I'm well enough. It doesn't take much effort to get on and off a train . . . Don't look so gloomy, Ossie! A week is not a long time.'

But for Osamu that week seemed interminable.

It was on his second day in Ilkley that the shingles appeared as numerous small blisters on one of Brian's eyelids. The following day the eye was red and constantly watered, and he felt an acute, burning pain. He said nothing to any of the family; when he went out to buy some pain-killers, he merely told them that he was going to stroll down to the post office.

'Oh, do let me go for you,' his sister-in-law, Mary, offered. There had been a time, after the sudden and mysterious death of Brian's wife, when she had hoped to marry him. Then she had settled for his house-agent brother, Luke.

'No, no! I'm no longer an invalid, you know. A little gentle exercise is good for me.'

At breakfast the next morning, Brian was aware that Andy was peering at him with those small, bright blue eyes which even now, in his eighty-seventh year, had lost nothing of their sharpness.

'Do you have to stare at me, father?'

'That eye looks really nasty. Let me drive you over to see old Bragg.'

'Fat lot of use that would be! It's just some local inflammation, that's all.'

Eventually, nagged not merely by Andy but by Luke and Mary, Brian consulted the old, vague, fragile doctor, so often Andy's ally in battles against those who wished to change the appearance of the town in which both of them had lived so long and which both of them loved so much.

'There's this new antiviral pill. I'll give you a prescription. And you'd better take a stronger pain-killer.'

'There you are, you see!' Andy was always glad to point out to others that he had been right and they wrong. 'I told you it wasn't just a simple infection, as you kept insisting.'

'You should have been a doctor, father.'

'Nonsense, I've never wanted to be anything but a soldier. In any case, I have awfully little faith in doctors. It took them more than a year to diagnose what was wrong with your mother and by then it was too late.'

The eye was slow to improve; and all the time Brian felt a crushing weariness, such as he had never experienced before in his life. More than once he repeated: 'Do you have to stare at me, father?' More than once he told Mary, as she fussed over him: 'I'm no longer an invalid, you know.' He would force himself to play bridge, go for walks or talk with others, when all that he craved was to lie out on his bed.

Luke looked up from the copy of *Country Life*, in which he had been examining the advertisements put in by firms in rivalry with his. 'That pneumonia seems to have hit you hard.'

'Oh, I'm all right now. I feel better every day.'

Luke shook his head, as though in disbelief, before once again looking down at the magazine.

Mary's high, clear voice, admonishing the children, could be heard from the bottom of the garden. 'I've told you – don't make so much noise! Be more considerate! Uncle Brian's still *far from well*.'

Andy approached the deck-chair, similar to the still unused one bought by Osamu, in which Brian lay out on the lawn. His pale face, forehead and upper lip freckled with perspiration, was upturned to the sun. His mouth was half-open in what, to Andy, looked like a grimace.

Andy squatted on the grass beside the chair.

Surprised, fretful, Brian turned to him, half sitting up. 'Yes?'

'You're still not well, are you, old boy?'

Brian said nothing. All at once he was wracked by the desire to tell everything, everything to his father, as he would have told him everything when a child. But he mustn't, mustn't. There were things that he could not tell him. And yet. And yet . . .

He sighed. 'Well, I haven't told you everything. You see . . . my illness was – is – more serious than I've let on. They tell me I have – leukaemia.' In the reference section of the Kensington Public Library he had hit on the disease the symptoms of which approximated most closely to those of his own. 'That's why I pick up all these opportunistic infections.'

'Oh, Christ! But that's bad, *bad*!'

Brian suddenly, gratefully, painfully realized: The old boy cares, he really cares.

'Not as bad as it used to be. There are all sorts of new ways of treating it. People survive with it for, oh, years and years. When I get back to London, I'll be starting a course of chemotherapy. There's this new cytotoxic drug, pioneered in America, new to this country.' It was easy to lie, far easier than he had feared. He was surprised how convincing he sounded.

'Why didn't you tell me? I *am* your father, for God's sake!'

'Oh, I don't know. I just don't want it broadcast.

You see, if it were known that I was seriously, chronically ill, it might, well, it might have a serious effect on my career.'

'But by telling me, you would hardly be *broadcasting* it! I know how to keep my mouth shut. Have all my life. I know innumerable secrets, government secrets, which even now I'd never divulge to anyone – not even to you.'

Brian covered his eyes with a hand, as though to shield them from a light unexpectedly shone in them. 'I know, father, I know. Sorry.'

'Do you want Luke to know?'

'No ... Strangely, I shouldn't mind if Mary did. But if she did, then eventually he would.'

'Mum's the word then.' Andy rose to his feet. With a tentative gesture, half-apprehensive and half-embarrassed, he put a hand out to his son's head, at once withdrew it, and then gave a brief caress to the back of his neck, where the greying hair was far longer and far more untidy than usual. The hair felt moist, as though Brian were running a fever. 'We're going to get the best advice and the best treatment possible for you.'

Brian had already had the best advice; and it had already been decided that, on his return to London, he was to start the best treatment.

'Do it for me, even if you don't think any good can come of it. There are all sorts of stories about the miracles she's performed. I'm as sceptical as the next man about most of these things. But it does seem ...'

Well, there was nothing to lose; and Brian was now in the state of mind to try anything on offer. 'I never imagined that you would ever be urging me to see a faith-healer.'

'Well, I've always believed that there are more things in heaven and earth . . . Even prayer – there have been so many occasions in my life when prayer has really seemed . . . You're laughing at me!'

'No, not laughing. Smiling. Oh, I wish I shared your faith.'

'You could, you know.'

'Acquiring faith is not like acquiring the ability to swim or ride a bicycle.'

'Isn't it? I'd have thought it rather similar.'

Mrs Walton was a jolly, eccentric Cockney, who lived in a cottage, marooned on a bleak spur of moorland, without either electricity or main drainage. She had moved out there from a council house when her husband, an Ilkley-born employee in the local refuse department, had mysteriously decamped, with no warning or explanation, to a job in Zambia. She lived on his occasional remittances, social security and her earnings from what she called 'my gift'. She kept three shaggy lurchers, which she would comb each evening while listening to the news on her ancient wireless. The wool so procured she would first spin and then knit into pullovers for sale at the next church jumble sale. People bought the pullovers, because they cherished Mrs Walton as a local character, but they rarely wore them.

Having abandoned the car in the lane, Andy and Brian walked up the steep path which, skirting brambles and a cairn-like assembly of boulders, led to the cottage. Brian was soon breathless. 'Take it easy, take it easy. No hurry,' Andy told him, pausing to lean on his stick. Far off the dogs had started barking.

Mrs Walton's grey hair had been parted in the middle of her forehead and then drawn back into a bun which looked like one of the balls of wool which she spun for her pullovers. She was wearing a pair of green corduroy trousers, with a man's fly in front, a grubby checked shirt open at the neck, and sturdy, flat brogues. As Andy called out 'Good afternoon, Mrs Walton!', she straightened up, trowel in hand, from the flower-bed at which she had been working. The dogs crowded, tails wagging, around Andy. Mysteriously, they left Brian alone.

Andy introduced Brian.

Mrs Walton's fierce green eyes narrowed as, unsmil-ing, she gazed at him. 'Yes, I remember you,' she said, 'from when you were just a little chap.' Brian had no recollection at all of her; but he did not dispute the statement. 'Come in then.'

At first it might have been no more than a social call. In the stuffy little parlour, with its smells of dogs, paraffin-oil and woodsmoke, Mrs Walton poured out strong Indian tea into pottery mugs and then rattled coconut biscuits in a rusty tin first at Andy and then at Brian. One of the dogs, slavering, put its chin on Andy's knee. He broke off a piece of biscuit. 'Oh, don't waste a biscuit on him!' Mrs Walton told him, her voice suddenly sharpened by irritation. 'He's a real greedy bugger.'

She and Andy began to talk about the 'new' vicar; about the drought of that summer in which one scorching day succeeded another, on and on, week after week; about the latest episode of 'The Archers' – 'It was plain daft,' Mrs Walton said, but what was plain daft, Brian, lost in a vague, apprehensive dream, did not take in.

Eventually the time came for what she called 'the treatment'. 'Shall we try the treatment then?' she asked, and Brian nodded: 'Yes, if you're ready.'

'He only half believes,' Andy said, as Mrs Walton began to drag the dog which she had called 'a greedy bugger' into the kitchen. 'We want these out of the way. We don't want no disturbance.' She dragged the remaining two dogs away simultaneously, a collar in each hand.

Then she stood, hands on ample hips, before the chair in which Andy was sitting, as though to confront him in some argument. 'So he only half believes?' she said. 'Well, I've had people here who didn't believe at all. But sometimes – not always, mind – sometimes things happened. Don't ask me how, don't ask me why. It's my gift, but how or why it comes to me ...'

She stood behind Brian's chair, so that he could not see her. Andy had got up and gone over to the small window, its panes obscured with cobwebs and dust, which gave on to the garden. He stared out, as though in the belief that, if he watched Mrs Walton, he would somehow nullify her magic.

Brian felt her hands on either side of his face. He felt them, as an emanating warmth, before their skin, dry and rough, had touched the skin, moist and smooth, of his cheeks, on which they eventually came to rest. The hands seemed to get hotter and hotter. In the end he had so strong a sensation of burning that he almost cried out. The warmth began to spread down his neck into his chest, along his arms, into his stomach. A tingling followed it.

Behind him he heard an exhalation of breath, then a little gasp.

'Well, that's it.' The voice was matter-of-fact.

Andy turned back from the window out of which he had been gazing. 'So quick.'

Mrs Walton sank into a chair. 'It takes it out of one,' she said. 'Like giving a blood-transfusion.'

Brian was indeed already feeling as he had felt when he had been given a blood-transfusion, lasting several hours, in hospital .... Oh, Christ, he would have to rush to the loo. These days he often had these peremptory summons.

'It's through and out of the kitchen into the yard and then round to the left. No mod cons, I'm afraid.'

'That's fine.'

As Brian opened the door from the kitchen into the small backyard, the dogs pushed past him. One scampered over to a rusty lawn-mower in the far corner and cocked a leg against it.

Mrs Walton got up and once again, hands on ample hips, stared at Andy as though in confrontation. Then she shook her head. 'Sorry, dear. It's not going to work.' She sighed.

'What do you mean? D'you already know ...?'

'Something always tells me – I can't say what. Nope.' Again she shook her head, then sank back into the chair. 'There's nothing I can do for him. Maybe someone else can, but I can't.'

Andy had the two ten-pound notes ready in an envelope. He placed the envelope on a corner of the cracked and stained wooden tray on which she had carried in the tea things. 'Anyway, that's for your trouble. It could be you're wrong.' He felt a sudden despair. He believed in Mrs Walton and her gift; and in any case she was only telling him something which, in some dark, dusty recess of his being, he had known all along.

'No, no! No need for that! No need at all!'

But Andy did not take back the envelope; and Mrs Walton made no further protest.

'All right then?' she asked Brian as he stumbled back into the room.

'All right, thank you.'

His voice was soft, hoarse. He did not look all right.

Osamu stretched himself out on the bed beside Brian. He threw an arm across him, then placed his head on his chest.

'Wouldn't you like to make love?'

'No. Sorry, darling. I just don't feel up to it.'

'You never feel up to it.'

'I know. I wish I did. But this illness – it drains one of all . . .' He ran the fingers of one hand through Osamu's hair. 'But it doesn't drain one of love. Not in the least. Not in the least.'

Brian was again in hospital. Osamu waited in the corridor outside his room, prowling up and down it, while the doctor was conducting an examination.

A sister and a nurse passed. The sister gave Osamu a hostile look from under half-lowered lids. Then she said to the nurse: 'I think he'll put Sir Brian' – she spoke the 'Sir' with a hint of derisiveness – 'on this AZT.'

Osamu had read of AZT. He stared after the two women, feeling suddenly dizzy and sick.

'But why didn't you tell me? Why? Why?'

He was holding Brian to him, lying across the bed. Once the sister had entered without knocking and had found the two of them like that, embracing each other. It was after that that her whole attitude, once so friendly, even coquettish, to Brian had changed. To Osamu, whom she had assumed to be some sort of employee, she had always been chilly.

'Because ... because ... Do you really want to know?'

'Yes, I really want to know. Why? Why?'

'Because I was afraid that, if you knew, you might leave me.'

'How could you think such a thing?'

How could he think such a thing? Alone in the flat, at the end of a day much of which had been spent with Brian, Osamu would go over that question again and again. Had Brian had so little faith in him? Had he imagined that he loved him so little?

Then, having asked himself the desolating question, he would begin to think of that telephone call from New York. Was it from George that Brian had caught the infection of certain death? Or was it from someone else? Osamu wanted, he so much wanted to ask Brian. But he knew that he must never do so.

He never did.

'I think that I must have a test?'

'A test?'

'To see if I am positive?'

'Oh, I hope not, I hope not! But do you really want to know?'

'I want to know.'

'But's what's the point of knowing? If you *are* positive, what can you do about it? Nothing.'

'I must know.'

The New Zealand girl who took Osamu's blood was extraordinarily kind and sympathetic. He thawed out, unstiffened, even smiled in gratitude as he pulled down his shirt-sleeve and began to button the cuff. He would hear the result from his doctor, she told him. The doctor was not in fact his – he had never needed a doctor – but Brian's.

'I'm sure everything will be all right,' she said, as she said to everyone who came for the test.

Everything was all right.

Osamu had expected to feel exhilaration but he felt only the depression of guilt. He was safe, Brian was dying. He had to force himself to walk from the bus-stop to the hospital and then to take the lift and then to make his way down the corridor.

Brian stared at Osamu's white, rigid face, the jaw clenched. 'Oh, God! ... What was the result?' At that moment Brian was certain that the result had been positive.

'Negative.' Osamu could hardly say it.

Suddenly Brian's whole body seemed to be irradiated with joy. 'Oh, darling!' He held out his arms. 'That's wonderful! That's terrific! Yesterday my father brought another two halves of champagne. The nurse put them in the fridge. Could you go and ask her for one? And for two glasses.'

Brian raised his glass.

'To us.'

Osamu could say nothing. He bowed his head, sipped, sipped again. He could hardly swallow. His throat ached with unshed tears.

'What's the matter?'

'Nothing. Nothing.'

For many months he had lived in Brian's love as in a small, cosy room. Now all at once the room had expanded, out and out, up and up, so that there was a totally unexpected grandeur about it, a totally unexpected nobility.

He had to say it. 'Brian – I do not know how to say this in English. Maybe I say it wrong.' He paused a moment, his face screwed up in an agony of thought. Then he said: 'You do not die your death. You live it.'

Since the start of Brian's illness, they had never used either the word 'die' or the word 'death' to each other.

Brian shrugged and pulled a little face. 'Well, one tries to do one's best.' He held out his glass. 'Give me another drop. Wonderful stuff!'

The tears suddenly spilled out of Osamu's eyes and began to run down his cheeks.

'Oh, come on, come on!'

Brian sounded angry.

With an effort, Osamu smiled through his tears.

IV

When Osamu arrived that afternoon, the room was empty. For a terrible moment he thought that, in his absence, Brian must have died. Then the familiar sight of the flotsam of haphazard objects which invariably gets washed up around a patient – the open copy of Ruth Rendell's latest novel, lying face downwards on the bed, the unopened box of Charbonnel and Walker chocolates, brought days before by Jeremy and Lucy, on the bedside table, the crumpled ball of a handkerchief on the floor, where it must have fallen – reassured him. They must have taken Brian off for one of those treatments or tests which he still, to Osamu's amazement, consented to endure.

Osamu sat down on the cold, slithery edge of the one armchair in the room and, head on one side as though listening for some far-off sound, gripped his clasped hands between his knees. He felt tired both from despair and anxiety and from the ferocious cleaning which he had given to the Highgate house in an attempt to convince himself that, in a day or two, Brian would return to it, as he kept insisting that he would.

The door suddenly opened. Osamu and Andy stared at each other.

Then Osamu jumped to his feet.

'Have I made a mistake? Have I come to the wrong room?' But as he asked the questions, Andy saw the Ruth Rendell novel on the bed before him. It was he who had brought it for Brian the day before. 'I was looking for Sir Brian Cobean.'

'This is his room. But he is not here. I think that maybe ... a test ...'

Osamu had never seen Andy; Andy had never heard of Osamu, much less seen him. Yet each was later to think, with bewildered wonder: Somehow it was as though I had known him for years and years.

Andy now walked into the room, his thumbs stuck into the pockets of his tweed jacket and his head high.

'You're waiting.' A statement, not a question.

Osamu nodded. Then he made a small gesture towards the armchair, as though he were pushing something invisible with the palm of his hand. 'Please.'

Without a word, Andy perched himself on the bed. He picked up the novel and stared down at the pages at which it had lain open. He felt his heart racing unpleasantly – tachycardia, Bragg had called it, when he had consulted him about it, nothing serious, probably due to the strain of poor old Brian's illness. He drew one deep breath and then another. He coughed.

'You're a friend of Brian's?'

'Yes, I am his friend.'

'And you're from . . .?'

'Japan.'

'I've never been to Japan. The nearest I ever got was when I put in a spell of duty in Hong Kong. I recently met the Japanese ambassador at a dinner party.'

'I do not know Japanese ambassador. I regret.'

'Did you and Brian meet each other when he went there on that case?'

'Case? No. We meet in London. In Holland Park.'

Andy got up from the bed and crossed to the window. He looked out through the double glazing at the traffic speeding over the Thames. He turned. 'Where do you live?'

'I live in Highgate. I live in Brian's house.'

The two men stared at each other.

'But I've never met you there. Brian never told me . . . I imagined . . .'

Osamu shook his head. He said nothing.

'Have you known each other a long time?'

Osamu again said nothing. Head now tilted side-ways on its long neck, he was gazing at the radiator.

At that moment Brian, supported by one of the Sisters, returned to the room.

'Father! I thought you said you wouldn't be coming until this evening . . .'

'That was the idea. But then I was asked to make up a four at bridge and so . . . Have I done the wrong thing?' He looked over at Osamu.

'No, of course not!' With a small groan, Brian eased his emaciated body first on to the edge of the bed and then across it. 'Thank you, Aileen,' he said to the nurse.

'Can I get you anything?' She had been slapping the pillows as though she wished to hurt them.

'Nothing, thank you.'

The nurse went.

'You two have never met. Osamu, this is my father.'
He left the introductions at that, putting his head back
on the pillows and closing his eyes.

'I guess that it is your father.'

Eyes still closed, Brian said: 'Ossie – would you
mind? There are things my father and I must talk about
... Could you wait for, well, half an hour?'

'I can wait.'

Osamu got to his feet, walked over to the door,
turned as though he were about to say something, and
then left.

Andy was often to wonder why he had never then
questioned Brian about the Japanese, as he was also
often to wonder why Brian had never made any
attempt to explain him.

'How are you, old boy?'

'Oh, a bit better, I think. What's the latest on the
Parkinson front?'

'Well, you won't believe this. Last Friday he actually
had the cheek to ask me for a rise ...'

It was, in essence, a conversation which they had
had each time that Andy had made a visit to the
hospital.

'Well, I suppose it had to happen some time or other.'

Osamu, seated on the bed with Brian's hand in his,
said: 'Yes, it had to happen.'

Brian sighed.

'Does it matter?' Osamu asked.

'Poor old boy! I wonder if he guessed what kind of
relationship it is.'

Osamu shrugged, as though he did not care whether

the old man had guessed or not. But he hoped that he had.

Andy had told Osamu that he would be back in the early afternoon. 'I'm meeting this old friend for luncheon at the club,' he had explained. Brian had now been in a coma for several hours, his eyes visible as no more than silvery half-moons under lids that would from time to time flutter like the wings of a moth in a killing-jar. More than once Osamu had stretched out a hand and placed it over those fluttering lids, in an attempt to still them. He had felt their convulsive movement not merely on the ball of his thumb and on his fingers but somewhere deep within him, like a new symptom of his grief.

'I will stay,' Osamu told Andy.

'Aren't you going to have a bite yourself? There's a little place just round the corner . . .'

For all his resentment of Osamu, Andy could not help also feeling admiration and gratitude. Nothing seemed to tire or deflect him; he looked after Brian even better than the nurses.

'I do not wish to eat.'

'I could bring you a sandwich when I come back.'

Osamu shook his head. Then, even before Andy had had time to leave the room, he leaned across the bed and again placed a hand over Brian's half-closed eyes.

Andy, mouth open to reveal teeth of which he would often boast 'Every bally one my own!', stared at Osamu, as the nurse and the young Thai intern were also staring at him. Osamu had somehow, by some miracle, made all three of them feel useless, unwanted, unneeded. There was blood on the front of his shirt, on his trousers at the knee, on his hands. He was holding Brian half propped up against the pillows and half propped up against him.

'He has died,' Osamu said. 'He died fifteen, twenty minutes ago.'

Briefly, united by shock and grief, they were comrades.

'We could have a drink at that pub round the corner. It's quiet at this hour.'

At any other time, Osamu would have said: 'Thank you, I do not drink.' But now he merely nodded. He had put on one of Brian's shirts, far too large for him, which he had found in the white chest-of-drawers in the now vacated room. He had repeatedly sponged at the blood-stain on his trousers with the new face-cloth which he had bought Brian only the day before, until it had dwindled to no more than a faint discoloration. 'Use cold water,' the young nurse had advised. She had always been sympathetic both to him and to Brian. By the bedside, hand over mouth, she had briefly sobbed.

Andy's hand rested on Osamu's shoulder to propel him first into the lift. 'Hate these places – even when, like this one, they're more like hotels than hospitals.'

There was a silence until they had emerged into the clamour and sunlight of the street. Then Andy said, as he had already said to the young intern: 'No one could really have wanted him to go on living in that state. If I were that ill, I'd just finish myself off – if no one else was prepared to do the job for me.'

'He was very brave. He fought to live. Always he fought.'

'Yes, of course he was brave! But brave for what, for what?'

There was a silence. Then Osamu said: 'I cannot explain.' He was afraid that, if he tried to explain, he would burst into tears.

Andy ordered his usual double Scotch, neat, and some Perrier for Osamu.

'Do you never drink?'

'Very seldom.'

'There'll be a lot of things to see to.'

He was amazed when Osamu said in a strong, steady voice: 'I will do.'

'Well, yes, but . . . I mean things like registering the death – and arranging the funeral – and . . .' At that moment he could think of nothing else; later, he was to think of many other things.

Osamu nodded. 'I will do. I am' – for a moment he could not remember the English for it – 'I am executor of will.'

Andy, glass raised, looked at him in stupefaction. 'My dear chap . . .' He laughed. The fellow must have got it wrong. 'You can't be – '

'Brian told me. I am executor. He made his will four, five days ago. The chaplain and that lady, the nurse, signed. True.' He nodded his head at Andy, as though at an uncomprehending child. Then he said: 'And I am sole beneficiary.'

Again Andy stared at him in stupefaction, the colour mounting into his cheeks and darkening there. Had Brian really done this crazy thing? Had he even omitted to leave any money to his godson, Luke's and Mary's eldest? Bloody hell! It couldn't be, it couldn't!

'I just don't believe this!'

'Tomorrow I will show you copy of the will. The will is in bank, Lloyds Bank, Kensington High Street.'

The calmness with which Osamu spoke only

intensified Andy's fury. 'But why, why, why? Why the fucking hell?'

Osamu shrugged. 'That is what Brian wished.'

Andy almost said: 'You must have got round him when he was too ill to resist you.' He almost said: 'Were you blackmailing him or something?' But he was too decent to allow himself to say either of these things.

He gulped at his Scotch, feeling it burn its way down into his gullet to add to the pain burning beneath his breastbone. 'Well, well, well.' He gave a short, explosive laugh. 'That's a turn-up for the book. That's certainly a turn-up for the book.'

'I am sorry.'

They sat on for a while in silence. Then Andy said: 'Anyway I'd better come with you to register the death. You might find yourself rather at sea with all that protocol and bumf.'

'If you wish.' Osamu did not want Andy to come with him; but he felt that he must make the concession.

The two men decided to meet at the hospital at eleven the next morning. Their first task would be to procure the death certificate.

As he creaked to his feet, Andy exclaimed: 'God, what hell all this is!' Osamu did not know whether he meant all the ordinary circumstances of any death, or all the extraordinary circumstances of this one. Nor did Andy himself know.

Out once again in the clamour and sunlight of the street, Andy asked: 'Where are you going now?'

'Home.'

'To Highgate?' It was as though Andy still could not believe that home for Osamu was the house which his son had bought so soon before his death.

'Yes. To Highgate.'

Andy was suddenly pierced by compassion for the

235

small, straight-backed, rigid-faced man before him. He wished that he did not feel this compassion. It was as though Osamu had somehow tricked him into it, as he had tricked his son into making that extraordinary will. 'Would you like me to come back with you?'

'Thank you. It is not necessary.'

Andy watched Osamu as he walked off, head still held high, to the bus-stop. Andy would also be taking a bus but he did not want to take the same one as the Japanese or even to stand waiting at the bus-stop with him. Then he shouted out: 'Oh, Mr Kawasaki! Mr Kawasaki!'

Osamu turned: 'Yes, General Cobean?'

'You'd better bring a small suitcase tomorrow. For Brian's things. I don't think they'll all fit into the one there.'

Osamu nodded. He had thought of that already.

Osamu had never understood why Brian had decided to give up the flat and buy the Highgate house. Admittedly, he had done it during the first of the two brief remissions which had preceded his death by a few months; but even then he must have known that he could not live for long. Even though the house, formerly owned by a colleague, was in excellent condition, and even though he had had Osamu to help him, why should a man in his frail state of health have deliberately submitted himself to all the problems of a move? Did he perhaps believe that, by changing his whole environment, he would by some miracle, also commute the life-sentence passed on him?

'Is it necessary?'

'No, it's not necessary. We're comfortable enough here. But think how wonderful it will be to have that large garden – and all those large rooms – and three bathrooms. You've always said that you wanted a dog and a cat. Now you can have both.'

It had been impossible to argue with him.

Now, as Osamu let himself into the house, he wished that he had acquired that dog and that cat.

He climbed the stairs, pausing once on the landing, a hand on the banister and his head cocked as though, once again, he were trying to hear some distant sound, and then pushed at the door to Brian's room, next to his own, and entered. He pulled open a drawer and then another drawer, peering down into each. He put out a hand, turned the key, and slowly pulled back one half of the large, mahogany, nineteenth-century breakfront wardrobe. He touched a suit. Stroked it. Then felt suddenly repelled by it, so inanimate, so inert, so rough. He had already decided what he would do with all Brian's possessions. He had seen an advertisement in the *Hampstead and Highgate Express*. He would make a telephone call, and then he would sell everything, and then he would send the money to the London Lighthouse.

He raced down the stairs to the kitchen, tore two heavy-duty dustbin bags off their roll in a corner, and raced upstairs with them. He tugged suits off their hangers and thrust them into one of the bags. He swept into it hairbrushes, combs, clothes-brush, after-shave lotion, stud-box, ashtray. From the drawers he grabbed socks, handkerchiefs, shirts, ties, some silk pyjamas bought during that visit of theirs to Florence.

Soon the refuse bag was full. He knotted it and then, grimacing under the weight, dragged it to the top of the staircase and began to descend.

All at once the bag split. Its contents cascaded downwards, the bottle of after-shave lotion smashing as it struck the stone floor.

Osamu stared down at the debris. It seemed to be the debris of their whole life together. Then he sank down on to the stairs and, forehead on knees and hands crossed over the nape of his neck, he burst into loud, gulping sobs.

It was soon after that that he telephoned to Anna Clive.

When, his face glistening with sweat, Andy entered the club, a small, hunched figure raised a hand to him, as though he were hailing a bus: 'Andy! Andy old boy! Long time no see!'

'Sorry, Dick. I'm in a frightful hurry. Sorry!' Andy rushed past.

In his room, he tore off his tweed jacket and tie, dropping them to the floor as, scrupulously tidy, he would never normally do, and then, seated on the bed, tugged at a shoe without undoing the laces. Oh, blast, blast, blast! Leaving the shoe on, he twisted his body round, until he lay with his face pressed into the pillow, hardly able to breathe. He wanted to suffocate himself. He wanted to suffocate all thought of Brian and that Jap.

Then he sat up, jumped off the bed and crossed to the washbasin. He twisted the cold tap on, held his hand under it and then, when the water had become an icy stream, splashed his lowered face repeatedly. He straightened. Water beaded his eyebrows, trickled down his face to his chin.

He frowned. It was as though, frantically, against the clock, he were trying to fit together the pieces of a jigsaw. Yes, that piece must go there, and that there, and that *there*. Of course! What a clot he had been. And Helen's mysterious fall in Agadir. And Brian's insistence, 'No, I don't want to have any children, that's the last thing I want.' And those holidays alone in Ceylon, the Greek Islands, Thailand. And the ...

What a clot, what a bloody clot he had been!

Later, he tried to telephone to Luke. But Luke was not there and it was Mary who answered the telephone.

'Oh, hello, Pop!' He hated that jocular 'Pop', it seemed somehow to demonstrate a lack of esteem for him. 'How are things?'

He told her the news of Brian's death.

Silence. Then in a clear, high voice, she said: 'Poor chap. Well, I suppose it was what is called a happy release.' She had long since prepared herself.

Andy had not intended to tell her about the will. But he could not stop himself from doing so; he had to tell someone. 'The most extraordinary thing! Unbelievable really.'

When he had finished, he asked: 'Well, what do you make of that?'

'It figures.'

'What do you mean?' He was astounded by the coolness of it. There was none of the expected amazement or indignation.

'Well, I'm not surprised.'

Extraordinary woman. A woman almost as extraordinary as the news which he had given her. He remained for several seconds in the stifling little telephone booth, a shoulder against one wall, while with the back of a hand he wiped the sweat off his forehead.

That evening, the old man who had waved to Andy as he had entered the club on his return from the hospital, limped over to his table. Oh, lordy, lordy! Silly old fart – Hodge, or Bodge, or Dodge, Andy could never remember his name. He had never thought anything of him: so many years in the Army and still only a major when early retirement was forced on him.

'May I join you?'

Andy grunted.

Even older than Andy, Dodge spent his days adrift on a mist-shrouded, constantly receding tide of memory. But since they had been fellow officers in the trenches, he never forgot Andy. He began to reminisce about those far-off, terrible days.

Suddenly, while chewing on some smoked salmon, Andy felt sick. He did not know whether what made him feel sick was the excessive salt of the fish, Dodge's quavering voice constantly asking 'Do you recall . . .?', or the shock of what he had learned about Brian. But he could not go on with the meal.

He put his napkin down on the table. 'Sorry. I'll have to leave you. Not feeling too good.'

'Oh, I say! Dear chap!'

But Andy had stridden off.

Out in Piccadilly the evening air was cool, drying off the sweat on his face and around his collar. As he crossed the street, a taxi-driver, hunched over his wheel as though with stomach-cramp, impatiently hooted at him. Oh, bugger off, bugger off, you stupid cunt! Then, on an impulse, he entered Green Park.

He sat on a bench, thin legs crossed and an arm extended along the wooden slats. The expression on his face was still one of exasperation, as though he had not yet forgotten that impatient hooting from the taxi. A small, fluffy dog of indeterminate breed came over to him, wagging its erect lavatory-brush of a tail. Although a dog-lover, he paid it no attention. 'Fritz,

Fritz! Come here!' its owner, a middle-aged, bald-headed man with a single earring, called.

Andy stared across the park, its grass a brownish-yellow after so many days of drought. Poor chap. They had never really got on, never really understood each other. He himself had so often been abroad or busy, so that it was natural that the boy and his mother should have grown so close. The classic recipe for that kind of thing, wasn't that what they said?

Suddenly he was aware that someone, a woman, had sat down beside him, even though at that late hour there were a number of other empty benches. She might have been Mary when her mother and father, neighbours in Ilkley, had brought her, a girl of seventeen, to a cocktail party. There was the same wide, candid face, with the low forehead and the slightly crooked nose; the same small hands, with stubby fingers; the same stocky figure. This girl was wearing a dark blue shantung suit with a white blouse and pale blue stockings.

'It's turned a bit fresher now.' The voice, with its trace of a West Country accent, was in no way like Mary's.

'Yes. Mercifully.'

She laughed. 'I like that. "Mercifully". It sounds so – old-fashioned, if you'll forgive me for saying so.' She drew a handkerchief out of her bag and pressed it to her upper lip. He could smell the scent on it. Then she said: 'Lonely?'

'No, not at all.'

These days tarts no longer looked like tarts. She could have been working late at some office in Whitehall and then have decided to walk home across first St James's Park and then Green Park before catching a train or bus to some little semi-detached in which she lived with a husband or her parents in the suburbs.

'You look – down.'

'I am down.'

'Well, then, how about letting me cheer you up?'

She had a two-roomed flat in Sussex Gardens. There was a huge rag doll in a mob-cap on the double bed – 'That's Mrs Bridges,' she said, chucking it on to an armchair. Lying flat on the dressing-table there was a photograph of a long-haired, sparsely bearded young man. The glass of the frame had a diagonal crack across it. The scent which had wafted from the handkerchief now seemed to impregnate everything: vaguely sickly, vaguely sickening.

He made love to her with such violence that more than once she remonstrated with him. (Steady on! ... Here, cut that out! ... Do you mind!) Fuck you, fuck you, fuck you, he was saying silently to himself, over and over again. He was fucking more, much more than this tart who looked so much like Mary when she was a girl.

'Well, that's generous of you, very generous! ... Would you like my card?'

'Why not? One never knows.'

Out of the house, he threw the card into the gutter.

I feel as though I'd been run over by a bus. A bloody bus. He massaged an arm, then stooped and massaged a leg, then massaged a cheek.

Under the desk the knees touched each other, the ankles touched each other. She shook a bell of hair and sucked on the end of her biro. 'I don't know what's happened to Dr Scott.' It was the third time that she had said that. 'Sorry. He said he'd be down at ten. The trouble is that we're so short of staff.' She was talking to Andy, because she had the weird sensation that Osamu, entirely still and entirely silent, was really no more than a cunning hologram projected there in a dark corner of her room.

Andy fanned himself with a free magazine, full of house agents' advertisements, which he had picked up off the table beside him.

'My apologies!' Dr Scott bustled in. 'An emergency.'

'Nothing serious, I hope.'

'Not too serious,' In fact, a patient had just died. He fingered the row of pens protruding from the breast-pocket of his white coat, as he sat down at a desk beside the one at which the girl was sitting. He had the physique of a rugger player but his face was pale and thin. 'Well, now, let's see, let's see.'

The girl handed him the file. He frowned down at it. 'Well, as you know, the immediate cause of death was meningitis. But' – he was apologetic, embarrassed – 'I'm afraid I have to put down the, well, basic cause.'

'Yes, I understand that,' Andy said, puzzled. 'Of course.'

'It was sad, so sad.' The doctor pulled out one of the pens and bent his head over the file. 'He was such a nice chap. When I had a moment to spare, I used to go into his room to chat to him. He knew so much – about everything. Always had something interesting to say.'

It was to Andy that he eventually handed the form. Throughout the interview he had avoided having to look at Osamu. 'There you go,' he said, suddenly jolly, as though he were a travel-agent handing over the tickets for a holiday abroad.

In the hall of the hospital, Osamu standing beside him, Andy looked down at the paper in his hand.

He turned to Osamu and asked angrily: 'What is this? What the hell is this? What has he written here?' He thrust the form towards the Japanese.

'That is how he died.'

'But he never ... Why did he ...? Why all that shit about leukaemia?'

'He did not wish you to know. He did not wish anyone to know.' Osamu put out a hand and placed it on the old man's shoulder. 'Sorry.'

Andy jerked away. Then he said: 'That's it! From now on you see to everything. You can do it without me. Here – take this!'

Osamu shrugged. He took the form.

Without another word, Andy strode out of the hospital.

From a seat, close to the driver, reserved for the elderly – usually he took a pride in avoiding such seats – Andy stared out. So many people and so many of them foreigners. It was no longer the London which he had known. Bloody city, bloody, bloody city. Bloody foreigners. Brian had probably been infected by that bloody little Jap nancy-boy. That was the most likely thing. God! Christ!

... But how brave he had been. Guts. Or bottle, as they called it nowadays. To keep up that pretence. And never to complain, never to cry out, never to ... And how he had suffered. Those fevers and chills. The constant tiredness. Those livid patches on his face. Skin and bone. The eventual blindness and then ...

They were in a traffic jam. The bus-driver had been watching him in a mirror.

'Cheer up, guvnor. It may never happen.'

'It has happened.'

You bloody fool – it *has* happened!

Soon after six the bell rang.

'Who can that be?' Wilfrid asked, looking up from the papers spread across the desk.

'It can't be the gasman. Too late.' Anna had waited in all day for the gasman's call.

'Osamu!' She could never bring herself to call him Ossie.

'I am sorry.' Despite her smiling greeting, he already knew that he was not welcome. He held out a huge bunch of flowers: 'For you.'

'Oh, Osamu, how lovely! But you shouldn't have! You shouldn't have!'

'You have been so kind to me.'

'Come in.'

Osamu edged into the sitting-room ahead of her.

'Wilfrid – look at these wonderful flowers which Osamu has brought me.'

'H'm.' Wilfrid inspected them over the rims of his glasses. 'Very nice. Very nice indeed.' With a sigh, he began gathering up the papers before him. Then, feeling a compunction, he looked across to Osamu: 'I was sorry to hear about your, er, friend. Sad, very sad.'

'He was very brave. For more than two years he knew that he was dying. But he told no one, only me.'

'Well, yes, that was brave.' Papers in hand, Wilfrid walked towards the door. 'You must excuse me. I had to bring back all this work from the office. There seems to be no end to it.'

'Please, please!'

'I'll just put these in some water,' Anna said. 'Oh, they are lovely.'

When she returned, Osamu was still standing in the centre of the room. She offered him a drink, a cup of coffee, a cup of tea, but he declined each of these suggestions. 'I do not wish to take up your time. You are very busy lady, I know.'

It was true. But she laughed and said: 'Not all that busy.'

'I have come to ask you for a favour, big favour.'

'Do sit down.' She pointed to the sofa.

But, ignoring her, he went on: 'I have told you of the funeral. Golders Green Crematorium.'

'Yes, I'll be there. I don't know if my husband will be able to make it – probably not. It's difficult for him to get away from his office in the middle of the morning.'

'It does not matter.' Osamu did not care whether Wilfrid attended or not. 'But I am happy that you will come.' Now at last he lowered himself on to the edge of an upright chair. Anna also seated herself. 'That is important to me. There will be many people unknown to me – colleagues of Brian, family of Brian. You will be my friend, my only friend.'

Looking at him, Anna thought how grey he looked. His face seemed even narrower and longer than ever, and his eyelids and lips had a mauvish sheen to them.

'Now I must ask you for the favour.' He paused.

'Anything. Anything I can do.' At that moment she was, indeed, prepared to do anything within her power for him.

He swallowed, his Adam's apple bobbing up and down in his long, thin neck. 'Brian – my friend – loved music very much. Unlike his family – father, brother – he did not believe in Christian religion. Once but no longer. But music – music he loved very much. Music was like religion to him. When he was ill' – his tongue ran over his lips – 'dying – he listened to music all the time. Once he loved opera, loved opera very, very much. But when he was dying, he listened only to Bach. Strange. Only to Bach.'

Anna nodded, leaning towards him, hands clasped.

'So . . .' He drew a deep breath. 'I remember coming here one day – many months ago – when we still lived in Kensington . . . And upstairs your daughter is playing, playing cello, playing Bach. Yes?'

Anna could not remember what Joanna had been playing. But she nodded. 'Yes, she often plays unaccompanied Bach.'

'So – I wonder . . . Big thing to ask. But maybe – maybe she will play at funeral? For five, ten minutes?' He looked at her, eyebrows raised above those lids which looked as if they had been smeared with some mauvish ointment. 'Is that possible?'

'Well . . . She's not a professional, you know. Only a student at the Royal College. Admittedly one of their best students, but still . . .'

'I should be happy if she consents.'

'She's not here now. She's out at a Prom. But I'll ask her, as soon as she gets back. And then I'll ring you, either this evening or first thing tomorrow.'

'You are very kind. You think she will say yes?'

'I hope she will say yes.'

Osamu, in a dark blue pinstripe suit which Anna had never seen before and which looked as if it were new, was standing, hands clasped before him, at the entrance to the chapel, like an usher. He stepped forward, greeted them and then took the cello, in its battered case, from Joanna. 'I will show you where to sit and where to play.' He was entirely composed. 'There is a programme of service. Brian was not believer but his family are believers,' he whispered as he conducted them up the aisle. Then he pointed. 'You will sit here.' 'Here' turned out to be the front row on the right-hand side of the chapel.

'Oh, not so near the front!'

'You are my closest – my only – friend.'

'Even so ...' Quickly Anna slipped into the third row, while Joanna followed Osamu up on to the dais, placed herself on the chair which he indicated, and then, head bowed, began to tune her cello. Her total composure had made Wilfrid comment at breakfast: 'Whether she has the talent to be a solo performer, only time will show. But she certainly has the temperament.'

Anna looked about her. At a first view the chapel seemed to be full of prosperous, grey-haired, bespectacled men in dark suits and ties. These must be lawyer colleagues of the dead man, she decided. Then, immediately across the aisle from her, she saw a red-cheeked old man, with sparse, closely cut white hair and a neatly clipped moustache; a plump, middle-aged woman in a black-and-white dress and a black straw hat; and a tall, balding man who, even as she was glancing at him, yawned and then yawned again, without bothering to cover his mouth with a hand. The trio must be Brian's father, brother and sister-in-law. Osamu had told her about them.

There was an atmosphere of increasing heat and stupor as the service progressed. The head of Brian's chambers, an eminent commercial lawyer noted for his after-dinner speeches, paid a tribute in which he included a few humorously intended anecdotes about the dead man. 'I shall never forget how Brian was determined to get to Glyndebourne for a performance of *Capriccio*, even though the case in which he was involved ...' one of these began; and another, 'As no doubt all of you will be aware, Brian laid great stress on convention in dress, so it was some surprise to me . . .'

In a bass, booming voice another colleague read Thomas Hardy's 'Afterwards', as though vaguely embarrassed by it.

There was a further tribute from a middle-aged woman, clearly suffering either from a cold or from hay-fever, who talked chiefly of Brian's voluntary work for Mencap. 'He was one of those who are not content with merely expressing sympathy with those less fortunate than themselves. He wanted to *do* something; and being the highly intelligent and efficient man that he was, he ensured that what he did was always something of value. I – we all – are going to miss his charm, his good humour, his kindness, his sense of fun. But above all we are going to miss his quality of *caring* . . .' She went on to speak of the dead man's closeness to his family – 'He relied so much on them and they on him. They were a truly united family. Our hearts go out to them in their tragic bereavement . . .'

As Joanna, her long, black hair swaying back and forth to shield her face from Anna's loving, apprehensive gaze, played a Bach unaccompanied suite, everyone seemed rapt. Even Anna, whom Joanna had so often teased about being so unmusical, felt mysteriously saddened and comforted at one and the same time.

Moving stiffly, his head held erect, Osamu mounted the dais, a single typed sheet of paper in one hand. For several seconds on end he surveyed the congregation, as though sizing them up. Then in his high, metallic voice, carrying to every corner of the chapel, he announced: 'As a tribute to my friend, my dear, my dearest friend Brian, I wish to read to you a passage from the *Confessions* of St Augustine. I am not Christian believer, I am not believer in any religion. My only God was Brian. But I believe in the beauty of love and the beauty of words. So I choose this passage, which Brian once read to me soon after we met. This passage tells of the feelings of St Augustine when, like me, he loses a beloved friend.' He cleared his throat, bowed his head. The hand holding the paper was wholly steady. 'I read,' he announced.

'"At this my heart was utterly darkened; and whatever I beheld was death. My native country was a torment to me, and my father's house a strange unhappiness; and whatever I had shared with him, for lack of him became a ghastly torture."'

Suddenly a memory flashed at Anna. She was seated at the wheel of the car, her head tilted sideways; she was staring at a darkened house. There were people in that house but all of them were strangers to her. Then another memory flashed. She was ringing at the bell of the house and, on the other side of the frosted glass panel of the door, she could make out a dark, amorphous shape. Why did that dark, amorphous shape not move? Why was it so slow to open to her?

'"Mine eyes sought him everywhere, but he was not granted to them; and I hated all things, since they held him not; nor could they now tell me, 'he is coming', as when he was alive and absent . . ."'

Anna had become aware of a growing unease in the audience, as at the first, faint tremors of an earthquake. Clutching her cello, Joanna was staring fixedly across at Osamu. Behind, a woman was coughing in sharp, nervous spasms. At the end of the row, one of the prosperous, grey-haired, bespectacled, dark-suited men was leaning sideways to whisper something inaudible into the ear of his female neighbour.

'". . . Wretched I was; and wretched is every soul bound by the love of perishable things; he is torn asunder when he loses them. So was I then; I wept most bitterly, and found my rest in bitterness. The direst weariness possessed me, and at the same time a fear of death, which had taken him from me ...'"

Suddenly Anna heard a clatter from the row across from hers. The old, red-cheeked man, Brian's father, had tumbled to his knees. Hands over face, he was praying. Then the plump woman beside him rested a consoling hand on his shoulder; pressed; pressed again. She was biting her lower lip. Her face was ashen.

'"... I marvelled that other mortal men should be alive, since he whom I had loved, as if he should never die, was dead; and I marvelled the more that I, since I was but his other self, should be alive when he was dead. Well hath one said of his friend, 'Thou half of my soul'; for I felt that his soul and my soul were one soul in two bodies; and therefore my life was horror to me, because I loathed that only half of me should be alive; and hence perchance I feared to die, lest he should wholly die, whom I had loved so much.'"

He stopped. Again he surveyed the congregation. Then, in the same high, metallic voice – a voice of titanium, Anna thought – he said: 'That is all.' He gave a little bow. 'Thank you. Thank you all. Thank you for attending.'

Suddenly it came to Anna: This has not been a funeral. This has been a wedding.

She looked across the aisle at the old man, who, clutching the back of the pew in front of him, was struggling to his feet. When the plump woman put out a hand to help him, he turned his face to look at her, not in gratitude or even in recognition, but as an accident victim, scarcely conscious, might squint through a daze of shock and pain at one of his unknown rescuers.

*

When Anna asked Osamu where he was going, he replied: 'Nowhere.' Then he gave a little, choking laugh. He was still clutching the sheet of paper from which he had read the passage from St Augustine. Would he like to come back for some lunch? Anna was thankful that Wilfrid would be at work. Osamu accepted eagerly.

In the car, beside Anna, he said little, as though becalmed in the middle of a lake of thoughts, with the two women waiting patiently for him far off on its shore.

At one moment he said to Joanna, who was seated in the back: 'You played beautifully, so beautifully. Brian would have been so happy if he had heard you.'

'Perhaps he did,' Anna said, although she did not really believe that.

Sadly he shook his head. 'No. Impossible.'

'There were so many people there,' Anna remarked at another moment. 'The place was packed.'

'So many friends of Brian. And I had never met one. And none knew that Brian's Ossie existed. Strange! Very strange!'

Anna wanted to say: 'Well, now they certainly know that Brian's Ossie existed!' But she restrained herself.

Luncheon passed in the same kind of torpid near-silence. From time to time Anna and Joanna discussed things that were no concern of Osamu's; from time to time one or other of them put to him a question – what were his plans for the future? would he be selling the house? did he ever think of visiting his family in Japan? – to which he gave abrupt, vague answers.

It was only as they were drinking their coffee that he suddenly leaned across the table and demanded of Anna: 'Mrs Clive – tell me – did I do right?'

'How do you mean, Osamu?'

'To read that passage from St Augustine, to speak as I did of Brian and myself.'

Anna considered. 'Do you want me to tell you what I really think?'

'Of course. Please.'

'Well . . .' Still she hesitated. But she was a woman for whom lying was always difficult. 'I'm afraid – I'm afraid I think it was – well, a mistake.'

He stared at her, the colour mounting into his cheeks to leave two hectic spots there. 'So you think . . . ?'

'I feel that at a funeral one must think not of what one wants oneself but of what the dead person would have wanted. From all that you've told me of your friend, I think that he wanted his life with you to be a secret. Perhaps he was wrong, yes, I'm sure he was wrong. But that's what he wanted. I think – I think that, had he been present, he would have been horrified.'

Mouth slightly open, he was still staring at her. Now the stare seemed to be one of incredulity, disgust, even hatred.

'Then there was his father. His brother, his brother's wife. All those colleagues of his. That woman from Mencap. Was it really necessary . . . ?' She broke off. Better not to go on.

'Yes, it was necessary. Very necessary.' He got up, angrily pushing at the table as he did so. Its edge banged against Anna's left hip. 'I go.'

'Oh, but Osamu . . . You asked me what I thought, you told me to tell you what I thought . . .'

He was gone.

Joanna jumped up and ran after him. She caught him up in the street. He wanted to escape from her but she grabbed him by the arm.

'I thought you were wonderful. Truly. So – so brave!

To tell all those smug colleagues of his and his family where they all got off! Oh, I loved it, loved it. And I loved you for it.'

Convulsively he took both her hands in his. 'Thank you! Thank you! We are same generation, we understand each other.'

Then he pulled free and began running, head lowered, away from her.

She thought of running after him, then abandoned the idea. He was running too fast.

She called after him: 'Osamu! One moment! Osamu!'

But he did not look back, although a number of other people did.

Anna saw Osamu only once after that.

She was crossing Paternoster Square and there he was, in only jeans and an open-necked, short-sleeved white shirt despite the chill of that autumn day. He was perched on his stool, his easel before him, painting St Paul's. It was the most obvious and conventional view of the cathedral, and she knew that he would be painting it in the most obvious and conventional way.

She halted a few feet behind him, wondering whether to go over, to speak to him, to try to make it up. But she felt – she did not know how or why – the intensity of his solitary absorption both in his work and in the life which he had chosen, a stranger in a country always strange to him. He would want, and would need, no contact with her or perhaps with anyone else.

She edged to one side; took a diagonal route; passed on and away.